05

Fool Erna Once

SPY CLASSROOM

code name
MEADOW

code name
PANDEMONIUM

SPY CLASSROOM 05

Fool Erna Once

Takemachi
ILLUSTRATION BY **Tomari**

YEN ON

New York

SPY CLASSROOM 05

Translation by Nathaniel Thrasher
Cover art by Tomari
Assistance with firearm research: Asaura

This book is a work of fiction. Names, characters, places, and incidents are the product of the author's imagination or are used fictitiously. Any resemblance to actual events, locales, or persons, living or dead, is coincidental.

SPY KYOSHITSU Vol. 5 <<GUJIN>> NO ERNA
©Takemachi, Tomari 2021
First published in Japan in 2021 by KADOKAWA CORPORATION, Tokyo.
English translation rights arranged with KADOKAWA CORPORATION, Tokyo through TUTTLE-MORI AGENCY, INC., Tokyo.

English translation © 2023 by Yen Press, LLC

Yen On
150 West 30th Street, 19th Floor
New York, NY 10001

Visit us at yenpress.com
facebook.com/yenpress
twitter.com/yenpress
yenpress.tumblr.com
instagram.com/yenpress

First Yen On Edition: May 2023
Edited by Yen On Editorial: Anna Powers
Designed by Yen Press Design: Andy Swist

Yen On is an imprint of Yen Press, LLC.
The Yen On name and logo are trademarks of Yen Press, LLC.

The publisher is not responsible for websites (or their content) that are not owned by the publisher.

Library of Congress Cataloging-in-Publication Data
Names: Takemachi, author. I Tomari, Meron, illustrator. I Thrasher, Nathaniel Hiroshi, translator.
Title: Spy classroom / Takemachi ; illustrated by Tomari ; translation by Nathaniel Thrasher.
Other titles: Spy kyoushitsu. English
Description: First Yen On edition. I New York, NY : Yen On, 2021.
Identifiers: LCCN 2021021119 I ISBN 9781975322403 (v. 1 ; trade paperback) I
    ISBN 9781975322427 (v. 2 ; trade paperback) I ISBN 9781975338824
    (v. 3 ; trade paperback) I ISBN 9781975338848 (v. 4 ; trade paperback) I
    ISBN 9781975343125 (v. 5 ; trade paperback)
Subjects: I CYAC: Spies—Fiction. I Schools—Fiction.
Classification: LCC PZ7.1.T343 Sp 2021 I DDC [Fic]—dc23
LC record available at https://lccn.loc.gov/2021021119

ISBNs: 978-1-9753-4312-5 (paperback)
       978-1-9753-4313-2 (ebook)

10 9 8 7 6 5 4 3 2 1

LSC-C

Printed in the United States of America

CONTENTS

SPY CLASSROOM
Specialized lessons for an impossible mission
Code name: Fool

Prologue

Longchon

Longchon was a small country in the region of the world known as the Far East. Compared to Western-Central countries like the United States of Mouzaia and the Lylat Kingdom, the Far East was relatively undeveloped. Its Republic of Ryuka had enjoyed nigh unrivaled prosperity during the Middle Ages, but even they had been helpless before the Western-Central powers' modernized armies. Nowadays, all but a small section of the Far East existed under Western-Central control.

Longchon, which sat directly adjacent to Ryuka, was one of the nations that had been invaded. Currently, it was a colony of the Fend Commonwealth.

In order to strengthen their control over the Far East, Fend had taken the small peninsula nation and poured vast sums of money and engineering resources into it in order to rapidly modernize its cities. In addition to building universities and banks, they also used educational institutions centered around Western-Central philosophies to drum the tenets of capitalism into the nation's people.

As a result, Longchon became a peculiar melting pot of both Western-Central and Ryuka culture and took on a new role—as the spot that connected the West to the East. People gathered there from the Fend Commonwealth, from other Western-Central nations that wanted to advance their incursions into the East, and from the Far East countries that had fallen under colonial rule. People who wanted to conquer, people who wanted to learn about developed nations' institutions, and people who wanted to break the shackles of oppression and control all gathered in Longchon with their various ideologies as though drawn there.

Politicians numbered among their ranks, as did journalists, academics, traders, refugees, soldiers, and revolutionaries. The list went on and on.

And behind the scenes, nations the world over sent spies in to do their work.

It was said that Longchon's heart was found in its nights.

The country was made up of two major sections. There was the mainland over on the continent side, and across the sea, there was Longchon Island.

The most prosperous part of the country was Longchon Island's waterfront, and the area around it, called the Great Harbor, was full of skyscrapers that cast their light across the gentle sea. Rows of Ryukese restaurants decorated with colorful red-and-yellow paper lanterns sat at the skyscrapers' bases, each of them filled to the brim with workers relieving themselves of their fatigue by chowing down on steamed buns and wonton noodles, and washing it all down with generous gulps of Shaoxing wine.

One of the restaurants was a popular spot for Western-Central businessmen, and in it, a man was drinking some oolong tea. He was a beautiful man with features so fair one could almost mistake him for a woman, but by wearing his hair long to hide his elegant features, he was able to blend in with the rest of the city and go all but unnoticed. When he casually sipped from his teacup beneath the red paper lantern, he was indistinguishable from any other young man visiting Longchon on business.

That man was "Bonfire" Klaus—a spy from the Din Republic.

He sat alone, doing nothing but eating his braised pork dinner.

In the seat behind his, there was a woman sitting with her back to him wearing a casual T-shirt. "It's been three months since the Tolfa

Economic Conference, so we're starting to see how each country made out," she said.

The woman was enjoying a glass of Fend-made whiskey.

Her hair was a striking combination of yellow and pink, and her face was decorated in heavy layers of eyeshadow. Her code name was Roaring Sea, and she was a messenger from Din's intelligence agency. Her job was to go out in person and deliver confidential information to their agents working abroad.

Roaring Sea hid her mouth behind her glass cup as she went on. "Bottom line is: The situation's about what we expected."

Her voice was hoarse and husky. When she drank, it went right to her throat.

"How so?" Klaus asked.

"There wasn't any obvious funny business that happened at the Tolfa Economic Conference. With one exception, mind you."

The two of them continued facing away from each other as they spoke.

"Ah," Klaus muttered.

The topic at hand was the showdown he'd had against Serpent in the United States of Mouzaia.

Upon discovering that Serpent had infiltrated a conference being held in Mouzaia, the world's leading economic superpower, Klaus took his subordinates and dove into the fray. After a long, hard-fought battle, they'd succeeded in capturing one of Serpent's members, but while they were busy with that, Serpent had largely had free rein to do their covert work.

The question was, were Serpent's actions going to end up reshaping the global situation now that the conference was over?

However, no major shifts seemed to have come about yet.

Roaring Sea's mouth curled into a thin smile. "As far as the conference itself went, the Allies finished carving up Tolfa with no big surprises to speak of. Everything seems pretty normal. Sheesh, your girl's feeling kinda let down."

For whatever reason, Roaring Sea liked to refer to herself as "your girl." Klaus had only known her a short while, and he had yet to get much of a handle on who she was or where she was from.

"Well, I guess that's spies for you," Roaring Sea said with a chuckle.

"Honestly, it's kind of creepy how good these Serpent guys are at getting stuff done behind closed doors."

"So what you're telling me is that we still have no idea what Serpent was after." Klaus couldn't help but let a touch of irritation creep into his voice. To him, Serpent was the most loathsome foe around. He'd loved Inferno like a family, and Serpent had annihilated them. "What about that data I got from the JJJ?" he asked. "Is the analysis finished yet?"

"That's gonna take a bit more time." Roaring Sea shrugged. "After all, I doubt the JJJ was feeling nice enough to just hand you all that information on a silver platter. I don't think they tried to play you or anything, but we still need to go over the intel with a fine-tooth comb before we can use it."

"Got it. And?"

"Hmm?"

"What was the funny business? You mentioned an exception."

"Oh yeah. You actually already know about it, though." Roaring Sea's voice went grim. "I was talking about the heavy losses all the intelligence agencies suffered…on account of Purple Ant's massacre."

"Ah, that," Klaus replied.

Purple Ant was a spy who worked for the Galgad Empire, and he was also a member of Serpent.

"I have to say, your girl was shook." Roaring Sea's voice was uncharacteristically somber. "You can't even call that intelligence work. I mean, single-handedly killing over a hundred spies and using human wave tactics to turn an entire city into a hunting ground? There isn't an intelligence agency out there that's not reeling right now. Everyone lost loads of their best people."

Purple Ant hadn't been messing around. He was a man who used torture to bend ordinary civilians to his will and mold them into assassins. Their orders were to murder any intelligence agents they found operating in Mitario—and to kill themselves if they failed. The man was like the devil incarnate, and he styled himself as Mitario's king.

Over the course of his reign, he had killed countless operatives with no regard for what nation they worked for. Rumors had swirled about exemplar spies from every nation under the sun meeting untimely ends, and one of the victims was even Klaus's de facto mother, Hearth.

"It was a massacre, is what it was. And thinking about how it all happened at the hands of a single man sends a chill down my spine. That sort of stuff just isn't supposed to be possible."

".........."

"At any rate, Serpent will be able to operate pretty freely for the time being," Roaring Sea said. "Purple Ant did what he set out to, and now the world is descending into chaos. It probably won't be long before Serpent begins making some serious moves, and if we let them get started, it'll already be too late."

".........."

"We're expecting great things from you, Bonfire. Or should I say... the Greatest Spy in the World?"

When she addressed him by his title, Klaus offered her no denial or modesty.

He hadn't taken the name out of arrogance. He'd done so out of self-confidence and his sense of duty. He'd been raised by the greatest teammates anyone could ask for, and the moniker was a symbol of his pride as a spy.

With Inferno gone, it was up to him to protect his homeland.

Roaring Sea stood up and began getting ready to head out.

"I have a message from the brass." The cloying smell of perfume drifted by as she made her final comment. "We'll figure out where Serpent is soon enough. Until then, just hold tight and take care of that other mission like we asked."

"Of course. I'll get it done as quickly as possible."

"Don't forget that this is an ask from your girl, too. As of right now, you're the only person the Republic can truly count on. Oh, and make sure you remember your other role, too, yeah?"

"Remind me."

"This one's pretty urgent. Purple Ant killed a lot of spies, and all the world's intelligence agencies are shorthanded right now. As a result, everyone's sending rookies out onto the front lines. And it's flipped the world's power dynamics on their head."

".........."

"A new era's coming. A younger one."

After sharing a few other pieces of information with him, Roaring Sea left for real.

Klaus was alone now, and he went back to sipping his tea and gazing out at the night sea. A number of ferries were making the trip between Longchon Island and the mainland.

Perhaps one of those ferries was carrying his subordinates at that very moment.

"A younger era, huh?" he murmured. "I just hope they find their place in it."

Chapter 1

Encounter

A dodgy-sounding conversation was audible through the wiretap.

"...*That's right, I'm in the market for some weapons. Bare minimum, I need a thousand SMGs.*"

"*Sure, no problem. I've got the best guns money can buy.*"

"*My god...you're a lifesaver! Now we can finally make that coup happen back home.*"

"*And you'll have our full support. We stand by your revolution, one hundred percent.*"

"*Th-thank you so much! So long, weak-kneed administration; hello, glorious crusade for the motherland! Oh, I'm so glad I came to Longchon! This is the happiest day of my life!*"

A secret meeting was taking place in a private room of a Longchon restaurant. A revolutionary from a small nation that had been colonized by the Lylat Kingdom had come to Longchon and was buying up every weapon he could get his hands on so he could overthrow his government and get his people out from beneath their first-world oppressor's heel. Now a Galgad arms dealer was offering to help further his goal.

The duo's gleeful voices crackled over the wiretap. Normally, this would be the point where they successfully ended their arms deal—

"Heh, tough luck! It takes a pretty nasty spy to support a doomed coup d'état as a way to throw another nation into chaos—but while God may forgive, I sure as heck don't!"

—but unfortunately for them, there was a girl grinning proudly before the wiretap.

She had silver hair that spread out gently to the sides, a face as adorable as a child's, and a large, plump bosom. At present, she was laying her hand atop said bosom and striking a rather daunting pose. She was wearing a bright-red Ryuka dress, a traditional piece of Longchon garb that clung tightly to the skin and had slits over the thighs.

The girl spoke loud and proud. "Lily, the gorgeously beautiful genius spy disguised as a waitress, is on the case!"

Her name was "Flower Garden" Lily, and she was a spy from the Din Republic.

She thrust her finger toward the restaurant storeroom ceiling. "It's been three months since the battle in Mitario, and once we became full-fledged spies, we began accomplishing great things around the globe and rapidly improving our skills. We're not just academy washouts anymore. Now our homeland is counting on us, and we've come to Longchon to go on our biggest rampage yet!"

Nobody had asked, but she laid out their background in detail anyway—

"All right, Annette, hit me!"

—and extended her palm.

"......................................."

The ash-pink-haired girl beside her stood motionless with a shallow smile plastered on her face. She had messily tied-up hair and a large eyepatch accenting her diminutive, angelically cute features. Her name was "Forgetter" Annette.

"I'm curious, Sis! What was the point of that speech just now?"

"You know, to get us fired up."

"I feel like it was pretty pointless, yo."

"But being a spy is so *boring* if you don't get to give speeches."

Lily tried to keep chatting, but Annette cut the conversation off right then and there. Instead, she rummaged around in her skirt and fished out a small rod. "This here is Lily's Spy Tool, prototype number sixty-eight!"

At a glance, the rod looked like little more than a stick.

Lily took the rod and gave it a few swings to get a feel for it. Then she tossed it in the air like an acrobat, let it spin a couple times, and struck another pose as she caught it. "At long last, it's finally finished, huh? You've been making me custom weapons ever since our mission in Mitario, and now it's time for this one to lead us to our first major success on our mission here in Longchon."

"I'm curious, yo! What was the point of saying all that?"

"I just said! It's to get us fired up." Lily tightened her grip on her weapon and sucked in a deep breath. "Now, let's do this, Annette! It's time to go crush the enemy spy's scheme!"

After getting far more fired up than necessary, the two of them charged out of the storeroom.

Their destination was the private room where the weapons deal was going down. They'd already gathered all the necessary information, so there was no need to let their enemy roam free any longer. Their goal now was to take swift control of the situation and capture the Imperial spy.

With a cry of "Prepare yourself, bubs!" Lily announced the mission's beginning—

"Sis, the prototype explodes if you swing it too hard."
"AHHHHHHHH!"

—and three seconds later, it ended in ignoble failure.

The world was awash in pain.

Ten years had passed since the end of the Great War, the largest war in human history. Seeing its horrors had driven the world's politicians to turn to spy work rather than military might as their preferred way of influencing other countries.

Nations the world over poured resources into their intelligence agencies, leading to an age of shadow wars fought between spies.

Lamplight was a spy team that fought on behalf of the Din Republic.

They started out as a band of academy washouts, but their skills improved by leaps and bounds over the course of their training and domestic missions, and once they completed their mission in Mitario, their boss Klaus declared that they were on par with academy graduates.

At the time, the recognition of their talents had filled the girls with delight.

"Let's keep this up and become the most invincible spy team around!" Lily declared.

""""""""Yeah!"""""""" the others cheered in agreement.

From then on, the girls had headed into all their missions like they were on cloud nine. After completing that grueling operation in Mitario, they felt like could do anything.

"At this point, it feels like any mission would be a breeze!" Lily said smugly.

Over the course of the next three months, though, they gradually came to realize how far off the mark those predictions were.

As it turned out, reality was a harsh mistress.

Lamplight's base of operations sat atop a hill on Longchon Island.

The building was a vacation home owned by the president of a Din jewelry company. Its open design took full advantage of Longchon's warm climate, and the large-leafed plants placed in every room made the whole place feel like a resort. Up on the second-floor terrace, the villa had a fantastic view of the buildings by the Great Harbor.

Lamplight's boss Klaus was staying there under the guise of being a relative of the president's, and there were a variety of excuses he used when the girls needed to come up to the villa. To the general public, he probably seemed like some sort of lecherous debauchee, but he realized there was really no getting around that.

Klaus kneaded his brow in the villa's study. "You let the target get away *again*? That makes for your eighth screwup in a row."

"Yes, sir. I'm really sorry..." "We bungled it big-time, yo!"

Lily and Annette stood across from him looking thoroughly disheartened. The two of them had just managed to blow themselves up and cause a sensation at the restaurant; after causing the explosion, keeping their identities hidden had taken so much effort that their target in the private room had managed to get away.

Lily looked like she was on the verge of tears, and Annette was grinning like the whole thing was one big joke.

It was a sight that was starting to feel painfully familiar.

Klaus frowned and tapped the transceiver lying in front of him. "On a related note, I heard some nonsense over the radio about 'becoming full-fledged spies and accomplishing great things around the globe.' What was that all about?"

"I made up a story to get us fired up."

"As I recall, that's sort of the opposite of how things have actually been going down."

"C'mon, you don't have to point it out. It's embarrassing..."

"...Anyhow, I'm just glad neither of you got hurt. Go ahead and spend the day resting up."

Klaus couldn't bring himself to get mad at them, and he chose his words as gently as he could.

"Thanks a million...," Lily replied, and she and Annette left the study.

Once they were gone, Klaus heaved a sigh.

Then he turned his gaze to the girl standing beside him. "Thea, how are we doing as far as cleaning up their mess?"

"Not to worry. I have it all under control," replied the dark-haired "Dreamspeaker" Thea. Her figure was attractively curvaceous, and her black hair was long and silky. Just like Klaus, she too was staying at the villa and helping him manage the team's operations. There was a map of Longchon hanging on the study wall, and she pointed out various spots on it as she gave her sitrep. "I sent in Monika's duo, and Grete will be joining to provide further backup. That should be more than enough to handle things."

"Still, that marks the fifth time we've needed to cover for them."

"True. They might be building up stress. I'll adjust the schedule to give them time to rest."

"...Well, it's not like Lily and Annette's op is even part of the main mission. Worst-case scenario, we can always hand it off to another team. Don't let anyone push themselves too hard."

"Of course. I made sure they all understood when to pull out."

Thea rearranged the pushpins on the maps as she efficiently gave her replies.

Thea's been improving tremendously these days.

Behind her, Klaus nodded.

Thea's confidence had been at rock bottom just before the Mitario mission began, but now she was holding her head high and carefully making sure that the team's members all got to where they needed to be.

Over these past three months, her skills had progressed at a blistering pace.

As a matter of fact, she'd even started proactively giving instructions to her teammates when Klaus was absent. Her true talent was in the sheer tonnage of interpersonal communication she was able to do. By sharing intimate conversations with her allies, she could find out their hopes and mental states and use that information to efficiently allocate the team's workload. There were plenty of people in Lamplight who required a careful touch, and the fact that Thea was able to lead them so well was a testament to her talent.

"Can you blame me for trying my hardest?" Thea seemed to have sensed Klaus's gaze. She laughed. "I was barely better than dead weight for ages, so I have to make up for lost time. And besides…"

"Besides, what?"

Thea answered Klaus's question with a smile. "If I don't get even stronger, how will I be able to keep being your partner?"

That was the role Thea had told him she wanted to maintain—his partner. Her skills were still lacking in some areas, but she was definitely on the right track.

There was only one word for it.

"Magnificent."

Seeing his subordinates improve was always a wonderful experience.

At the same time, though, Klaus had worries aplenty.

I've got no problems with Thea, but aside from her…

After the showdown in Mitario, Lamplight went on to complete missions in nations the world over. To be honest, even Klaus had been optimistic. He assumed that the team's major issues were behind them, and now that the girls had improved, they wouldn't need his backup anymore.

However, he soon realized he'd given them too much credit.

Long story short, they were a mess.

Lily made blunders left and right, and Sybilla frequently forgot details about their operations. Meanwhile, each invention Annette made was more bizarre than the last, Erna managed to trip at all the worst moments, and Sara spent half her time fretting about how much danger her teammates were in. Monika and Grete were both reliable, but the two of them had to devote so much attention to backing up the others that they couldn't take full advantage of their talents.

Furthermore, Klaus found himself unable to give them anything in the way of specific guidance.

The thing was: He'd been bad at teaching from the get-go. The wisdom he had to offer them started and ended at abstract concepts like "do it correctly" and "stay in sync," and despite the girls' constant blunders, he could never manage to give them any proper advice.

As a result, the girls kept on screwing up, and Klaus was forced to step in and address their shortcomings the hard way. It never stopped.

Klaus pondered the situation and reached a conclusion.

The problem is: They've plateaued.

Even keeping up with their original training regimen hadn't given rise to any dramatic improvements. However, perhaps that was to be expected. It would have been nice if doing the same training exercises over and over had been enough for them to reach the loftiest peaks of skill, but there was obviously no way that was going to happen.

…What to do, what to do. Should I go back to handling all the missions solo like I used to…? Well, they're managing to get by, even if just barely, so should I wait and see what'll—?

As the team's boss, it was up to him to make the call.

No mission was without its danger. Should he pull them out before one of them got hurt, or considering that none of their blunders had proven truly disastrous, should he give them time to forge their skills through the course of their missions?

As he agonized over what to do, a certain someone's words flashed back through his head.

"Just barely getting by is the most dangerous thing you can do, you know."

"I tell you, Young Klaus, you're rubbish at relying on people. Now, stand back, young'un. All you're fit for doing is my chores."

The voice itself was gentle, but the way it was used was as harsh as could be.

It belonged to a member of Klaus's old team, Inferno.

"Firewalker" Gerde wasn't as kind as the team's boss, Hearth, nor did she actively guide him the way his mentor Guido did. She was simply the strictest woman around, and she'd scolded Klaus incessantly.

Every time I find myself at a loss, I appreciate Granny G's wisdom a little more.

Klaus thought about his late teammate, then shook his head.

Between that and this nasty feeling I have, I should at least start by revisiting the way I've set up our missions.

Just like that, he had his answer.

For the time being, he ought to let the girls rest.

"Thea, I want you to get the others, and—"

Right when Klaus was about to deliver his verdict, Thea beat him to the punch. "Teach, do you have a minute?" she asked.

There was a touch of panic in her voice.

"What is it?"

"Would you mind going and doing a quick check-in?" Thea looked worriedly at the clock. "Sybilla and Erna were supposed to be back by now, but they're not here…"

Something must have gone wrong.

"On it," Klaus replied succinctly as he rose to his feet.

He felt a faint chill run across his skin. His spy's intuition was warning him of danger.

Over on its mainland side, Longchon was home to a bustling cotton mill.

The mill was a massive compound filled with rows of Fend-made steam turbines that let out dull mechanical noises as they spun. Raw cotton was dirt cheap in the Ryuka cultural sphere, and it was turned into cloth in these facilities before getting shipped off to Western-Central nations. With how cheap land and labor was in that part of the world, the developed nations saw the mills as veritable money printers.

In the middle of the mill, there was an eight-story administrative building. That was where all the mill's systems were controlled from, and its towering height let it overlook the entire compound.

At the moment, there were no employees to be seen there. Not only was it a holiday, but the floors were scheduled to be waxed that evening, so even the people working through the holiday weren't doing so from the admin building itself.

Naturally, that meant that the director's office on the eighth floor was empty of workers as well. Sculptures modeled after tigers and dragons sat side by side atop its silk carpet, and a goldfish swam leisurely around in the bowl on its desk. The room was equipped with a cutting-edge security system, and without a special key, you couldn't even get in. Its bulwark of a door was the sole way in or out, and even its ventilation ducts could only be opened by manually operating them from an office down on the third floor.

Despite all that, though, a pair of girls stood in that very office.

The two of them were hard at work rummaging around and searching the room.

"Hmm, I'm not finding anything at the bottom of the goldfish bowl."

"Fool" Erna's sleeves were getting thoroughly soaked as she dug around in the fishbowl. Erna was blond and had skin as fair and delicate as a doll's.

"Nothin' by this wooden tiger, either. Where the hell's that classified document?" replied "Pandemonium" Sybilla. She had a sharp look in her eyes and muscles as toned as a wild animal's.

It probably goes without saying, but the two of them were in the middle of a mission.

The Din embassy had conducted an investigation into the colonial situation in Longchon, but the report had been leaked, and when one of their diplomats tried to figure out who had gotten ahold of it, he was assassinated for his troubles. Lamplight had been dispatched to pick up where he left off, and at present, they were infiltrating the mill's admin building to try to pin down the document's location.

After a whole lot of careful prep work, the girls had successfully breached the security system of the director's office. No matter how hard they searched the room, though, the crucial document was nowhere to be found.

Sybilla kicked the wooden tiger statue in frustration and clutched her head. "AHHHHH! Why can't we find this goddamn thing?!"

"Yeep! The goldfish bowl toppled over!"

"Shit, sorry for spookin' you... Aw, crap! The carpet's soaked!"

"Wh-what should I do about the little fishy?"

"M-move it to another tank! Quick!"

Things weren't going too hot for them.

After rescuing the goldfish, the two let out heavy sighs.

The carpet was drenched, and the goldfish bowl had lost much of its water. So much for keeping their break-in a secret.

"Well, we can at least dry the carpet out," Sybilla muttered as she opened the office's curtains. She would've liked to open the windows as well, but they were fixed shut. The office's security really was top-notch.

When she saw the light of the setting sun, it suddenly struck her just how much time had passed. It was going to be evening soon, and that was when the janitors were going to come in to wax the floors.

Sybilla planted her hands on her waist.

Things just keep on goin' south lately, huh?

She, too, had noticed the slump that Lamplight was in. Their missions just kept refusing to go smoothly. It was like the team's gears were out of sync or something. They kept on screwing up, and their big victory in Mitario was starting to feel like a distant memory.

Where does it keep goin' wrong? I'm tryin' my best out here...

It wasn't like she was being negligent about her training or anything, either. The constant missions were putting a strain on her schedule, but she was still keeping up with her independent training, and she was making sure to regularly attack Klaus, too.

When it came to actual missions, though, she just couldn't stop screwing up.

She clapped herself on the cheeks.

Welp, no point worryin' about all that in here. Right now, I gotta act.

She quickly shifted back to her usual positive mindset.

"C'mon, Erna, let's retreat downstairs for a bit. We'll fall back to the seventh floor, and once the janitors finish waxing floor eight, we'll come back up. Don't worry. We'll get through this."

".."

Erna was holding the bowl she'd transferred the goldfish to with her head hung low.

"Erna, you with me?" Sybilla asked.

"Yeep!" Erna flinched. "R-right. We should start by escaping."

She set down the bowl and hurried over to Sybilla.

"What's wrong? You tired?" Sybilla patted Erna's head. "We can take a quick breather in the room next door first, if you want. We've got some time before the wax folks get started."

Erna nodded. "...Yeah. That'd be nice."

If they rushed out carelessly, they ran the risk of bumping into the janitors.

Once they discreetly left the director's office, Sybilla shut the door behind them, taking care not to let it make a sound.

Erna audibly gulped.

Just like they'd feared, the janitors were already on-site. A man and a woman in cleaning uniforms were coming up the stairs with equipment in tow. Apparently, they were planning on starting from the top floor and working their way down.

Sybilla and Erna quickly headed away from the director's office and took refuge in the nearby storeroom. Once they got there, they took a short break. Erna settled herself down on the floor and began taking deep breaths. All their recent failures were starting to wear her down. After taking all the time they needed, the two of them waited for the perfect moment to emerge.

Eventually, they slipped out and quietly headed to the back end of the building.

An emergency exit sat at the end of the hallway. It was connected to the building's external emergency stairs. Anyone outside would have been able to see them as plain as day, but using it to go down just a single floor seemed safe enough.

Sybilla and Erna exchanged a silent nod, then stepped out into the emergency staircase.

An alarm began ringing.

"Yeep?" "What?!"

Their eyes went wide.

A shrill alarm was going off and buzzing through the entire admin building. It wasn't clear if someone had seen them and set it off, or if the emergency stairs had been booby-trapped.

Why...?! Why'd it go off just now?

Something unforeseen had happened. That much was clear.

Sybilla clicked her tongue, and the two of them went back inside. Every pair of eyes in the mill would be on the admin building right now. The stairs were too exposed to use.

They could hear the sound of people starting to gather on the lower floors.

"L-let's head back to the director's office for now!"

The suggestion came from Erna.

"Why there?" Sybilla asked.

"Because the normal employees won't be able to get in!"

It was a logical decision.

The director's office was heavily secured, and nobody but the director and his secretary could get in. Given that they had nowhere to run, hiding out in the director's office for the time being was the best option available to them.

Erna rushed off.

"Right." Sybilla nodded and followed after her.

As the sound of the employees coming toward the eighth floor grew ever louder, Erna reached the director's office, re-disabled the security, and opened the door.

The two of them stepped forward to go in—

"Hold up!"

—but then Erna screamed.

"Huh?" Sybilla grunted.

The moment Sybilla tried to step inside, Erna yanked on her jacket. Sybilla reacted instantly and leaped backward, and Erna followed up by throwing herself on top of Sybilla to protect her.

A fiery explosion blasted forth.

Flames burst out from inside the director's office and sprayed fire out into the hallway. It wasn't the kind of fire that destroyed everything in its path, but it was still fierce enough. The hallway was smothered in red.

The Lamplight duo had just barely managed to dodge it, but if they'd taken a direct hit, they probably wouldn't have survived.

What's up with the fire? We disabled all the traps, so why...?

Questions swirled through Sybilla's head as she sat on her rump.

Once again, something had gone wrong in a wholly unexpected way.

The one silver lining was that the building was made of reinforced concrete, so they weren't in any danger of having the whole thing go up in flames. The fire seemed to be contained to the carpet inside the director's office.

Suddenly, Sybilla let out a gasp. "Erna, you okay? Erna?!"

Beside her, Erna was collapsed on the ground with her face contorted in pain. She was clutching her upper arm like it was burned, and she must have hit her head during her fall, too, as there was blood trickling down her forehead.

Erna let out a hoarse, unintelligible moan. Then her body went limp. Sybilla tried calling her name again and again, but she got no reply. Even when she shook Erna's body, her teammate's lips didn't move.

Erna was unconscious.

Sybilla frantically checked to make sure she was breathing. Erna's small chest was rising and falling; she was alive. However, Sybilla needed to get her somewhere safe, and she needed to do it now.

All the while, the employees' footsteps just kept on getting closer. After hearing the fiery explosion just now, they knew that something was wrong. A group of men were shouting angrily.

Sybilla was in big trouble.

The employees were gathering in the eighth-floor hallway, she had nowhere to run, and her partner was lying unconscious beside her.

"Sorry, Erna," Sybilla said to her sleeping teammate. "This is gonna be bumpy. Hope you don't mind."

As the words left her mouth, she picked up Erna and hoisted her onto her back. Then, while carrying her teammate, Sybilla crouched down and lowered her center of gravity.

Getting out was going to require taking some risks.

Realizing that, Sybilla *kicked in the hallway window.*

Then, in the same motion, she leaped out the eighth-story window—with Erna still on her back.

She knew that someone might spot them, but getting her teammate to safety was priority number one. Now she was going to have to perform a technique she'd never even practiced and nail it on the first try.

Let's hope this top-story dive thing works!

It was a trick she never would have even considered using if it weren't such an emergency, especially not when it was going to endanger one of her teammates' lives on top of her own. By pushing her body to its limit, she was able to spin around in midair and fire a wire out from her wrist just before they started falling in earnest. The wire hooked around one of the building's external drainpipes and killed her downward momentum.

The idea was that she would act like a pendulum. By shifting her trajectory from "falling" to "swinging," she could avoid having them become smears on the pavement. However, that was precisely what was about to happen if Sybilla had made even the slightest of errors in the timing or length of her wire. Her body traced an arc through the air so forcefully it felt like it was going to tear her apart, and she could feel the air being squeezed from her lungs.

As the ground rose up to meet her, a terrible chill ran through her body.

A moment before impact, though, Sybilla rose back up into the air. The tips of Erna's hair scraped against the ground.

Sybilla continued swinging back and forth until the pendulum motion had killed enough of their momentum to leave them dangling in the air. After safely landing back on solid ground, she let out a massive sigh of relief.

Looks like I pulled it off...

Then she took off across the facility so the other employees wouldn't find them. She headed toward the edge of the premises, scaled the fence, and went into the alley across the street. The alley was about ten feet wide and flanked on both sides by tall buildings. Once she got there, Sybilla looked over her shoulder and gave Erna a smile. "That should be far enough, yeah?" Sadly, she got no reply.

As Sybilla caught her breath amid the darkness, she was greeted by an unexpected duo.

"I'm here to save you, yo!" "Hey, hey, hey! I filled up on sweets, so my head's back in the game."

It was Annette and Lily. They came rushing over from the other side of the alley.

When Sybilla and Erna didn't return when they were supposed to, the others had gotten worried and come to help.

"...Y'know, I could've sworn I just saw an orangutan leap off an eight-story building and use trapeze artist tricks to stick the landing," Lily said.

"Oh, shaddap," Sybilla shot back. "This is no time for your nonsense. Hurry up and get Erna some first aid."

"Wait, Erna's hurt?"

"Yeah, she's out like a light. We need to patch her up and get her somewhere safe, pronto."

"I brought a first aid kit!" Annette piped up. She shook her skirt, and tons of bandages, disinfectant, and the like came pouring out.

Lily and Sybilla quickly got to work treating Erna. By the time they were done sloppily winding the bandages around her head, her forehead looked like a large, misshapen lump.

Their intention was to carry Erna off to their base posthaste—

"Don't move an inch, *ladies*."

—but as it turned out, they weren't out of the woods just yet.

All of a sudden, a new person showed up in the alleyway.

Sybilla whirled around.

Over in the direction of the mill, there was a man wearing a janitor uniform. He'd appeared so suddenly and with so little warning that it was almost like he'd materialized out of thin air. The girls had been preoccupied, but even so, that wasn't the kind of thing that happened every day.

Sybilla recognized his face, and the smell of wax coming from the mop resting atop his shoulder was a familiar one as well.

Huh? The janitor who was just in the admin building...? Why'd he follow us?

"Who are you people?" the young man asked threateningly. He had short brown hair and looked to be in his early twenties. His dark, gloomy gaze was fixed right on them.

Sybilla was the first to react. She closed in on the man so fast and so hard her foot left an imprint on the ground. She didn't know what he was after, but the safest thing to do was to start by overpowering him. After closing the gap faster than he could possibly react, she pressed her knife against his throat. "Sorry about this, but we're on the clock, too," she said in a menacing tone.

The man said nothing, but his eyes widened a little.

"That was quick, Sis," Annette said, sounding audibly impressed.

Sybilla had demonstrated it in her escape, too, but her athletic abilities had improved even more over the past three months. In any sort of one-on-one fight, there wasn't an amateur around who could hold a candle to her.

"Don't scream," she said, still holding her knife against the man's throat. "I don't wanna have to hurt a civvy, so this is what you're gonna do. You're not gonna report this to anyone. You're not even gonna tell anyone. In fact, just forget this ever happened. If you can promise me that, I'll let you go. We cool?"

"................"

The man dispassionately returned Sybilla's gaze, offering her little in the way of a reaction.

Sybilla tilted her head in confusion. She'd been expecting him to be scared or to start tearing up. "...What? At least say *somethin'*."

His stare remained just as apathetic, and his entire body was slack. He didn't seem tense in the slightest. It was the way you'd expect someone to act if they were watching a play that bored them.

Did he not understand the situation he was in?

"Maybe your face is so scary he can't work up the nerve to reply?" Lily quietly offered.

Sybilla didn't love the way she'd phrased it, but Lily's theory had some merit. "I mean, we *are* kinda the bad guys here. Sorry for gettin' you caught up in our shit. Still, I hope we can count on you."

She smiled and slipped a coin into the man's pocket as compensation for his troubles.

"This is insipid."

As the unsettling voice echoed out, the janitor bent back.

After dropping himself backward to escape from Sybilla's knife, he leaped into the air with his body still tilted and launched a football-style bicycle kick at the side of Sybilla's head.

He had started resisting completely out of the blue, and what's more, he'd chosen an incredibly acrobatic way to do so. "You little shit," Sybilla grunted, then got to work trying to pin the man down. As she did, Lily charged forward with a poison needle, and Annette leaped in with her stun gun.

They were attacking him from three directions at once, and the janitor was still in midair. There was no way he could dodge—or at least, there shouldn't have been.

"I'm code name Flock—and it's time to gouge clean through."

The janitor's self-introduction echoed in their ears.

He slammed his mop into the ground like a cane, then turned aside in midair and nimbly avoided the three-pronged attack. It was a feat that had required incredible core strength.

As he spun, a shower of knives came pouring off of his body. Sensing danger, the girls retreated—at which point, they all slipped and fell.

Sybilla's eyes went wide. *Wax?!*

The man had spread it from the mop he was carrying.

From there, the rest happened in a flash.

As soon as the man landed, he leaped into the air again. It was like watching a spring. By using both hands and taking advantage of his long reach, he was able to utilize his knives to pin the off-balance girls to the ground by their clothes. He was so fast they got crucified before they ever had a chance to dodge.

Sybilla was powerless to do anything but gawk as she collapsed onto the ground.

Beside her, Lily's eyes were wide. "Wh—?"

They'd been completely physically overpowered. Despite their numerical advantage, they'd gotten manhandled. The girls had been just a tiny bit careless, and the man had taken full advantage of it.

He shot the three of them a pointed glare as they lay on the ground. "You people are obnoxious. Maybe the world could use fewer of you."

In his hand, he was holding a knife.

He turned its blade toward Sybilla.

"Let's start with you."

Without a moment's hesitation, he swung his knife down at her.

"Vindo, wait!"

The knife froze right before it reached Sybilla's throat.

She broke into a cold sweat. What she'd just experienced was the unmistakable specter of death.

Her heart was pounding out of her chest.

If this guy wanted to—

She could picture it clear as day.

—he coulda killed me. Right there, right then.

Her knees rattled. Even so, she looked up to survey the situation.

Someone else had just joined them in the alley.

The newcomer was a young woman with large glasses. Her jade green hair was done up in a ponytail, and the look on her face was willful and determined. She was the other janitor from back in the admin area.

"Those girls aren't our enemies," she snapped. "We're on the same side."

"Oh? Are we, now?" The young man named Vindo frowned. "This is even more insipid." He stowed his knife away.

The jade-haired girl let out a deep sigh, like the air was pouring out from the very bottom of her lungs. "Oh, thank goodness you stopped in time... You nearly stabbed one of our own allies, you know that?"

Vindo gave the woman a cold look. "Shut up, Qulle. Even if you hadn't stepped in, I would've stopped anyway."

"Huh?"

"Up above. You shouldn't need me to point out these things."

Sybilla followed Vindo's lead and looked at the building's roof.

Klaus was standing atop it.

He was holding a gun in one hand and a knife in the other. His long hair was tied back, and he was gazing down at them ready for war. Sybilla gasped. So did everyone else, Vindo included.

The air was heavy with raw hostility.

The young woman named Qulle let out a small shriek and shrank back a step.

If Klaus wanted to, he could've had everyone there dead and gone within seconds.

"I recognize that guy... So that's Bonfire, huh?"

The only person feeling uncowed by Klaus's hostility was Vindo, who glowered back boldly.

Klaus leaped off the roof and landed soundlessly beside Sybilla. The building was five stories tall, but he didn't so much as wince. After a short silence, he turned his gaze toward Vindo. "It would seem I don't need to introduce myself."

"No. I know you by name, if nothing else," Vindo replied curtly. "I'm code name Flock, alias Vindo."

"I see. And you?"

"Y-yeek! I—I, um, I'm G-Glide. My alias is Qulle."

The girl who'd introduced herself as Qulle gave Klaus a nervous bow.

"Let's split up for now," Klaus said calmly. "It's not secure here."

"Roger that," Vindo replied. He took his mop and headed back to the admin building with Qulle.

"""" .... """"

The girls could do nothing but stare as they found themselves completely left in the dust.

It would appear that they were safe now, but they still had no idea who that duo actually was. However, it seemed like Klaus knew something...

Sybilla decided to be the one to ask. "Who the hell were they?"

"Allies. Fellow spies from the Din Republic," Klaus promptly replied.

Then he followed up with a piece of info that came as a shock to all of them.

"They took the top six students out of all the spy academies and made them into a new team called Avian."

Roaring Sea had already told Klaus all about Avian.

For a time after Klaus's mentor, "Torchlight" Guido, betrayed them, the Din Republic's spy network lay in shambles. Guido was more than just your ordinary spy, and when he double-crossed Din and joined the

Galgad Empire, he brought massive amounts of intel on the Republic along with him.

As a spy, having your information leaked like that meant constant peril.

Guido's betrayal was like something out of the Republic's worst nightmares. After he handed intel on their best spies over to the enemy, many people perished. It wasn't just Inferno; the Republic lost a huge number of other valuable personnel, as well. And the spies they sent in to stem the bleeding all had their information leaked, too. It was looking like checkmate.

The only reason they were able to recover—

"Well, there's two reasons. One was the fine work you did, Bonfire. The way you put together Lamplight and beautifully filled Inferno's shoes was like a ray of light in the midst of our darkest despair," Roaring Sea had explained. "And the other was the way the cream of the crop from our academies really stepped up."

The Republic had been faced with an unprecedented crisis, and they'd reacted by hurriedly sending academy students to the front lines. Klaus had been concerned that high-performing students would have had their information leaked, too, so he chose to build Lamplight out of washouts and get results that way. But all the while, the top students were taking their graduation exams and heading into battle as well. The logic was that not even Guido could have memorized full dossiers on *every* promising student.

"Not all the newbies succeeded, of course. Guido leaked intel on a fair chunk of them. A *lot* of them didn't make it. But there was one team that kept putting up outstanding results one after another, almost like they were trying to get revenge for their comrades who weren't so lucky. And that team was Avian."

It was Klaus's first time hearing the name, but he assumed they were a recently formed spy team.

"I'm telling you, these guys are the real deal. We've got over three thousand academy students, and after Inferno went down, we took all the best ones and put them through a graduation exam. Avian is a dream team made up of the top six scorers."

"The best six out of a field of three thousand, hmm?"

"They've already got a pretty hefty backlog of finished missions under their belt. We haven't been giving them any of the real gnarly ones yet..." Roaring Sea sounded like she was enjoying herself. "...but as far as their raw count goes, Avian's got Lamplight beat."

The group carried Erna to Klaus's base.

They immediately called for a local doctor, who told them that she would wake up just fine after she got some rest. At the moment, Erna hadn't regained consciousness yet and was sleeping in one of the beds. Every so often, she let out a pained-sounding groan. Aside from her burns, she'd also suffered a concussion when she fell over. That said, it came as a huge relief to the Lamplight members to know that her life wasn't in danger.

After all the others left, Sybilla stayed right by Erna's side.

"I'm sorry, Erna. I screwed up, bad..."

She mopped away the sweat running across Erna's forehead. After offering that brief apology, she stood up from the bed. Her stomach was rumbling something fierce. She still felt like shit, but hunger was calling to her all the same.

The sun had already set, and it was just about dinnertime.

"So basically, the two teams' missions ended up overlapping?"

Over in the combination kitchen–dining room, Lily was getting a sitrep.

The eight-seat table was piled high with all sorts of Ryukese takeout. There was roast chicken, *gyoza*, boiled prawns, five-color *xiaolongbao*, and peach *manju*. Every dish looked delicious.

All of it was leftovers from the restaurant Lily had infiltrated. If there was one thing she took seriously, it was getting her hands on grub.

Thea, Lily, and Annette were already at the table, and Sybilla went over to join them.

"Apparently, yes," Thea explained. She delicately peeled the shell off one of her prawns. "Avian and Lamplight were going after different targets, but we ended up in the same place. These things are rare, but they do happen."

"Hmph. For spies who hog all their intel to themselves, sure," Lily said, stuffing her face full of *xiaolongbao*.

Annette bit into a peach *manju*. "I think it'd be better if we all just shared our info, yo."

Thea nodded. "You're right. And over in the study, that's precisely what Teach is coordinating."

The girls turned their gazes toward the study.

Vindo and Qulle had stopped by the villa not long ago, and that was where they were now. Instead of their janitor outfits, they were wearing school uniforms. Their cover story was that they were exchange students who'd come to Longchon on a study abroad program.

At the moment, Avian and Lamplight were probably sharing all sorts of information.

"Sheesh, man..." Sybilla let out a dejected sigh. "I mean, the top six academy students?"

"You can say that again," Thea agreed, looking just as glum.

Klaus had already given them the basic rundown on Avian. Word was, they were the elite of the elite from the academies.

"Rrrrrrrrrrrrrrrrrgh!" All of a sudden, Lily began writhing in agony. "All sorts of horrible memories are resurfaciiiiiiiiiiing!"

A pained expression crossed her face, and she wasn't the only one. Sybilla and Thea were in the same boat. All of a sudden, they lost their appetites. The only person unaffected was Annette, who was happily stacking the peach *manju* on top of each other.

Lamplight was the exact opposite of Avian—they were a team made up of academy washouts. For a variety of reasons—poor grades, interpersonal problems, bad behavior, individual setbacks—each person in Lamplight had failed to thrive in the academy environment. The whole roster had been on the verge of dropping out.

"Yeah, that dredges up a whole bunch of nasty memories," Sybilla muttered.

"Oh, I feel you," Thea agreed. "To be frank, the experience left me traumatized. I had hoped to leave the whole thing behind me."

"Plus, runnin' into them when things haven't been goin' too hot for us just makes it feel that much worse," Sybilla added.

""How unlucky..."" They all sighed in perfect unison.

A heavy silence descended on the table.

The sound of the ceiling fan's motor echoed lifelessly through the room.

"H-hey, look on the bright side!" With that, Lily rose to her feet. "W-we've changed since our academy days! You're looking at Super-Agent Lily, a girl who's trained with Teach and completed Impossible Missions!"

"Y-yeah... Yeah, that's a good point." Spurred on by Lily's enthusiasm, Sybilla stood up a few beats after her. "Hell yeah! Lily's right. All that washout stuff is in the past! Hell, our own boss told us about how academy success is too narrow to judge someone's worth off of!"

The other two stood up as well.

"Wh-why, I'm a perfect example of that," Thea said. "After all, I wasn't being graded fairly on my merits!"

"And those stupid instructors treated all my awesome inventions like garbage, yo!" Annette agreed.

It sure felt like they were putting on a show of false bravado, but they all began raising their voices. Once they had themselves well and truly pumped up, Lily broke into a shout. "We'll never give up our jobs to a bunch of a highfalutin elites! If Avian wants to bring it, then I say let's let 'em!"

"""Yeahhhhhhhhh!"""

They raised their fists in the air with great gusto.

"I see the ladies of Lamplight are in a good mood."

A deep voice echoed from behind them.

The girls didn't like where this was going. They whirled around to find Vindo, who was looking at them coldly, and Qulle, who chuckled awkwardly. "Ha-ha-ha..."

The discussion in the study had reached its conclusion.

Vindo stood there with both hands in his pockets and laid on the pressure. "So what was that about Avian? You got something you want to say? Come on, let's hear that shout again."

"""" .... """""

Now that they were face-to-face with the real deal, the girls shut up in a hurry. Their expressions froze.

Eventually, Lily was the first to turn traitor. "I think *Sybilla* had something she wanted to say." "Th-that's right," Thea agreed, and Annette lit the fuse even further. "Go on, Sis, tell them all those horrible things you said."

Sybilla glared at her teammates. "You're all dead to me."

"Do at least try to comport yourselves with dignity." At that point, Klaus arrived in the kitchen–dining room as well. "I just got finished making arrangements with Avian. While we're in Longchon, our team and theirs are going to be completing our missions together. Don't go getting territorial on them."

Qulle gave them a wave. "I'm looking forward to working together."

Vindo said nothing.

The Lamplight girls' faces flushed red, and they bowed in return.

"Huh? Wait a sec," Sybilla said. "What're you two doin' here yourselves? For stuff like this, wouldn't it make more sense to have the two team's bosses hash it out?"

"Normally, yes," Klaus said. "In this case, though—"

"I wanted to see it with my own two eyes," Vindo said, cutting him off. "I'd heard the rumors here and there. About a team of academy washouts who completed an Impossible Mission. At first, I thought it was just misinformation the instructors spread to get us fired up."

There was an unusually intimidating air to Vindo's voice. He closed in on the girls one step at a time until he was right in front of their faces. His razor-sharp gaze seemed to be appraising them as well. The girls let out small whimpers.

"Are the stories true? Did you really finish an Impossible Mission?"

"...Y-yeah. Yeah, that's right." The reply came from Lily. She was sweating bullets, but she threw out her chest all the same. "We completed a couple. And hoo boy, we had to fight some nasty battles. Especially that infiltration mission in Galgad. If not for our flawless teamwork, we never would've been able to—"

"In the state you're in?" Vindo's voice was as cold as ice.

Lily grimaced and went quiet.

Vindo turned away as though to say he had no more use for them now that he'd gotten his answer. He turned toward Klaus, his hands never once leaving his pockets. "Bonfire, I want in on the mission tonight. That good with you?"

"Be my guest."

"I appreciate it. I'll be there at the time we discussed."

Now that his business there was done, Vindo headed briskly for the entrance. He paid the Lamplight girls no further heed.

Qulle hurried after him, apologetically pressing her hands together. "Er, sorry about that. Vindo can be a bit much sometimes," she said as she headed out, too.

A series of mixed feelings welled up within the girls as they stared at the door the pair had left through.

"Th-that guy was kinda scary...," Lily murmured.

"F-for sure," Sybilla agreed.

Vindo was intense in a whole different way than the other spies they'd met to date. There had been overachievers at the girls' academies too, of course, but even compared to them, there was something special about Vindo. For one, none of the overachievers the girls could think of had been anywhere near that unfriendly.

"He has the mindset of a professional," Klaus said. "Perhaps too much so, but staying vigilant is never a bad thing. Perhaps you all should consider taking a page from his book. Tonight we'll be starting our joint mission with Avian. Sybilla, get prepped—and make it quick. Lily will be providing you with backup in Erna's place."

"Huh?" "What?"

Sybilla's and Lily's eyes went wide at the unexpected assignment.

"No matter what happens, the mission goes on," Klaus told them firmly. "I've got another job I need to take care of tonight, so I'm counting on you two. I wrote notes with some advice for you, just in case."

"O-okay." "Y-you got it..."

Hearing Klaus's calm voice helped bring the girls back to their senses. He was right; they were still in the middle of a mission. This was no time to be shuddering over recollections of past academy traumas.

"Feels like nothing ever breaks your focus, huh, Teach?" Lily noted.

"Of course not. I'm a professional," Klaus replied.

He handed them each a folded piece of paper. Therein lay the advice he had for his two floundering pupils.

They unfolded their papers and found short messages written in awful handwriting.

Pilfer as a rainbow does when crossing the moon.

Be like the full moon and be your full self.

For some reason, Klaus looked terribly proud of himself. "Because I'm a professional, all you have to do is follow my advice, and you too will be able to—"

"Your instructions aren't professional for shit!" Sybilla roared.

A few hours later, Sybilla and Lily stood in front of the cotton mill once more.

It was already past ten PM, but the mill was still chugging away. Muffled noises echoed across the grounds, and though more than half the lights in the admin building were off, a couple of the rooms were still lit and occupied. Some of the employees were pulling all-nighters. The girls had heard stories about how abusive the management practices there were.

Lily turned to the person walking beside them. "So how much does Avian know about what's really going on in the mill?"

"Everything," Vindo replied concisely. He was back to wearing his cleaner's uniform.

He'd infiltrated the admin building a couple weeks ago by getting a part-time job there as a janitor. Thanks to his guidance, Sybilla and Lily had been able to enter the premises without running into any trouble.

The two of them continued following Vindo across the mill. All they were doing was walking straight through the darkness, but for whatever reason, nobody was crossing their path.

Notably, Qulle was operating separately at the moment. Sybilla, Lily, and Vindo were the only ones on the infiltration op.

"The mill is secretly backed by the local mafia. Here in Longchon, everyone knows that information is worth its weight in gold. The mafia bribes foreign diplomats for intel, then sells it to the highest bidder. They're basically information brokers. And this cotton mill is one of their fronts."

Much to the girls' surprise, Vindo dutifully explained the situation. He might not have been the friendliest guy around, but he did an excellent job laying out the information they needed to know.

"This area is their home turf, and they have eyes all around the city. Even just trying to tail someone here can prove fatal. We can assume that the classified document you were after has already been moved off-site."

"Yeah, I figured as much. So how're we gonna play this?" Sybilla asked. "You got some idea of how we're supposed to track down the new location? Honestly, I dunno who we'd even need to shake down to find out where it is."

"...You have a point. They've ratcheted up security on account of the commotion you kicked up. Now *our* carefully orchestrated plan is useless."

"Urk. Sorry about that..."

"We're going to have to get a little crude. We did have a plan for this eventuality."

During their conversation, they'd made it all the way to the base of the admin building.

Vindo casually picked up a rock about the size of his fist from the ground, then muttered something. "...By the way, what happened to the blond?"

"Huh?"

"You know, the kid. The one you were carrying."

Vindo stared at Sybilla. His face betrayed no emotions, but from the sound of it, he was worried about Erna.

"She got knocked out during our mission, so she's resting now. Some sort of explosion went off in the director's office... Come to think of it, what was that? Did you guys lay some kind of trap?" Sybilla asked.

"...No, I don't know anything about that. Must've been something else."

There was an odd pause before he gave his answer. Sybilla didn't know what to make of it.

Vindo turned the rock over in his hand and inspected its shape. "Still, I get where you stand. I'll handle your missing blond's part."

As soon as the words left his mouth, he hurled the rock through one of the admin building's windows.

Sybilla and Lily stared at him in shock. ""?!""

The hell does this guy think he's doin'?!

The window shattered, and unsurprisingly, an alarm bell began loudly ringing. They could hear the roar of sirens and the footsteps of guards rushing their way.

"Keep your cool. The enemy won't kill us; not before they get us to sing." Vindo remained utterly composed under the girls' aghast stares. "Just keep your mouths shut—and watch how we do things in Avian."

His voice carried an unsettling degree of confidence.

The guards rushed over and captured the three of them just the way Vindo had planned. The worst-case scenario would have been if the guards took them straight to the police, but they chose to haul them into the admin building instead.

Sybilla hadn't noticed until she saw them up close, but it was obvious just from looking at the cotton mill's guards that they didn't exactly live on the straight and narrow. They certainly looked the part of mafia underlings, and they each had a pistol hidden in their pocket.

After tying the spy trio's hands behind their backs with rope, the guards took the three of them to a room inside the building.

"Is this...?" Lily whispered. "Is this the director's office?"

Sure enough, the three of them found themselves getting shoved into the same office from that afternoon. Its carpet and many of its sculptures had been burned to a crisp, and the air was thick with the smell of charcoal. That said, the room had been given a cursory cleaning, and everything in the middle of the room had been completely cleared out.

Vindo looked unconcerned. This is where he'd expected the guards to bring them.

Ah, that makes sense, Sybilla thought.

With how intense the director's office's security system was, it was pretty much completely sealed off from the outside world. None of the factory workers would be coming near it, and no matter how much they screamed, none of it would be audible from outside. It was the perfect place to use as a torture chamber. The goons here didn't want to get the cops involved; they wanted to interrogate Vindo and the girls themselves.

The guards threw them roughly onto the floor.

There were ten men standing in the room, several of whom were sporting sadistic grins. It was clear to see how thrilled they were at having successfully captured their prey.

Eventually, the clicking of high heels echoed out, and a woman strode forth from among the men.

"I never imagined we'd end up reeling in a couple of youngsters like you."

Sybilla recognized her; she was the mill's executive secretary. The young woman was wearing a tight suit and had that particular air about her exclusive to those who operated in the world of violence. Now there was really no doubt about how deep the mill's ties to the local mafia ran.

Vindo closed his eyes as though he was bored out of his mind.

"........."

"I take it you're the leader of this merry little bunch?" The secretary laughed in amusement. "Tell me, are you kids the ones who started that fire in the office earlier today? Do tell. And I must say, dressing as a janitor was an unexpected touch. Who are you working for?"

Vindo didn't open his eyes. "You really think I'd tell you?"

"Oh dear, I'm afraid that's the wrong attitude to take with me. Tight-lipped spies have a habit of dying in this room."

As she spoke, one of her henchmen stepped forward holding an iron whip. He started by punching Vindo in the head, then began showering him with blows. Again and again and again the iron lumps slammed into Vindo's body, and with each strike, the dull sound of metal striking bone echoed through the room.

Eventually, the man with the whip stopped to give his arm a break.

Sybilla and Lily could do nothing but stare speechlessly. Intentionally letting themselves get captured was feeling like a worse idea by the minute.

"Did he go overboard, I wonder?" the woman said, sounding rather satisfied. "That might have been too much. Was it too much? Though, I suppose even if worse comes to worst, and the man dies, we still have the two girls to get answers out of—"

"This is insipid. Not that I'm surprised." Vindo sat up.

The men surrounding him let out shocked gasps.

With his hands still bound, Vindo rose to his feet. His balance didn't seem hindered in the slightest, and for that matter, there wasn't a wound visible on his body. He looked calm and collected.

The secretary's shock was evident in her voice. "...How can you be uninjured after taking all those blows?"

Sybilla was familiar with the technique, as Klaus had used it on numerous occasions. There was a way to ward off attacks that made it look like you were still being hit even though you weren't taking any real damage. However, she'd never seen it performed with anything close to the finesse Vindo had just shown.

"I had hoped to hold out for a bigger player, but I guess you're the best I'm going to get." Vindo let out a small sigh. "What a buzzkill. Well, consider it an honor. Not many people of your ilk get to hit me like that."

"What are you babbling on about—?"

"By the way," Vindo said, "haven't you noticed how hot it's getting in here?"

Suddenly, they heard a woman shouting. "Fire! There's a fire coming this way!"

One of the henchmen dashed out of the room. "It's true! The building's burning!" he reported.

The mafia members in the director's office froze. They were panicking. The sudden emergency left them with too many factors they needed to consider—Did they need to evacuate? Should they go ahead and kill the captured spies now?—and their minds turned as fast as they could.

A mocking comment rose up to fill the void. "This is even more insipid."

It was Vindo.

"I'm code name Flock—and it's time to gouge clean through."

Even with his hands still bound, his body rose into the air as though unrestrained by gravity.

Blood went flying.

The first person he slashed was the grunt with the iron whip. The man let out a dumbfounded gasp as the concealed knife in Vindo's shoe tore through his throat.

It was Sybilla's second time seeing Vindo pull that stunt. He was using his entire body like a spring, and no matter what position he was in, his raw arm and leg strength always seemed to be sufficient to propel him off the ground so he could send knives soaring through the air. That was the power of the man who'd dominated the academy student rankings—paired with beautiful knife work, he executed movements too unpredictable to even illicit a reaction from anyone!

In the blink of an eye, Vindo cut down two more men who'd been standing near him. At some point, he'd also found the time to undo his restraints. The next time he jumped, it was to thrust a knife into the heart of another foe, and by the time one of the other goons drew his gun to take advantage of how open Vindo was in the air, Vindo had already used his latest corpse as a springboard to relocate to safety.

His jumping was giving him and his knives free rein over the entire director's office.

"R-run for it!" someone shouted. "If we stay here, we'll just burn to death either way!"

With that, the dam broke, and the full cohort that had been in the office flooded out the door.

Lily had been a little late to the party in undoing her restraints, but now she was free, too. "You ain't goin' nowhere," she declared as she drew her gun.

"Don't bother, Silver." However, Vindo stopped her before she could give chase. "Those guys are idiots. They've already forgotten who applied the wax this afternoon."

Suddenly, the sound of air bursting exploded in from the hallway, followed by the sound of the men screaming.

Sybilla could hear them being burned alive.

Now it all made sense. Vindo's plan had revolved around that fire from the get-go. By mixing chemicals into the flammable wax, he'd basically created a fuse for the fire to follow. Qulle was probably the one who'd started it. Come to think of it, that first person who shouted "Fire!" had sounded an awful lot like her.

As it so happened, the three of them and the secretary were now the only ones left in the office.

Vindo twirled a knife in his hand. "Now it's just you."

"Th-this is insane..." The secretary sank to her knees. "You can all burn... At least you're going down with me..."

"This office is treated to be fire-resistant, and the fire is following a prearranged path. It'll take a while before the carbon monoxide poisoning does us in."

"Ulp..."

"You have to know where that classified document got to. Tell me, and I'll spare your life."

The secretary bit down on her lip, but eventually, she made up her mind. "...Fine." She told them where the document was. Her fear drove her to speak quickly, and in the end, she even told them where the mafia boss's hideout was. "...That's everything I know," she whimpered.

"Got it. Then we're done here." Vindo readied his knife.

"Huh?"

"You actually thought I was going to let you live?" Vindo said dispassionately as he raised the knife aloft. "Two months ago, your men killed a good woman. She was protecting an innocent kid, and they shot her dead. I'll have to live with that regret for the rest of my life."

"Wait!" the secretary screamed. "I have a son and two daughters waiting for—"

"Maybe you'll find dignity in death."

Vindo swung his arm down and hurled the knife straight into the secretary's throat. Her eyes went wide, and after convulsing for a bit, she crumpled lifelessly to the ground.

All Sybilla and Lily could do was watch it play out from the side.

Between his infiltration technique, his physical abilities, his calculations, and his cold resolve, Vindo had pulled it off perfectly. He'd tracked down the document's location, and everyone who'd seen their faces was dead. Vindo had told the two of them to "watch how Avian did things," and sure enough, he'd put on a stunningly efficient master class.

It was early in the morning when Erna finally woke up.

When Sybilla and Lily got back from the cotton mill, they found that Annette was still awake. "Erna's up, yo!" she cheerily informed them.

The two of them charged into the bedroom, each wanting to be the first one to get there. Inside, Thea was sitting by the bed and looking after Erna. Sybilla and Lily let out a nonsensical "WHOOO!" and started hugging Erna's head and poking her cheeks. When Erna groaned, "Th-that hurts...!" they switched to tossing her into the air, which earned them a sharp, "She needs *complete bedrest*!" from Thea.

Once they were done getting carried away, the two malfeasants took some deep breaths.

"Are you okay? You don't have amnesia or anything?" Lily asked.

"I would certainly hope not," Erna replied.

"What do you remember about Sybilla?"

"She's a dummy, but in a good way."

Without a word, Sybilla gave Erna's cheeks a gentle pinch. "Yeep!" Erna yelped in delight.

The bottom line was that she didn't seem to have suffered any brain damage. A wave of relief washed over the team. Things had been looking dicey there for a minute, but now they could finally breathe easy.

"B-by the way..." Erna got a little louder. "What happened with the mission?" She sounded pretty worried, and there was something almost frantic about her voice.

For a moment, everyone around her froze up.

Sybilla glanced around evasively. "R-right. About that..."

"There's kind of a lot that's happened since then," Lily said with an awkward smile.

After deciding it would be faster for her to see for herself, the girls took Erna to the dining room. She cocked her head in puzzlement but followed along anyhow.

Over in the dining room, there were two people sitting in the dim morning light.

"...Ah. The blond."

"Oh, you must be Erna. It's nice to meet you."

Namely, Vindo and Qulle.

The two of them had come to the villa as well, in part to report the result of the mission to Klaus. Right now they were eating the breakfast sandwiches Thea had made for them. Vindo was stuffing his cheeks full, whereas Qulle was taking small, modest bites.

After Erna mumbled "Yeep?" in confusion, Sybilla and Lily filled her in, both about Avian and the mission they had completed over in the admin building.

"I'm tellin' you, it was nuts. It was like magic, the way they got it all done!"

"It really was! I was totally blown away!"

Sybilla and Lily gesticulated wildly as they regaled Erna with tales of Avian's exploits. They were so excited they were talking a mile a minute, and Erna was flustered by the raw zeal in their voices.

"These top academy student guys are the real deal! They've totally turned me around on 'em."

"Yeah! I've never even seen spies like that except for Teach!"

They meant every word of praise they were showering on Avian. The murders Vindo committed had surprised them in the moment, but looking back at the situation objectively, they understood that it had been the right call. Besides, all the people he'd killed had been criminals who did evil deeds on behalf of the mafia.

What impressed them most of all, though, was how deeply honed his talents were.

I mean, it sucks to have to admit, but after that display he put on, I can't lie, Sybilla thought, having rather mixed feelings about the whole thing. *The fact is, these guys are on a whole different level.*

She had no choice but to discard any sense of rivalry she'd felt toward them. The skills Avian had up their sleeves were proof positive of their elite status.

"I-it was…Vindo and Qulle…right?" Now that Erna was up to speed on the situation, she pushed through her shyness and gave them a timid bow. "Thank you for filling in for me on the mission."

"Don't mention it," Vindo replied curtly. Then he looked at the girls gathered around the table. "It's too noisy in here," he declared, then grabbed another sandwich slice and rose to his feet. From the look of it, he planned on finishing his breakfast elsewhere.

The girls stared in bafflement, but Qulle spoke up in Vindo's defense. "Don't take it personally. He's like that with everyone."

After that, the Lamplight girls decided to have breakfast as well. The sun had begun making its ascent, and the dining room had a fantastic view of the purple-streaked sky. They gobbled down sandwiches, filled with that special satisfaction that came after a mission well done.

Unsurprisingly, the topic dominating their conversation was Avian. The girls crowded around Qulle and showered her with compliments.

"You know, you really shouldn't talk Avian up like that." Midway through, Qulle gave her cheek an embarrassed scratch. "The way I see it, Lamplight's just as impressive. It makes me feel kinda bad to hear you compliment us so much."

Sybilla tilted her head in confusion. "Wait, you figure?"

"Absolutely. I hear you're each a little overspecialized, but even so, you're still strong enough to pass the academy graduation exam. Looking at you, it's hard to believe you used to be washouts. You should be proud of how far you've come."

Sybilla gave her a small bow. "Th-that's nice of you to say."

The girls' faces went red. They weren't used to receiving praise. It had been a good long while since anyone other than Klaus had complimented them.

Thea joined in on the conversation. "Still, it feels like it's been one failure after another," she said. "I'm ashamed to admit it, but things haven't been going too well for us lately. I wonder what it is we're doing wrong?"

"Wrong? I think that's pretty normal."

"How so?"

"Lamplight just reached the level of academy graduates. And that's wonderful, don't get me wrong, but in our world, that's only the starting line. I wouldn't expect a fresh graduate to be able to pull their weight right off the bat."

"Ah, that's a fair point."

"If anything, I'd say you just got lucky for things to go as smoothly as they did before."

It was an unbiased assessment, but it didn't help solve the girls' problem. They had been overcome with joy when Klaus had informed them of their graduation, but all it actually meant was that they'd reached the minimum threshold to even be called spies. There was a long road ahead, and they'd only just taken their first step.

"It's not like everything always goes well for us, either. We've certainly had our share of bitter failures."

Qulle traced her finger around the rim of her teacup as she reminisced.

"I'd love to hear the details, if you don't mind," Thea said.

"Sure. I'd be happy to tell you all about it," Qulle readily replied. "It's pretty nice, getting a chance to chat with people my age aside from just my teammates for a change. Why don't we all share, then? I can tell you about my missions, and you can tell me about yours."

The girls relocated to the nearby chairs and listened attentively as Qulle shared her stories. They were dying to know what kind of missions the elites had been on.

Everything in the dining room was calm and friendly.

So much so, in fact, that none of them paid any attention to the fact that Vindo had yet to return.

Klaus returned from his mission as well, and he took a short breather over in the study.

As he partook in a traditional Longchon breakfast of unflavored rice porridge with chicken, he flipped through a nearby document. It was some data on Avian he'd picked up from Roaring Sea after finishing his late-night mission.

By and large, spies weren't kept abreast of what other teams were up to, a policy that was designed to safeguard against leaks. Aside from legacy old-timers like "Torchlight" Guido and "Hearth" Veronika, the only person who knew the full details of the nation's spy network was their spymaster, C.

In the short period of time Klaus had to work with, not even he had been able to get his hands on more than a few scraps of information. That said, even just those tidbits were enough to show him how ripe with potential Avian was.

They really are an excellent team. I don't see any meaningful shortcomings.

That was one big difference between them and Lamplight. Unlike Lamplight, which had clearly defined strengths and weaknesses, Avian had no flaws to speak of. They had trained diligently to be able to handle any mission they might come across. And of the team's members, the person whose skills stood out the most—

—was the first-place scorer on the graduation exam, "Flock" Vindo. I had no idea there was someone with talents like his in the academies. I have a hard time believing that Guido simply overlooked him. Did he first enroll in the last two years, maybe?

There was nothing particularly novel about his full-body spring movement, his knife skills, or his outstanding acting abilities, but they all spoke to his excellent fundamentals. That put him in sharp contrast with Lamplight's members, each of whom was something of a one-trick pony.

Apparently, he was acting as Avian's team leader.

Then we have the fourth-place scorer, "Glide" Qulle. I got the sense that she had a knack for providing rearguard support, but even so, fourth place is impressive.

There were another four members that Klaus hadn't met in person, but looking at the data gave him a pretty good idea of how powerful they were. In all likelihood, the second-, third-, fifth-, and sixth-place scorers all had skills that far outstripped the average Lamplight member as well.

Even if I'm being generous, the only people we have who could compete with them are Monika and Grete. Annette might have a chance if she was motivated, but she's so fickle...and the others would be straight-up outmatched.

That was his objective assessment of the two teams. If nothing else, the collective strength of Lamplight's members was far below that of Avian's. Klaus felt a pang of chagrin. Perhaps that was his pride as an instructor talking.

What is it? What is it that makes Avian so different from Lamplight?

Klaus stared at his document.

If I'm going to improve their skills, what is it I need to—?

As soon as he turned his attention to the intelligence contained therein, there was a knock on the study door.

Vindo stuck his head in a little.

Klaus was the first to speak. "Did you need something?"

"Just a small bit of business," Vindo replied. "Could I have a minute of your time?"

"Of course."

"Much obliged. I'll make it quick."

Vindo gave Klaus a small bow, then faced him head-on. After combing back his hair, he fixed his gaze on Klaus with an air of great formality.

And as for the next words that came out of his mouth...

"The fact is, your team is garbage. They're worse than useless."

Qulle was a masterful orator.

She broke down Avian's missions in easy-to-follow terms. Some of her tales kept the girls in breathless suspense, and others filled them with wholehearted delight, but they found lessons to take away from all of them. One of the big things that made Avian hum was the friendly rivalry its members had with each other, and the Lamplight girls were taken with how the incredibly cool Avian members vied for supremacy.

"I think that about covers it," Qulle said bashfully once she was finished.

Lily, who'd been diligently listening and jotting down notes from right beside her, rose to her feet—

"That was incredible. I feel like I learned so much!"

—and let out a shout before grabbing Qulle's hand and vigorously shaking it.

The rest of the girls had been just as transfixed. Erna gave Qulle a small round of applause, and Annette's eye gleamed like she'd just found a fun new toy. She handed Qulle a homemade peanut gun, ostensibly as her way of thanking her.

"You know, it's weird." Qulle patted Annette's head as one would a child's. "I never would have expected to run into fellow countrymen so far away from the academy. Maybe this is fate at work..."

"Now that you mention it," Lily asked, "did you go to the same school as anyone from Lamplight?"

As it so happened, each Lamplight member had come from a different academy.

Qulle tilted her head. "Ummm, I'm not sure..."

"By the way, the three members who aren't here right now are Daughter Dearest, Glint, and Meadow."

"You really shouldn't hand out intel so freely..."

After lightly admonishing her, Qulle turned her eyes upward in thought—

"But yeah, I think I remember there being a girl named Daughter Dearest. We didn't interact much, though."

—then replied.

Her answer made a lot of sense to the girls. Odds were, there might be other people in Avian who'd gone to school with Lamplight members, as well.

Qulle touched her bangs, looking a little mournful. "Actually, I had something I wanted to ask you all."

"What's that?"

"Do you ever wish you could go back somewhere safer?"

The unexpected question earned her some quizzical looks.

"Just now it struck me all over again," Qulle explained. "You all are really good people. I don't want you to die. I want you to live, you know?"

Lily still wasn't sure what she was getting at. "Uh...huh... I mean, nothing beats staying safe, I guess...," she answered noncommittally.

"Right?" Qulle said, nodding in relief. "Oh, I'm so glad."

It was then that Sybilla realized that something felt off. *Hmm?*

She could feel ominous goose bumps running all across her skin.

There were the over-the-top levels of hatred Vindo had shown toward their enemy during the joint mission. There was the look of sadness that had crossed Qulle's face when the topic of failures came up. And there was the way Avian's boss never showed up, even when they were coordinating their missions. What was the root cause behind all those oddities?

Before Sybilla had a chance to act on her doubts, Thea beat her to the punch. "Say, would you mind if I asked you something, too?" she said, cutting Qulle off with a question. "What kind of person is Avian's boss? What are they doing right now?"

"'Sky Monk' Adi," Qulle replied. "I can't think of a woman I admire more. She was witty and cheerful and just an all-around wonderful person."

"'Was'?"

"She died. Two months ago."

The Lamplight girls were at a loss for words. That "good woman" Vindo had mentioned back with the secretary had been Avian's boss.

The first emotion that filled their hearts was compassion toward Avian.

"So you guys have been operating without a boss this whole time?" Lily asked worriedly.

"Yup," said Qulle. "Din's been too short on personnel lately to assign us a new one, so we've all been working together to fill in the gaps. And Vindo's the one who's been stepping up most of all. He's been working really hard and putting his leadership skills to the test."

"...That's got to be stressful for him. No wonder he's so snippy."

"That probably has a lot to do with it, yeah. But it's all good. We're just about out of the woods." There was something deeply suspicious about the way Qulle took off her glasses. It almost felt like she was mocking them, like she'd just finished buying all the time she needed to. "We just found someone great—someone perfectly suited to become our new boss."

On hearing that, a long-overdue realization dawned on the girls.

Vindo had left a while ago, and he still wasn't back.

◇◇◇

Sybilla took the lead as the girls dashed toward Klaus's study. After charging in so hard they could have broken the door, the five of them ended up in a tangled pile on the floor.

Inside, Vindo coldly looked down at them. "You really are a noisy lot."

He had both his hands in his pockets, and everything about his pose seemed to radiate contempt.

Across from him, Klaus was frowning. His was the face of a man who'd just been given some uncomfortable news.

The girls rose to their feet and glared daggers at Vindo.

"Looks like you figured out what's up," he said, practically spitting out the words.

"We just finished wrapping up our negotiations. Bonfire's going to become my team's new boss."

The girls gasped at how accurate their fears had been. At the same time, rage began welling up inside them at the overfamiliar way Klaus's code name sounded coming out of Vindo's mouth.

Lily took a step forward. "B-but why…?"

"It's really not that strange." Vindo's voice was downright frigid. "If anything, it's the only rational choice. Bonfire's place is with other talented spies. All you people are doing is holding him back."

There was no joy in Vindo's eyes. The gaze he gave the girls was sharp and fierce.

His words had hit Lamplight right where it hurt, and their hearts ached all the more for having known it all along. The best thing for their motherland would have been for Klaus to focus wholly on his missions, but as things stood, he was spending huge chunks of his time training the girls and cleaning up after their messes. It was hardly fitting work for the Foreign Intelligence Office's mightiest spy, but the girls had turned a blind eye to that fact and continued taking advantage of his kindness.

"B-but…," Lily stammered back. "Even if that's true, why should you guys get him?"

"Avian is far more capable than Lamplight. I think we've made that perfectly evident."

He was talking about the night prior. He and Qulle had cleared a mission with ease that Sybilla and Erna had failed.

"Not only did you fail a trivial mission, one of you even got knocked out and put you all in peril, and Bonfire had to go out of his way to come bail you out. If that doesn't count as holding him back, then I don't know what would."

Erna let out a pained little moan.

"Then we went in and cleared it all on our own. What more proof could you possibly need?"

"That was your goal all along, huh?" Sybilla immediately snapped. "So much for 'handling Erna's part for us.' You fuckin' played us."

"It's your own fault for letting yourself get played," Vindo said, gesturing rudely with his chin. "As of right now we're the nation's best spies whose intel hasn't been leaked to the Galgad Empire. The best thing for us would be to have Bonfire join forces with Avian. It's as simple as that."

"I-if I may." This time, it was Qulle who spoke up from behind the girls. "This really isn't as bad a deal as it sounds. What do you say to having Lamplight take a break from fighting on the front lines for a while? You've improved a lot, but your skills are still pretty shaky, and that puts you all in a lot of danger."

She went on.

"You should really consider going back to your academies."

Her tone sounded almost consoling, like she was trying to show that she didn't harbor any animosity toward them. That it wasn't anything personal—it was just business.

Seeing her attitude made the girls' bodies go red-hot. They'd "improved"? Qulle didn't see them as equals, not one bit. All those compliments she'd paid them had come from a place of smug superiority, and the way she looked at them like misbehaving children rubbed each and every one of them the wrong way.

"T-Teach, where do you fall in all this?" Lily said, forcing the conversation in a new direction. "Are you seriously buying into this nonsense?"

The whole time they'd been arguing with the Avian duo, Klaus had merely listened in silence. The girls' hearts swelled. Surely, Klaus would reject Vindo and Qulle's proposal and declare that he was going to remain Lamplight's boss.

"If nothing else..." However, Klaus's expression was hard. "...I've given them the green light."

"____!"

"To be honest, they have a point. Having me become Avian's boss is the best option we have available to us right now. It's in our nation's best interests to pair the most skilled boss with the most skilled subordinates and have them complete missions together."

There was a dark gloom in Klaus's eyes that none of them had ever seen before.

"And as for what you all will do once you don't have a boss anymore, going back to your academies for a time might not be such a bad idea."

The words coming out of his mouth were as cold as ice. The girls could practically *feel* a chill run down their spines.

That was Klaus's stance—as a spy, he respected the legitimacy of Avian's argument.

"They've already provided me with compensation, too. Vindo taught me about a technique that Lamplight was lacking. I have to say, it was fascinating to hear his viewpoint. Sharing his findings with you will be my parting gift to you all."

"And there you have it," Vindo said with a brief nod. "We've already finished our negotiations. If you don't like it, then come up with a rational, logical reason to convince us otherwise. Go on, make an argument worthy of a spy."

He glowered at them.

"And if you can't...then give us your boss."

"........."

The girls gulped as the words refused to come to them. They wanted to give Vindo a verbal smackdown, but that desire accomplished nothing for them except making their heads go even hotter.

What should they say?

That they had good synergy with Klaus? No. They had no way of objectively demonstrating that, nor could they refute the possibility that Klaus might have good synergy with Avian, too. That they'd successfully completed Impossible Missions? No. Not after the three months they'd just spent failing over and over and dragging Klaus down. That they had skilled members like Monika and Grete? No, that would be a poor move. That would just end in Monika and Grete getting transferred to Avian, too.

They couldn't come up with any spy-worthy arguments.

But if they didn't do *something*, Lamplight was going to fall apart. Klaus was going to leave them, and they were all going to get separated when they went back to their academies. Even just picturing it was enough for grief to run through them like someone had gouged a hole in their hearts. However, no rebuttals came to mind, and all the girls could do was mumble incoherently.

Vindo went on, appearing almost bored. "Sounds like you don't have any counterarguments. In that case, I'll get in touch with our superiors and recommend that—"

"Oh, but we do."

A clear, resonant voice split the air.

"You're really trying to rush this along, aren't you? I must say, impatient men aren't really my type."

An indomitable smile rested on Thea's lips. She swept back her hair, then brushed Lily aside as she took a step forward.

"Hmph." Vindo raised his jaw. "What are you saying?"

"Just that I have some spy talk for you. And it's logical, just the way you like it."

"Go on."

"I say we have no defense. Teach is all yours. Go ahead, make him Avian's boss."

Every girl present stared at Thea in horror.

Vindo gave her a suspicious frown. "How oddly understanding of you. I have to imagine you're plotting something."

"Oh, perish the thought." Thea smiled amicably. "I'm just curious about what you wanted to do for your onboarding."

"Our...onboarding?"

"That's what I said. Sybilla and Lily, could you give me your papers from last night?"

Sybilla hadn't understood what Thea was up to at first, but when she stuck her hand in her pocket, it finally dawned on her. Lily pulled out her paper as well.

After collecting them, Thea handed them to Vindo. "These are the instructions Teach gave the two of them for last night."

"...So?"

"Once you read them, I think you'll understand why an onboarding process is necessary."

On the papers, there was some bizarre advice.

Pilfer as a rainbow does when crossing the moon.

Be like the full moon and be your full self.

"...............What?" Vindo frowned.

When Qulle looked at the papers, her eyes went wide. "Yikes," she exclaimed.

"When it comes to explaining things, Teach is as terrible as they come," Thea declared triumphantly.

That was Klaus's big weakness—his inability to properly convey the specifics of things like spy techniques. Naturally, he was no good at giving concrete orders during missions, either.

"That's why I assumed you were going to need some onboarding. What do you say?" Thea asked with a smile.

Vindo clenched the instructions in his hand, then silently whirled around. "...Did you actually write these, Bonfire?"

"I did."

"Are they poems?"

"It's some advice I left for them."

"Why'd you encode it, then?"

"I didn't."

"......................"

Just this once, the girls couldn't help but feel a little sympathy toward Vindo. That must have come completely out of left field for him.

Thea gently made her case, making sure to frame it like she was doing Avian a favor. "There are some tricks of the trade you need to know if you want to work with the Greatest Spy in the World. What would you say to working together until the mission's finished? That way, we can help get you up to speed."

Vindo sank into contemplative silence. After shifting his stony gaze back and forth between Klaus and the instructions, he eventually let out a small sigh and clicked his tongue. "...Fine. We'll do it your way."

"Wonderful. We'll teach you everything you need to know," Thea replied.

"I expect you to give us your all," said Vindo. "It won't be long until we have that mission done."

The corners of Thea's eyes twitched a little at his provocative tone, but that was all. She refused to lose the cover her geniality afforded her.

"I'd say this conversation is over," Vindo snapped. He headed to leave the study. On his way to the door, he exchanged vicious glares with Sybilla and Lily.

Qulle followed a step behind. "It's really nothing personal, you know," she said.

Then Thea called after them. "By the way, there's just one thing I want to confirm."

"Oh yeah?" Vindo stopped in his tracks. "What's that?"

"Oh, it's just a little detail. But if, hypothetically, *Lamplight is able to demonstrate that we're better than Avian during the onboarding period*, I'm sure we can agree to just forget this whole thing about you taking Teach. After all, you'd have lost the whole foundation for your argument."

"It's a moot point. *That could never happen in a million years.*"

After that final verbal clash, Vindo and Qulle left the villa.

The sound from the front door closing behind them seemed to echo unnaturally loudly.

"""""
....
....
.... """""

For a little while, the girls said nothing. It was taking them some time to digest the implications of Thea and Vindo's last exchange.

Eventually, Thea let out a big sigh and smiled. "I trust I handled that the way you hoped I would, Teach."

"That's right, Thea. That was magnificent."

A cheer of "Theaaaaaaaaaa!" exploded up from the girls, and they rushed over and leaped at her. Lily hugged her neck, Sybilla gave her a thump on the shoulder, and Erna and Annette rubbed their heads against her belly.

She'd executed her play flawlessly.

The girls could all feel it—they still had a tiny shred of hope. They'd successfully bought themselves some time and avoided the worst-case scenario of losing Klaus right there and then. One of the core tenets of negotiation was that you needed to find common ground rather than verbally beat the other side into submission, and Thea had done that with flying colors. For now, Klaus was still Lamplight's boss.

Klaus gave her a round of applause. "That was some fantastic work you did there. If I'd tried to bring up an onboarding period myself, it would have come across as unnatural."

"I told you, didn't I? When I said I was going to become your partner, I meant every word of it," Thea declared, sounding tickled pink with herself. "If I couldn't stay in harmony with you on things like this, how could I ever hope to remain by your side?"

The others fawned over Thea for a good while longer until Lily and Annette eventually got carried away and made her mad by tickling her sides.

After they finished basking in their feelings of exultation, Sybilla looked up. "Th-there's one thing I don't get," she said, turning her gaze over toward Klaus. "Tell me, where's your head at with all this? You seriously thinkin' about goin' with Avian?"

Upon hearing her question, the rest of the girls all said "Ah" and stopped their idle chatter. Sybilla had a point. They'd delayed the issue at hand, but they still hadn't actually solved anything.

Klaus nodded. "...I am. I am a spy, after all. And I have a duty to protect the nation that Inferno loved. If it becomes clear that it's the best choice available, I'm prepared to set aside my personal feelings and take charge of Avian. If that happens, and you all end up without a boss, then having you go back to the academies might be for the best."

"Yeep..." Over beside Sybilla, Erna hung her head.

The others understood all too well how she felt. They knew it was spoiled of them, but even so, they didn't want to accept that this was happening. The thought of Klaus leaving and the team getting torn apart was just too unthinkable. If there was anything they could have said to prevent it, they would have, but—

"But remember this. When I first assembled my team, I didn't pick any of those Avian members. I picked you," Klaus said decisively. "And from there, I trained you myself. Now these Johnny-come-latelies think they're better than you? As if. All you have to do now is go out there and prove them wrong. Take those Avian punks as fuel for your own growth."

With a start, Sybilla realized she'd been looking at it all wrong. There *was* a way to avoid that horrible future. All they had to do was prove one thing during the onboarding period—that they were the ones who deserved that spot by Klaus's side!

"But of course!" Lily said, sounding oddly excited. "Ooh, now I'm fired up. Behold the awakening of Lily, Washout Extraordinaire!"

Sybilla immediately clenched her fists. "Yeah! I might've been on a losin' streak, but that ends today!"

The two of them exchanged a fist bump as the others starting chiming in as well.

"I've still got loads and loads of pranks I want to try out on Bro, yo!" Annette chirped.

"L-let's do this!" Erna declared. "If they want to steal Teach away from me, then they've got another thing coming!"

"Don't you worry about a thing, Teach," Thea said, laying a hand atop her chest. "We'll surpass Avian right before your eyes. Heh-heh. After all, you wouldn't want to be separated from me, either, would you? Why, you're so taken with my ravishing body that you can barely stop yourself from thinking of ways to get me and Grete into your bed so you can—"

"And to think, you would have almost been respectable if not for all the sexual harassment."

"I'm plenty respectable!"

"Still, that energy—that unshakable spirit of rebellion you all possess—is your first and foremost weapon."

He was right, and the girls knew it. Losing wasn't an option. They had their pride, after all. They couldn't afford to lose Klaus, and like hell were they going back to those damned academies.

It was time to win, and if they had to take down some academy elites to do it, then so be it.

"Just now, I was able to extract some information that will help you overcome Avian." Klaus's voice was firm and resolute. "There's a final lesson the academies give, one that you never got to take. And it's about an espionage fighting style called liecraft."

Chapter 2

Liecraft

The Din Republic's intelligence agency, the Foreign Intelligence Office, ran twenty-seven different spy academies. Each one had just over a hundred students, and their ages ranged all the way from eight to twenty-two.

In order to get in, you had to receive a recommendation from one of the myriad scouts and spies scattered across the nation. Any children they found promising would then abandon their old identities and head to an academy to live in a dorm sequestered from the rest of the world.

Then, in order to graduate, they had to pass one of the academies' semiannual graduation exams. It generally took students six years to graduate, but the lion's share of them didn't even get the chance to try. About 80 percent of the students ended up flunking out due to poor grades in the periodic exams well before then.

The reason why so many of the students failed out was because of the sheer breadth of knowledge the academies wanted them to retain. They were expected to cram in every foundational skill a spy needed. Naturally, that included learning several languages, and on top of that, the students needed the physical abilities to infiltrate anywhere they might have to, the conversational and acting skills required to engage with whoever they might need to, and the marksmanship and close-quarters prowess to carry out assassinations, to name a few. And the list just went on from there.

For the students, Monday morning through Wednesday afternoon was all outdoors training. Their instructors would drop them off deep in the mountains and force them to walk dozens of miles all through the night. Then Thursday and Friday were filled with nonstop language and cultural lessons, and on Saturdays, they had lectures on specialized topics like cooking and dance. Most of the students spent their Sundays sleeping like corpses. The hellish curriculum wore away at their minds and bodies, and one in ten students fled before the six-month mark even rolled around. Even those who remained often found themselves unable to clear the periodic exams' hurdles, and slowly but surely, the students' ranks dwindled.

Amid that brutal environment, there were two groups of people who became spies through vastly contrasting paths.

Avian's members were standouts from the start. Take "Flock" Vindo, for example.

Vindo was eighteen when he first enrolled. During his time in the Naval Intelligence Department, his outstanding successes caught the attention of a major player in the Foreign Intelligence Office. From there, he left the navy and entered one of the Foreign Intelligence Office's academies. After passing all his periodic exams with ease, he decided to take the graduation exam just a single year after enrolling. The best and brightest students from every academy were there, but even so, he secured the highest score in brilliant form.

Thanks to his hard work and honed talents, Vindo entered the world of espionage through the official path. And most of the Avian members' stories were a lot like his.

Then you had the hodgepodge of special cases that made up Lamplight. Take "Flower Garden" Lily, for example.

Lily was only nine when she first enrolled, making her one of the younger students at her academy. People initially had high hopes for her due to her natural resistance to poison, but she had one fatal flaw: She was a giant klutz. She got great grades on her written exams, but on her practical exams, she made one huge blunder after another. If not for the potential her diligent attitude toward her training and unique physiology represented, she would have long since gotten expelled. And the rest of the team's experiences largely mirrored Lily's.

"Daughter Dearest" Grete was a bona fide master of disguise, but her fear of men kept her from using her talent to its fullest. She often suffered from poor mental health, and her physical health wasn't anything to write home about, either.

"Meadow" Sara had a talent for rearing animals, but what she didn't have was a disposition suited for espionage. She was timid and indecisive, and while her instructors decided not to expel her during her first year out of compassion, they'd all but decided that her second year would be her last.

"Pandemonium" Sybilla's athletic skills were fantastic, but she always had big problems on her written exams. Plus, after the injuries she caused during a certain incident, her ability to cooperate with the other students began falling apart, and she started becoming a washout.

"Forgetter" Annette didn't give a whit about the rules, "Dreamspeaker" Thea got in hot water with her instructors for her extracurricular lovemaking training, "Glint" Monika started cutting corners after suffering a setback, and "Fool" Erna found herself isolated due to her poor communication skills.

All the girls Klaus found and recruited into Lamplight had been a hair's breadth away from expulsion.

Avian and Lamplight were as different as could be, and there in Longchon, the two teams were coming to a head.

Avian's base of operations was over in the Longchon mainland's business district. Longchon had been steadily growing, and the nation had responded to its population influx by building a series of large-scale apartment complexes. Each one had a restaurant on its ground floor, and from there on up was a series of sketchy apartments piled atop one another with each hallway blanketed in ads for dentists, traditional herbalists, and the like.

At the moment, Avian was renting one of those studio apartments.

Having a mixed-gender group of six all living together in a single room would normally have made for a pretty cramped living environment, but with how rare it was for all six of them to be there at the same time, it wasn't too bad.

When Vindo and Qulle returned, they found the apartment empty.

As soon as they were inside, Vindo slammed his fist into the wall. The beer bottles scattered across the floor toppled over from the shock. "Damn you, Bonfire," he snapped with a small click of the tongue.

Qulle let out a surprised yelp. It was the first time she'd ever seen Vindo so mad. "Huh? Did Mr. Klaus do something to you?"

"That bastard wants to use us as *tools* to train his students with." Vindo plopped himself down on the bottom bunk bed. "That was what he was after the whole damn time. When I made my demand, he said he'd only accept it if I told him about the techniques that Lamplight hadn't learned yet. I knew he'd see through me if I tried lying, so I had to tell him, and not a moment later, they drop that nonsense about an onboarding period."

"………"

"He thinks he can play us for fools. I have to say, it's been a while since the last time I felt so belittled."

"Nothing's ever easy, is it?"

On the surface, it looked like the negotiations had gone their way, but there were moves being made behind the scenes. Klaus came across as amiable, but apparently, he had a hell of a stubborn streak.

"Are we going to have a problem, do you think?" Qulle asked. "Is he going to break his promise?"

"I doubt we have to worry about that. There's no way he gets sentimental enough to embarrass himself by staying in Lamplight after we're done demonstrating how much better we are."

"So you're saying that our goal—"

"Hasn't changed. We have to prove that Avian's better than Lamplight. That's all."

Once they were done sorting through the situation, Vindo said "…I'm going to turn in for a bit" and got a bottle of beer out of the fridge. He bit into someone else's half-eaten *xiaolongbao* and washed it down with the beer.

After finishing his light meal, he began pulling off his clothes.

Qulle drank from her glass of grape juice and gave him a disparaging look. "I'm right here, you know."

"Oh, get used it already," Vindo replied unconcernedly as he tossed his outerwear into the laundry basket.

Qulle took another sip of her juice. "Why are men such animals?" she mumbled quietly.

"When I wake up, it's go time," Vindo said, naked from the waist up. "While we're doing this mission with Lamplight, I want to gather intel on them. Make sure the others know the score. I don't want to leave a single stone unturned."

"Are you sure we can't just do this peacefully? I feel like we'd be just fine, even without going all out."

"Don't underestimate them. They might look like a mess, but they've cleared multiple Impossible Missions. There must be a reason for that." Vindo cracked his knuckles. "No mercy. I want us taking Lamplight to the *cleaners.*"

"..............."

Qulle could tell he was really fixated on this. Them not having a boss was a problem, of course, and she wanted to fix it, too. Elites or not, they were still rookies, and it would have been great to have someone more experienced there to guide them. For Vindo, though, there was clearly more to it than just that. It was like he wanted Bonfire badly enough that he was willing to do whatever it took to get him, and whatever his reason was, Qulle was pretty sure it was something he hadn't shared with her yet.

She thought about asking him about it, but Vindo had already burrowed into his mattress.

As it turned out, the members of Avian weren't the only ones renting an apartment in Longchon. The other apartment in question was also a tiny studio, and though at a glance it felt more spacious than Avian's, that was only because of how meticulously clean its cerulean-haired resident kept it.

The morning light streamed down on the three girls sharing a meal there. They were eating pasta, which was about as far from being a staple of Longchon cuisine as you could get. No matter where in the world the cerulean-haired girl was stationed, she never changed her diet. She liked to have things just so, and if not for how flexible her brown-haired roommate was, their cohabitation would have quickly ended in disaster.

The girls were seated around a circular table.

"Avian, huh? There they go, making big decisions without me again," the blue-haired girl—"Glint" Monika—grumbled. She had a medium build and had gone to some lengths to strip herself of any distinctive physical characteristics. The one notable aspect of her appearance was the way her asymmetrical hairstyle hung down and covered her right eye.

"Top academy students? Oh no. I don't think I'm going to like this at all," "Meadow" Sara said, nervously cradling her head. Her brown permed hair peeked out from beneath her drooping newsboy cap, as did her skittish, squirrel-like eyes.

"I agree. Things have taken quite an unexpected turn...," redheaded "Daughter Dearest" Grete muttered gloomily. Her limbs were so slender they looked liable to shatter if handled too roughly, lending her the kind of ephemeral air one would expect of a glass sculpture. She wore her hair bobbed.

The three of them had been off on a separate op, so they hadn't been consulted on the Avian issue. The others had only just radioed over to inform them that they were in the middle of a winner-takes-Klaus battle, and they were feeling more than a little blindsided by the news.

Of the trio, Grete's expression was the most brooding of them all. "To think that people would come try to steal away the boss... I suppose it makes sense once you consider how endearing he is, but still..."

By that point, the fact that she was in love with Klaus was common knowledge.

Monika waved her hand mockingly. "I mean, those Avian guys have a point. There's no denying that, as things stand, Lamplight's just an anchor weighing Klaus down."

When Monika put that out there, Grete agreed. "You're aren't wrong," she replied. "But oh, what to do... I haven't even completed the first step of my plan to deepen my camaraderie with the boss..."

"Just for the record, what step is that?"

"Getting him into bed with me."

"And who was it that came up with this plan?"

"Thea. Isn't she wise?"

"I swear, I'm gonna punch that girl."

Monika began loudly popping her knuckles, but Sara hurriedly chided her. "W-we need to start by freeing Miss Grete from her brainwashing!" That said, she didn't voice any specific objections about the "hitting Thea" part.

After their standard little back-and-forth, Grete got the conversation back on track. "...For now we should go over to the boss's base so we can get a better handle on the situation."

"Yeah, good call." "You got it."

After settling on a course of action, they finished their meal and headed out.

During their stay in Longchon, the three of them hadn't spent much time at Klaus's villa. It wasn't a good idea to have a group of undercover spies all gather in the same place too often, and besides, they'd been up to their necks helping out the other squads anyhow.

This was going to be Grete's first time seeing Klaus in a good long while, so she was all smiles.

As the three of them walked through the city, Monika offered a suggestion. "So what do you say we make a bet of it?" she said. "Let's predict what the others are up to right now. The winner gets everyone's share of ice cream tonight."

"You really love gambling, don't you?" Sara said, putting her hand to her mouth in amusement. "My guess is that they're training. We'll need to work hard if we want to beat Avian."

"Oh yeah?" Monika replied. "I figure they've all buried themselves in bed after having their old traumas revisited."

"...In that case, I'll predict that they're engaged in acts of sabotage," Grete said. "Now that Avian is trying to steal the boss away, I imagine the others will want to do whatever it takes to obstruct them."

After each of them finished making their bets, they arrived at Klaus's villa. Given the time, they assumed the others would all be there. This was going to be the first time in two full weeks that all of Lamplight was together under one roof.

Monika used the knocker hanging on the front door. However, no one came out to greet them. She knocked again, but the result was no different. All she got for her troubles was the loud sound of the knocker's clanging echoing fruitlessly through the air.

"URRRRRRRRRRRRRRRRRRRRRRRRRRRRRGH!"

Then they heard a low, animalistic groaning coming from inside.

"Hmm?" Monika tilted her head in puzzlement, then tried the doorknob and found that the door was unlocked.

Inside, in the living room just past the entrance, there were five girls sprawled out on the floor.

"URRRRRRRRRRRRRRRRRRRRRRRRRGH!" Lily groaned.

"HRAAAAH! GRAAAAAAAH!" Sybilla screamed as she repeatedly smashed her fists into the ground.

"When the man's finger reached the girl's maidenly fruit, she could no longer stop herself from letting out an obscene cry—," Thea said, reading aloud from an erotic novel.

"Yo… I'm sleepy…," mumbled Annette, who was in fact fast asleep.

"I'm adorable. ♪ Hee-hee—and so sparkly," Erna said with a strange smile.

It was abject chaos.

""""What am I even looking at?"""" the three newcomers said in unison. None of their predictions had been anywhere close to the mark.

As the three of them stared at the others in bewilderment, Erna mumbled "I—I—I'm pretty…" and walked over to them. Her face was pale, and her eyes were out of focus. She spun in place twice in a row, then toppled over to the side.

Sara rushed over and caught her. "Oh, be careful!"

As Erna lay in Sara's arms, she let out a groan. "Yeeeeep…" Something was clearly wrong with her.

Monika frowned. "What are you all doing?" she asked.

Erna's pallid lips trembled as she gave her answer. "T-trying to learn liecraft…"

""""Liecraft?"""" the other three parroted back.

Sure enough, not a single person in Lamplight had so much as heard of it before.

After splashing water on her collapsed teammates, Monika forced them to give her a sitrep.

According to the others, Klaus had gotten Vindo to tell him about a concept called liecraft.

"To be honest, this is a way of looking at things I'd never really considered before. The academies were the ones who came up with it, so what I'm about to tell you will mostly be me repeating what I heard from Vindo verbatim," Klaus had explained to the five girls. *"First of all, liecraft is a concept that the academies only teach students when they're right on the verge of graduation. There would be no point to learning it without building up your other skills first."*

"Ah... So that explains why we didn't know about it," Lily interjected. By the sound of it, none of Lamplight's members had gotten far enough to reach that particular lesson. They'd all run into their stumbling blocks well before getting to the graduation exam, and they'd gotten recruited into Lamplight before they had a chance to learn about liecraft. *"It sounds super cool, though. Is it, like, some sort of crazy secret technique?"*

"It's nothing nearly that complex. At its core, a liecraft is a way of deceiving people." Klaus looked around the circle. *"Up through now, how have you each been deceiving your enemies?"*

Looks of confusion crossed the girls' faces at the unanticipated question.

"...I've just kinda been winging it," Lily replied.

"Yeah, I've mostly been goin' with the flow," agreed Sybilla.

"I've been telling real good lies, yo!" Annette declared.

Klaus sighed in exasperation. *"Your explanations could use some work. A lot of work."*

"Goodness, I wonder who we learned that from?" Thea commented.

"Still, that's pretty normal," Klaus continued. *"I've never given much thought to how I deceive people. I just do it."*

The girls agreed. Deception wasn't really the sort of thing you could explain.

"However, the word deception *actually contains a wide variety of sub-categories. You can deceive people through acting, through theft, through tools, through hiding, through omission alone, by tampering with objects, by playing dumb, by leading them astray through seduction—the list goes on and on."*

"Now that you mention it, you're right," Thea murmured.

The girls had tried to deceive Klaus on countless occasions, but they'd done so in all sorts of different ways. If they tried to classify all the different things they'd tried, they could probably come up with over a hundred different categories.

"Here's another question for you." Klaus raised his index finger. *"What type of deception is the one that best lets each of you leverage your skills?"*

"""""" .... """""""

The girls didn't have immediate answers for that one.

"Do you not know?" Klaus asked. *"Because I'm sure there is one. What type of deception do you always turn to when you're up against the wall? Alternatively, what type of deception ties in most closely with your strengths?"*

His voice was beginning to pick up in intensity. They were starting to get to the heart of the explanation.

Sybilla spoke up. *"So wait, you're sayin' that liecraft is—"*

"Exactly." Klaus nodded. *"Your liecraft is* the type of deception that synergizes best with your unique talents."

It was a simple concept, when you got down to it.

Each of the girls had a special skill they could use better than anyone else. Between their poison, theft, disguise, negotiation, rearing, tinkering, and accidents, they were basically a group of extreme specialists. However, the way they used those talents was far from perfect. For example, Lily had been relentless about trying to spray Klaus with her poison gas, but he'd evaded it each and every time.

What they needed to do was *multiply their talents by their deception.*

They'd been unconsciously trying to pair the two, of course, but none of them had ever given the idea any serious thought.

"*Here, I'll put it in real-world terms,*" Klaus offered. "*Let's use Vindo's liecraft as our example.*"

"*Ooh,*" the girls cooed. They leaned in, spellbound.

They'd been made painfully aware of what a powerful spy Vindo was twice over now, and even the girls who hadn't been there personally had no choice but to acknowledge his skills.

Klaus took a piece of paper and wrote something resembling a formula on it.

Knife Skills × *Pretending to Lose* = *Instakill Counterattack.*

"*.........*"

"*This is the trick behind Vindo's strength.*"

The girls stared at the formula.

Then Lily quietly raised her hand. "*So Vindo's liecraft is 'pretending to lose'?*"

"*Apparently. When he told me, he went into more detail,*" Klaus replied. "*It's a simple trick but a powerful one. In order to take advantage of his advanced knife skills, he needs to start by getting in range. To do that, he puts on a clever show. By pretending to lose and getting in close, he can use his explosive, springlike movement to take down his opponent before they can react. It's a combo he's used to complete many of his missions.*"

Sybilla and Lily immediately understood what Klaus was talking about. They'd each seen it with their own two eyes. Vindo had refined his tactic, and once his foes fell for his trap, there was nothing they could do. When Vindo had launched that surprise attack when he was supposed to be wounded, his enemies had fallen into disarray and become helpless prey for his knives.

"*As spies, you all have only just reached the starting line,*" Klaus told them. "*And your skills are still lacking. Even if you hit your opponents with one hundred percent of what your honed special abilities are capable of, there will be plenty of times where that's not enough to best them. If you want to win in spite of that fact, you'll have to deftly use lies and falsehoods to engineer situations where your abilities can operate at three hundred percent of their capacity.*"

He was absolutely right. If they wanted to get stronger, they couldn't just sit around waiting for it to happen. Their special talents were weapons. They'd acquired them over the course of their lives, and they'd

68 Spy Classroom: Fool Erna Once, Vol. 5

honed them through their training with Klaus. What they needed now was a new fighting style—one that let them use those weapons to their fullest!

As the girls listened with bated breath, Klaus wrapped up his lecture. His voice rang with conviction. *"Now, find the type of deception that'll let you shine brightest. Once you do, you'll improve by leaps and bounds."*

That marked the lesson's conclusion.

For a strange, short little while, Klaus and the girls just stared at each other.

"............................"

«««««««   »»»»»»»»
....

"............................"

«««««««   »»»»»»»»
....

"............................"

«««««««   »»»»»»»»
....

"............................"

«««««««   »»»»»»»»
....

"............................"

«««««««   »»»»»»»»
....

".........That's what he said to me, but still," Klaus said, sounding deeply moved. *"That was inspiring. For the first time ever, I actually managed to give a lecture like a proper instructor. I have to say, it felt kind of nice."*

"That's what we were just thinking!" Lily bellowed.

There stood Klaus, deeply proud of having done nothing more than repeat what Vindo had said word for word.

◇◇◇

"The type of deception that will let us shine brightest, huh…," Sara said after sitting through the long explanation. "I guess I never gave it much thought…"

The eight of them were all still on the living room's leather sofa. It was their first time getting back together in a while, but the mood was hardly festive. The girls' exhaustion was written all over their faces.

Liecraft—that concept was going to take Lamplight to the next level.

I guess we all graduated before we had a chance to learn about it...,
Sara thought. It made sense. Based on the fact that Klaus hadn't heard
of liecraft, either, the idea must have come from the academies. Klaus
had learned to do the same thing, but in his case, he'd done it more or
less subconsciously.

"So that's the idea, huh? I don't hate it," Monika commented. "It
makes your deception more predictable, but I guess having no struc-
ture has problems, too. And a lot of us have been in the habit of just
firing off our special abilities without putting any thought into it. Some
of us could definitely do with some introspection."

After calmly laying out her analysis, she shifted her gaze.

"So what was all that groaning about?"

"I was groaning 'cause I can't figure out what my liecraft should be!"
Lily cried, pounding the sofa. "I don't know what kind of deception fits
me best! The thought never even crossed my mind before, so I barely
even know where to start. I mean, I have *some* ideas, but like..."

"Ideas like what?"

"Poison × Covert Ops! Like, where I hide in the shadows, then catch
my opponent by surprise by spraying poison."

"Nope. Don't you hate sitting still?"

"Poison × Crocodile Tears! I could cry like a baby, then stab my opponent with a poison needle when they let down their guard."

"See, now you're just being pathetic."

"Stop wounding me with your words!" Lily wailed, then collapsed
onto the floor. She let out a quiet sob. "I *know* they're no good."

The question Lily and the others had been racking their brains to
solve was, what kind of liecraft would suit them best? They understood
liecraft as a concept, but they still needed to figure out how exactly they
were going to make it work for them. It was a tough task, especially
considering that this was their first time even thinking about it.

"We can't afford to put this off," Thea explained. "Our battle with
Avian is right around the corner. I'll fill you all in with the specifics
later, but the gist is, we are going to be competing against Avian over
a classified document. Whoever gets their hands on it will prove that
they're the more competent team. And we only have a week left until
the battle begins."

"So you're saying we need to learn our liecrafts before then?" Monika asked.

"If we don't, Lamplight will fall. We'll lose Teach, and we'll all end up back at the academies."

Thea's voice rang with a sense of urgency. Earlier, Vindo had taken out three Lamplight members single-handedly, and including Qulle, Avian had another five whole elites on its roster.

A stifling air hung over the living room. None of them voiced it, but the team's members all shared the same feeling of unease. Their mouths were dry at the way the word *defeat* loomed over them.

"I'm having it rough, too...," Erna moaned to Sara, who was sitting beside her. "I'm no good at tricking people with my words, so I can't find a single type of deception that suits me."

"I don't blame you...," Sara softly replied. She patted Erna's head.

Incidentally, Erna had been testing out Accidents × Cutesy. The idea was that she could adorably approach her target, then ensnare them in one of her accidents. Thea was the one who'd come up with it. Considering how ill-matched Erna was with the deception technique she was practicing, it wasn't hard to see just how far off course the team had strayed.

"...And I need to work harder than anyone."

"Hmm?" Sara tilted her head to the side. She hadn't quite caught Erna's murmur.

What did she mean by that?

Before Sara had a chance to ask her to repeat herself, though, Annette presented Sara with her head and said "Pat me too, yo," so Sara missed her window.

When Sara replied "Roger that" and began patting Annette's head as well, Erna closed her eyes.

At that point, Monika stood up and called over to her. "Sara, we gotta go."

"Wait, where are we going? I wanted to pat their heads a little longer...," Sara asked, still patting Erna and Annette at the same time.

"...I swear, it really is like they're your kids."

"Oh, it's very relaxing. Would you like to give it a try, Miss Monika?"

"Don't you have something a *little* more important on your schedule right now? Especially considering our battle with Avian is just around the corner," Monika said in exasperation. "You've got intensive train-ing to get to."

Monika had first started training Sara right after their mission in Mitario.

It had all started because of their darts match against Purple Ant's minion Miranda. Sara herself didn't feel like she'd provided very good backup, but either way, it had been enough to earn Monika's respect. After they got back to Din, Monika began showing her the ropes.

"Everyone else on the team is either a kid or an idiot. I'm gonna need you to help pick up their slack, and it's not like I can count on Klaus to teach you squat."

That complaint of Monika's began something of a regular refrain.

Sara wasn't sure she quite agreed with Monika's assessment of the team, but she also didn't turn her down. Sara badly needed someone to help her find and patch the holes in her skill set, and she was over-joyed to have someone as talented as Monika willing to fill that role.

However, the training regimen she found herself thrust into was downright spartan. Not only did Monika make her do long training runs on the daily, she also assigned Sara five books a week to memo-rize. "But that's impossible!" she cried over and over—but Monika was doing the exact same training.

The most grueling part of all, though, was Monika's hands-on com-bat training.

They conducted their sessions on the roof of the apartment complex they were staying in, and today their bout ended in Monika flinging Sara away with a beautiful throw.

"Good work," Monika said. "We should probably head out for our mission now."

"I can't... I can't... M-my legs won't work anymore," Sara moaned, still lying prone on the roof.

Despite the fact that they had a mission right afterward, Monika hadn't pulled her punches even a little.

"Oh yeah?" Monika coolly replied. "In that case, we can take five. That means *five*."

She was a devil in teacher's clothing.

That said, all her lessons were exacting in both their pertinence and accuracy. Unlike Klaus, whose laissez-faire teaching style revolved around positive reinforcement, Monika's lessons were harsh but specific and useful.

"It's been nearly three months since we started your training, huh."

Monika pulled out a canteen of lemon water and handed it to Sara. Sara thanked her and glugged it down. "Y-you're right," she said with a nod once she was done drinking. "H-have I gotten a little stronger, do you think? At least enough that I'm not getting in everyone else's way?"

"Nope. You're useless."

"Y-you could at least be nicer about it…"

"Your job's to provide backup, but you're not even dependable enough for *that* yet. Honestly, I have some serious doubts about whether you and Lily have actually reached academy graduate level."

"I—I see…"

Sara's shoulders slumped at the harsh appraisal. Monika was the one person willing to say what the others wouldn't—that out of all of Lamplight's members, Sara's skills were the most lacking.

Each of them had their strengths and weaknesses, of course, so it was a little like comparing apples to oranges, but over the many months they'd spent together, something akin to a hierarchy had become evident. And Sara was the weakest of them all. In practical terms, she didn't have a single major accomplishment under her belt. All she'd done so far was hide in the others' shadows and use her animals to help them out. Compared to the other girls, there were far fewer situations where she could make herself useful.

"You are getting stronger, though. I'll give you that," Monika said matter-of-factly. "You just haven't hit the benchmarks I need you to."

"I—I see…"

"How's that assignment I gave you going? You think you'll be able to train that animal of yours to do it?"

"I-I'm still giving it my best, but I'm not making much progress…"

"Well, keep at it. If you can get Johnny to pull it off, it'll hugely expand your strategic options. Make sure he gets it. It'll go a long way toward letting you pull your weight. Maybe go ahead and try it out on someone?"

Johnny was the name of Sara's puppy, and there was a specific trick Monika had ordered her to teach him. Aside from just Sara's training regimen, Monika had been giving her specific instructions about other things, too. Monika came across as blunt, but she was actually really caring.

"For now, though, I guess you should focus on your liecraft. Hmm... you're not really the type to specialize in just going up and lying to people. And with your 'rearing' ability... Huh. I wonder what'd be best for you?"

Monika crossed her arms and sank into thought like she was pondering her own skills. Instead of working on her own liecraft, she was prioritizing helping Sara figure out hers.

However, Sara wasn't able to muster up much of a response. "A-am I really going to be okay...?" she asked, her voice trembling.

"Hmm?"

"I'm just a little anxious... How is someone like me supposed to go up against Avian?"

"What?" Monika dropped her voice an octave. "You seriously that freaked out?"

Sara nodded. She fidgeted restlessly with her fingertips as she spoke. "I—I really don't know if I'm going to be up to this... Back when I went to my academy, the top students shone like the stars. It was like they had this whole different aura about them, like everything about them was just better than me, and those feelings turned to an ache inside me like a wound that never healed..."

The painful memories from her academy days rested heavy in her heart.

There had been tons of students at her academy with incredible talents. In the time it took her to commit a single book to memory, the top students memorized ten. When it took everything Sara had just to decode a cipher at all, the top students finished in a third of the time. Even now, Sara started fading if she stayed up for more than twenty straight hours, but the top students had been able to complete their training after a full fifty hours of sleep deprivation.

When Sara watched them, it made her realize just how much of a washout she was. In her mind, those six people who stood above all the other top students may as well have existed in a whole different dimension.

She rubbed her fingers back and forth against each other. "He said we needed to find a type of deception that would let us shine, but...I can't even begin to picture what that would look like..."

This was the final technique conferred only to students about to graduate. As someone who'd stumbled well, well before reaching that line, Sara found it difficult to imagine herself successfully mastering it.

Monika quietly muttered a few words. "...There you go, still thinking of yourself as ordinary."

Sara looked up with a start and turned her gaze toward Monika. She could tell that her teammate hadn't meant it as a compliment.

A look of contempt loomed in Monika's eyes. She frowned wearily, swept back her hair, and let out a deep sigh. Then she began rapping her fingers against her thighs. "It pisses me off. You're still stuck in that headspace? After all that coaching I gave you?"

"Huh?"

"I mean, I felt the same way when I first joined Lamplight, but you have to realize by now that that won't fly anymore. Remember how the self-proclaimed World's Strongest, Klaus, recruited and praised us? There's no way we're just ordinary. We're not allowed to be."

"........."

"If we were, Avian would be right to make that demand of theirs. Klaus doesn't need ordinary people working with him." Monika flicked Sara in the shoulder. "You need to hurry up and get it through your head that *you're a prodigy, too.*"

Sara gulped. She had no reply to that. It felt like Monika had just socked her right in the spoiled part of her heart.

"You're sitting out today's mission," Monika declared. "I'll be fine on my own. You, just stay out of it."

"........."

After unilaterally making the call, Monika walked off toward the roof's entrance.

Sara could do nothing but watch her go as despair swelled within her.

Sara slumped over.

Oh no, I made Miss Monika mad...

Things with Monika had generally been going pretty well, but it would seem that she'd finally exhausted Monika's patience. Sara's heart still stung from the disdainful look Monika had given her right before she left. Everything she'd said was true. At the end of the day, Sara's resolve was lacking. She didn't have strong positive feelings about the spy profession like Thea or Lily, and she couldn't make herself believe she was a prodigy.

I don't even have a proper motive for wanting to be a spy in the first place...

On top of her mediocre abilities, even her mentality was weak. Looking at the situation objectively, it was no wonder Monika had abandoned her.

Sara headed back to the apartment with heavy footsteps.

Inside, Grete was organizing their data by looking at the photos of their targets they'd stuck on the wall and jotting down notes. She glanced over at Sara. "Monika told me what happened," she said gently. "I'll make the arrangements to have Monika handle the mission this afternoon on her own. Please, do take the day off. I can't imagine you've had much time to rest lately."

"Okay, but...I know I need to do better."

"...You mustn't take it so hard. I'm sure Monika is just on edge because of how tired she is."

The only response Sara could offer to Grete's consolatory words was an appreciative bow. Then a question sprang to her mind. "T-tell me, Miss Grete, do you think of yourself as a prodigy?"

".........?"

"Oh, no, it's nothing important. I was just wondering if you were at all afraid about going up against Avian."

Grete must have been an academy washout, too, and Sara was curious how she was confronting her old demons.

"That's a fair question..." Grete stroked the corners of her lips. "I would be lying if I said I wasn't anxious. I have a lot of unpleasant memories about my academy days..."

"I—I can imagine."

"But when I was brought into Lamplight, I met the boss. He sensed all the days I'd spent agonizing and all the nights I'd spent crying in confusion, and in his compassion, he offered me the most wonderful encouragement."

"........."

"Because of him, I'm prepared to give this battle everything I have. I know that all I have to do is take advantage of the skills I spent my time with the boss cultivating."

To Sara, there was something dazzling about the unashamed way Grete gave her answer. *I'm no match for Miss Grete, am I?* she couldn't help but think.

Grete was proud of herself, just the way she ought to be.

Klaus had complimented Sara, too, of course. He'd called her magnificent, and consequently, she'd started becoming slightly more assertive with her teammates. However, she had yet to make any bold plays during any of their missions.

Sara thanked Grete and left the apartment. Now that she'd been ordered to take the day off, there was nothing for her to do but rest up. She headed outside so she wouldn't get in her teammates' way, thinking that perhaps she could go out and let her hair down a bit alongside her pets. As she recalled, there was a kind of treat called an egg tart that had made its way onto the scene lately, and she really wanted to try one.

When she got to the ground floor, she was still mulling over how best to spend her break.

That was when she ran into someone unexpected. "Huh? What are you doing here, Miss Erna?"

Down on the first floor, Erna was standing in front of the complex's communal letterbox and frowning in consternation. It looked like she'd forgotten which apartment Sara and the others were staying in.

Erna's face lit up. "Oh, Big Sis Sara! Perfect timing!"

"Did you need me?"

Now that she thought about it, it had felt like Erna had wanted something from her earlier, too.

Erna practically hopped her way over to Sara. "If you wouldn't mind," she said, "I'd like your help. There's something I really want to try out so I can hopefully figure out my liecraft."

"Y-your liecraft, huh? That's all well and good, but what exactly were you thinking?"

"Isn't it obvious? When Lamplight wants to train, there's just one thing for us to do." As Erna went on, her voice boomed with excitement. "I want us to attack Teach! You and me, together!"

It probably went without saying by that point, but attacking Klaus was the way the girls trained. As the team's boss, he'd given his subordinates one simple training exercise—"Defeat me." Their missions had kept them so busy lately that they hadn't gotten as many chances to go after him, but the assignment was still ongoing. In a sense, it was going better than ever, as it gave them an opportunity to get extra reps with techniques that hadn't worked out for them during missions.

Sara decided to tag along with Erna. She hadn't settled on an itinerary for her day yet, so she had no particular reason to turn down the request.

"Are you sure you're okay to do this? I don't want to get in the way of your mission...," Erna asked.

"Y-yeah, it's all good," Sara replied with an evasive smile.

She really didn't want to have to explain how Monika had sidelined her for the day.

The two of them made their way away from the middle of Longchon to a spot on the outskirts of its mainland side. After a one-hour bus ride, they arrived in a town close to Longchon's border with the Republic of Ryuka. Unlike the more central parts of Longchon, the outskirts hadn't received any urban planning whatsoever, and they were lined with buildings of all sorts of mismatched heights and widths. Signs were scattered about written in Ryukese characters, and as disorderly as the townscape was, it spoke to the vibrance and energy of the people who lived there.

The air was thick with the fragrant smell of spices, and Sara's puppy twitched his nose in irritation. According to Erna, this was where Klaus was carrying out his mission. "By sneakily watching Teach work, we can figure out how to take him down," she'd explained.

The reason she'd recruited Sara was because she needed help tracking Klaus's position. If she tried tailing Klaus by conventional means, he'd sniff her out for sure, but with Sara's puppy's nose, they could follow him from far enough away that he wouldn't notice them. The puppy wasn't loving all the spices in the air, but he dutifully followed Klaus's trail all the same.

"You're really fired up, aren't you, Miss Erna?" Sara noted as they followed along after the pup. "You must be so busy with your missions, and here you are, using what little free time you have to train more."

Erna nodded deeply. "I mean...of course I am."

"What makes you say that?"

"At the end of the day, the whole reason we're in this mess is because I screwed up the mission back at the cotton mill."

"Ah." Now Sara finally got it. After successfully completing the mission that Sybilla and Erna had bungled, Vindo and Qulle had used that as evidence to make their case that Avian was stronger than Lamplight. As part of that, they'd referenced the way that Erna had gotten knocked out.

Sara could only imagine how guilty Erna must have felt about that. In her opinion, Erna was making it out to be bigger than it actually was, but Erna's voice was brimming with fervor. "I have to make things right... I'm going to come up with an awesome liecraft and use it to trounce Avian!"

Erna was taking long strides. Even her gait spoke to how unusually determined she was.

From the sound of it, Erna wasn't scared of Avian, either.

"That'd be nice...," Sara replied, trying to hide how mixed-up she felt about the whole thing.

"I've come up with loads of potential options," Erna said, sounding quite serious. "My plan is to pick one based on the situation and hit Teach with it."

"Oh, what kind of options?"

"Accidents × Seduction. I can lure enemies to their doom by seducing them the way Big Sis Thea does!"

"I think that might be hard for you, what with how shy you are."

"Accidents × Babbling. I'll guide them to where I want them to go by telling them clever lies like *Good fortune awaits you to the north*."

"These ideas are starting to sound as bad as Miss Lily's."

Sure enough, Erna was well and truly lost. All Sara saw in her imminent future was failure. However, there was something truly courageous about how proactive Erna was being about coming up with ideas.

She's really giving this her all...

Sara couldn't help but compare Erna against herself. She had yet to come up with a single decent idea for her liecraft.

What would even work for me? What kind of deception pairs well with animals? Bluffs? Could I tell someone The monster I reared will swallow you whole? *Masquerading? Could I dress up my pets to make them look like different animals than they actually are...?*

She gave it some more thought, but none of those options seemed likely to work. She just couldn't picture a washout like her successfully taking on a group of elites. She wasn't even the kind of person who battled her enemies head-on in the first place. She was terrible at fighting.

But...if I don't, Miss Monika is going to get mad at me again...

Sara was sick and tired of what a coward she was, but rooting out a deep-seated inferiority complex was easier said than done. She hung her head.

Ahead of them, Johnny the puppy came to a stop. He carefully swiveled his head from side to side, then began walking circles in place. Eventually, he turned to the side and headed down a small path.

They soon arrived at a hill road made up of cobbled stone steps. The path curved sharply to the left, so it was impossible to see what lay beyond. The sides of the road were lined with abandoned buildings with signboards that said things like FORBIDDEN ROSE HOTEL and ENTRAIL MEDICINES. They appeared to be hotels and pharmacies and the like, but there was something unmistakably shady about them, and the air was ripe with the sickly sweet smell of narcotics.

Erna gulped a little. "B-Big Sis Sara... Looking around, I think we're in a pretty bad neighborhood."

"I know it's a little late to be asking, but what did the boss come here to do?"

"I think...he was meeting someone...? Oh, now I remember..." Erna went on softly.

"...he's here to negotiate with the Longchon mafia."

The moment the two of them set foot down the path, they spotted a small table by the side of the road. It was barely visible behind the signboard.

CRYSTAL DIVINATION

According to the sign, it was a fortune teller. It wasn't an uncommon sight; it felt like there were fortune tellers down just about every alleyway in Longchon. However, the part that caught Sara's attention was the method the fortune teller used. Palm readings and bamboo divining sticks were much more in vogue in Longchon, so you rarely saw fortune tellers who used crystal balls. Sara had learned that from one of the books Monika made her memorize.

As it turned out, she was right to be suspicious. All of a sudden, the fortune teller rose to her feet and swung something straight at Sara's head.

""_____?!""

That something was an iron fan. Right away, Sara and Erna evaded the attack. As they leaped to the left, they reached for their guns.

"Oh-ho! You dodged it!" the woman crowed. She shed her shabby-looking fortune teller getup to reveal her red *dogi*, the outfit worn by practitioners of traditional Ryukese martial arts. Her long hair was tied back in three braids, leaving her broad forehead fully exposed. Based on the lively energy of her smile, she was probably still pretty young— early twenties, maybe. "I attack any suspicious characters who pass me by, but you two are the first to ever react in time! I can tell you're no amateurs. Are you covert operatives from abroad, perchance? Villains, come to trample Longchon beneath your boots? How intriguing! I think I'd best capture you for an interrogation!" After rather arbitrarily making her assessment, she spread the iron fans she was dual-wielding out wide. "My name is Reirin, proud member of the Jewel Family Eight!"

"".........""

Sara and Erna stared in disbelief at the woman calling herself Reirin. If the introduction she'd just given was true, that would make her a member of the Longchon mafia.

"...She seems like she could be dangerous," said Erna.

Sara nodded. "I feel like interacting with her would be more work than it's worth."

As an aside, the two of them were talking in Din's national language. Reirin was ostensibly a Longchon native, so there was no danger of her understanding them. She gave them a puzzled look.

Sara and Erna inched backward and got ready to make a break for it.

"Hmm? I introduce myself, and you try to leave without reciprocating?" Reirin made a pouty face. "So discourteous. I suppose you must be spies. Cowards, that's what you are!"

Sara saw little point in lending her an ear. Instead, she told Erna her plan. "I–I'm going to shoot. Just to scare her a little. When I do, we run."

She didn't want to cause a commotion, but it was more important that they get away from that woman.

Sara quietly produced her gun and leveled it at Reirin.

"Hmph. You'd do well not to look down on Reirin, proud member of the Jewel Family Eight!"

That woman seemed to *really* like introducing herself. "You already told us that part!" Sara retorted as she placed her finger on the trigger.

The moment she did, Reirin somersaulted backward and hid behind one of the signboards. With how nimbly she moved, it was clear that her *dogi* wasn't just for show. From where she was, she vanished off down the far end of the street.

Erna cocked her head. "She ran away...?"

Sara decided not to fire and lowered her gun. If Reirin was going to flee all on her own, there was no need for them to go out of their way to fight her.

"It looks like it... For now we should run away, too, then—"

Before Sara could finish her sentence, something struck her in the shoulder. "——?!" she gasped as the air rushed from her lungs.

Whatever had just hit her was hard and blunt. She lost her balance and crumpled to her knees.

"Big Sis Sara?" Erna yelped.

Sara hadn't caught so much as a glimpse of the attack. However, she knew which direction it had come from.

"...B-behind us," she choked.

The two of them whirled around in unison and saw Reirin with her iron fan held aloft.

"Too slow, scoundrels!"

Before Reirin had a chance to swing her fan down, Sara hurriedly did a forward roll to get out of harm's way. Her combat training with Monika was paying dividends. As she came out of the roll, she tugged Erna by the hand and broke into a run.

They made their way up the winding hill road, turning at what looked like a dentist's office and heading across a road filled with even more small shops. There was a signboard blocking the path, which was pretty obnoxious considering what a hurry they were in.

"What happened back there...?" Erna asked as they ran. "We blinked, and she was all the way behind us!"

"I—I don't know!"

That was just the thing—Reirin's movements didn't make sense. One moment, she disappeared down a path in front of them, and the next, she was right behind them. No human could have covered that much ground that fast on foot. It just wasn't possible. Sara hadn't even had time to ready her gun.

As Sara racked her brain over how she'd done it, Reirin strode out from behind the LIU XIONG BOOKS sign straight in front of them.

Erna and Sara skidded to a stop.

Once again, Reirin had traveled impossibly fast—and this time, she'd cut them off.

"It's an art called earth-shrinking." Reirin laughed proudly at the girls' bewilderment. "I learned it through dutiful study, and now all I have to do is shrink the earth and connect your location with mine. It's a trivial technique; any of the Jewel Family Eight could perform it."

With that, she swung her fans hard to the side.

At that point, there was still a good ten feet between her and the girls.

"With it, my attacks can *transcend distance*!"

A dull pain shot through Sara's knee. Something had just hit her again, and this time, it came from the side. She hadn't been expecting to get attacked from that angle, so she hadn't even been watching.

"You can't escape me. And know that I, Reirin, offer no mercy to those who would defile my beloved homeland!" Reirin readied her fans. She was winding up to do that invisible attack again.

Sara spoke as loud as she could muster. "W-we don't mean this country any harm. We're just a couple of tourists with a little bit of combat training, that's all. And this gun is only for self-defense..."

"If you think I'm going to fall for that, think again! You spies are a foul lot—you lie as easy as you breathe!"

"......!"

"Though I'll admit, I can see that you *are* terrified of me!"

Reirin flashed them a combative grin. When a real mafia member decided to do someone in, they didn't pull punches. Sara wasn't going to be able to fib her way out of this one.

I should have given it more thought... I should have considered what kind of operation the boss was on!

She'd already known that their current mission involved the Longchon mafia. By tailing him so carelessly, they'd wandered right into mafia-controlled territory.

"Yeep!"

Beside Sara, Erna pointed her gun at Reirin.

Reirin laughed mockingly. "No matter how much time you buy for yourself, this will always end the same way."

Before Erna could pull the trigger, Reirin somersaulted back behind the signboard. The area was full of things she could use for cover, and based on how she was moving, she knew them all like the back of her hand.

"Now's our chance! Run!"

Sara grabbed Erna's arm and dashed off once more. Yet again, they made their way along the curved hill road. There were signboards all over the place, so their ability to see their surroundings wasn't great. Due to all the clotheslines the buildings' residents had hung up, the area barely even got any sunlight.

In all likelihood, Reirin was moving to cut them off again. Sara didn't know if her earth-shrinking ability was real, but regardless, she definitely had *some* sort of incomprehensible movement technique at her disposal.

Sara's breath ran ragged as she diligently kept running. Her injured leg hurt, but she had no choice but to grit her way through the pain.

I'm sure Miss Thea could have figured out how to negotiate well enough to avoid a fight... Miss Grete could have used her disguises to escape... And I doubt Miss Monika or Miss Sybilla would have lost to her in a fight...

She couldn't help but think of the absent members of the team. She didn't have the tools to escape this dilemma. That was the painful truth, and she couldn't stand it.

Then Erna grabbed Sara by the sleeve. "Let's stop here, Big Sis Sara."

Huh? It didn't make sense to Sara. The spot Erna had chosen for them to stop in had terrible visibility. The road was narrow, and the buildings had all sorts of signboards sticking out of them. Given that they were up against a martial artist who liked to show up from unexpected angles, waiting for her there seemed like a terrible idea.

Before long, Reirin made her appearance, chasing after them by leaping from one signboard to the next like she was running across the sky. Sure enough, her movement was still blisteringly fast. She brandished her fans from a good distance away.

Erna leaned against Sara. "Anyone who bullies you is going to have me to answer to."

After making it so that the two of them would fall over together, she took her gun in both hands and fired.

The shock wave from the blast slammed Sara head-on. Erna's gun was a massive revolver, and its magnum round ripped through the air. Erna's body was too petite to withstand the shot's force, and with a "Yeep!" she collapsed backward.

Sara gently caught her as she fell.

Above them, Reirin recoiled a little at the gun's thunderous roar, but she soon broke into a mocking sneer. "Were you even *trying* to hit—?"

"I'm code name Fool—and it's time to kill with everything."

The moment Erna's lips moved, the sound of metal snapping rang out. It might have been because of the magnum round's impact, or it might have been because of the sound waves from the gun's discharge, but either way, the worn and fatigued iron signboards were at their limit. An avalanche of surrounding signboards cascaded down.

"Wh—?!"

Reirin's eyes went wide, and she frantically dodged away.

That was the last thing Sara saw of her. She was shocked, too, and she wrapped her arms around Erna's head and protectively cradled it. As she did, though, Erna just casually stared upward. She wasn't fazed in the slightest.

Sara thought back to Erna's ability.

Erna was so intropunitive and drawn to misfortune that she'd gained the ability to sense ill omens before they came to pass. That was why she'd fired that shot—she realized that the signboards were on the verge of collapsing.

The sound of metal getting crushed boomed out as the signboards continued crashing all around them. However, not a single one of them landed on Sara.

When the noise eventually stopped, Sara timidly raised her head. There was a mountain of debris surrounding them on all sides.

"~~~~~~~~!"

Sara let out a voiceless shriek. No matter how many times she saw Erna's ability at work, it never failed to inspire awe.

She was a little worried that Reirin might be dead, but she didn't see any bodies beneath the signboards, just a few scraps of Reirin's outfit. It didn't look like she'd been crushed, so she'd probably retreated for the time being.

"Well, it looks like we're out of danger for now," Erna said. Then one last bolt came tumbling out of the sky and hit her right on the head with a big *clunk*. "How unlucky…," she groaned as she hunched over.

"Y-you're right. Reirin's gone for now, so we should run away, too."

Reirin was a skilled martial artist. Sara didn't know who the Jewel Family Eight were, but they seemed like trouble.

She massaged her injured knee and rose to her feet.

"W-we should go back to the base for now," Erna said worriedly. "I'm sorry, Big Sis Sara. You got hurt, and it's all my fault…"

Midway through her sentence, she started getting choked up. As soon as tears began welling in her eyes, Sara patted her head. "It's fine," she said. "It's really not your fault. There's nothing to worry about."

"But…"

"Plus, there's no need to head straight back. I wasn't just running away at random, you know." Sara gave her puzzled comrade a big smile. "Mr. Johnny's been following the boss's scent—and we're really close."

All of a sudden, the black-furred puppy popped his head out from the alley where he'd been hiding. He rushed over to Sara, nudged her, then clambered atop her head, wagging his tail all the while.

Erna's eyes went wide. "Oh!" Now she understood the situation.

Mafia stronghold or not, it didn't matter. The Greatest Spy in the World was close by, and that meant that they were as safe as could be.

Apparently, Klaus was inside a massive mansion.

When they followed the puppy's nose there, they were greeted by a towering scarlet gate flanked on each side by a bronze statue of a dragon. The building inside was downright palatial, and it was surrounded by walls made of stacks of glazed orange roof tiles. Whoever lived there was clearly a big deal.

As Sara recalled, Klaus's mission had involved going and negotiating with the mafia. This must be where the boss lived, and the mansion was designed to keep outsiders away.

"I had no idea just tailing him was going to be so hard…," Sara murmured.

"Me neither. But the fact that we got this far is proof of how much we've grown," Erna declared proudly.

Sara agreed with Erna's optimistic view of the situation. And it wasn't just their regular training with Klaus—the intensive spartan training Monika had put her through was paying off, too. If not for that, they never would have escaped from Reirin.

Over at the gate, there was no gatekeeper to be seen.

"But what in the world do we do now?" Sara looked over at Erna. "Should we give up on the training and just ask the boss to protect us?"

Their original plan had been to threaten or attack Klaus once they'd tracked him down, but they'd worn themselves out just getting there. And to make matters worse, if they weren't careful about what they did next, Reirin might well attack them again.

"After we came all this way? I still want to give it a go."

Erna puffed up her cheeks in displeasure, but Sara couldn't bring herself to agree. "But we've already gotten in loads of training. Trying to take things further now would be dangerous."

"………Fine." Erna nodded, but she didn't look happy about it.

Miss Erna seems almost desperate…

A flash of unease ran through her upon seeing how much pain her teammate was in. The same behavior that had seemed courageous just moments ago now filled Sara with worry. It was like Erna didn't even care about how much danger she was putting herself in.

"Let's join up with the boss and figure the rest out from there," Sara urged her.

Having decided on the objective, the two of them headed around the side of the gate. It wasn't like they could just march in the front door and demand to see Klaus, but as spies, infiltration fell well within their wheelhouse.

After circling around to the building's flank, they scaled the wall and used their binoculars to check out the situation inside. Fortunately, the spot they'd chosen had a pretty clear view. There was a big pond in the middle of the yard, so there were no trees to block their line of sight. The garden around it had been carefully maintained.

""Huh…?""

Still holding their binoculars, the two of them simultaneously tilted their heads.

A pond sat in front of the gorgeous scarlet building with ten different bridges of varying sizes stretched over it, and the garden was full of long-weathered boulders, pavilions, and well-sculpted shrubs. It was a truly elegant space, but there was something bizarre scattered across the ground in it.

Namely, an unconscious horde.

Eyeballing it, there were nearly a hundred people collapsed in the garden, all still clutching their guns and falchions. It was evident from their lolling tongues that they were unconscious.

And there, standing in the middle of it all, was Klaus.

He leaned against one of the bridge's handrails, looked up at the sky, and muttered a few words to himself.

By reading his lips, the girls could tell what he was saying.

"...I had no idea that negotiating would be this difficult."

His expression was marked with sadness.

"Who would have thought that three mafia families would all join up and try to kill me without even listening to what I had to say? I guess they don't much care for foreign spies, not after all the years spies have been running roughshod over Longchon... I suppose it was a mistake for me to come to them openly as a show of good faith."

Waaaait, wait, wait, wait, wait, wait! Sara and Erna thought in unison.

Klaus had just taken down three entire mafia families. From the sound of it, he'd decided to try negotiating with them directly instead of secretly pilfering information from them. He said he'd meant it as a show of good faith, but the move was so audacious it had backfired and merely pissed them off. As a result, he'd had to knock out over a hundred mafia members.

As per usual, the scale he operated on was outrageous. It was starting to get to be a little bit much.

But.........

Sara looked up from her binoculars.

This is the world the boss lives in...

As a man who carried their entire nation's safety on his back, Klaus was constantly getting more responsibilities dumped in his lap. He often had little time to work with, and sometimes that meant having to take aggressive measures like he had there.

It was as if he and they lived in totally different worlds. As things stood, Lamplight was only capable of providing him with backup, nothing more.

Erna let out a sad "Yeep..." as that realization sank in. She clutched at the hem of Sara's clothes.

The two of them had just witnessed the sheer gulf that existed between them and Klaus. Then right as they felt their chests start to tighten—

"Vindo and Vics have the north side of the building under control, Mr. Klaus."

—they spotted a jade-haired girl in a ponytail rush over to Klaus.
"That's Qulle," Erna murmured. Avian was here.
Qulle pursed her lips with a touch of proud excitement.
Klaus, who'd been waiting for her on one of the bridges, gave her a nod, then spoke.

"Good work. Just to be sure, they didn't kill anyone, right?"
"Nope, just like you said. The one thing is, we couldn't find the guard who's supposed to be the go-between for the Steel Urn Group and the Jewel Family... If we'd just been able to talk with her first, this would all have gone a lot smoother."
"She's out on patrol right now."
"Wait, you know where she is?"
"One of the guys I knocked out just told me. She's supposedly quite fickle, so he didn't have any idea when she'd be getting back."
"Ah, I see. Should we go sweep the area, then?"
"That would be great. Having you all here has been a big help. This'll be a lot easier than trying to clean this all up myself."
"...Wh-what? No, no, you're too kind! Besides, it was nothing. Vindo and the others barely broke a sweat taking down the Jewel Family Eight."

Klaus and Qulle were chatting away like old friends. Apparently, Klaus was carrying out his current mission together with Avian. That was no surprise; after all, this was supposed to be an onboarding period so they could work together better in the future.
From there, Klaus and Qulle began carefully coordinating what the next steps in their op were going to be. Sara couldn't make out the specifics of their conversation, but it was obvious how in sync the two of them were.

"...................."

Her chest hurt, and her fingers drifted up to curl into her shirt. Each time she looked at the scene before her, she could feel her heartbeat pound faster.

Now I finally understand why Miss Erna felt so desperate...

Sara looked over at Klaus off in the distance.

His most immediately noticeable trait was his eccentricity, but he was also open-minded enough to accept all of Lamplight's members as they were. If not for that, he never would have agreed to work as the boss of a team as riddled with problem children as theirs. However, teaming up with Avian wouldn't stop him from being able to put his superhuman powers to use. Sara knew that all too well. Klaus was special to the girls, but to him, there was nothing special about them.

Avian really is skilled... It took everything we had just escaping from that mafia member, but they were able to stand proud and defeat loads of them...

The question was, who deserved that spot by Klaus's side more—the elites or them? By now, though, the answer was plain as day. It was Avian. She and Erna had come to ask Klaus to save them, whereas Avian had been strong enough to fight by his side.

Avian would make a far better group of subordinates for the Greatest Spy in the World. Sara understood that, and yet...

It hurts, Boss... I can't stand the thought of losing you to some other team...

Seeing him like that made it all feel terribly real.

Klaus was really going to leave Lamplight. They weren't going to have him around anymore. He was going to go become another team's boss, and they were going to have to part ways.

No! a voice in her heart shouted.

A moment later, she realized that that voice was her own. *No, no, no, no, no, no, no, no, no, no, no!* her heart pathetically screamed.

Sara broke into a run.

"Huh?" Erna said, but Sara didn't hear her.

She fled the mansion, and with it, that horrible sight.

◇◇◇

Sara never had a strong reason for becoming a spy.

She was born in a small coastal region of Din. Her parents happily ran a restaurant there, and one thing she loved to do as their only child was feed leftover food to the local dogs and cats.

Her childhood was, by all accounts, an ordinary one. There was just one unusual event in her life, and that was when she found an injured hawk by the side of the road and nursed it back to health and tamed it. After that, she developed a strange knack for getting along with animals.

When she chose to become a spy, she did so to avoid financially burdening her family. There was no deeper motive than that. Her parents' restaurant had gotten caught in the crossfire during a spy battle. Rumor had it that the fight was between an Imperial spy and the Military Intelligence Department, but in any case, there was a big flashy firefight that left the restaurant all but demolished. Her parents didn't have the savings to repair it, so they had no choice but to close up shop, and before long, the expenses associated with raising a child got to be too much for them.

That was when a Foreign Intelligence Office scout who'd heard about her through the grapevine approached her and asked if she wanted to enroll in a spy academy. With no other way to put food on the table, she decided to take the path of least resistance and accept the offer.

As a result, Sara didn't have anything driving her. She wasn't particularly motivated by the idea of protecting her nation, and she didn't even have an ideal in mind of what kind of spy she wanted to become. When her academy branded her as a washout, she figured she deserved it.

At the end of the day, she didn't really care about being a spy.

She was immature in body, mind, and resolve alike, and with how unmotivated she was, there wasn't a single person who expected anything out of her.

Sara's thoughts turned as she dashed down the curved hill road.

Then, after becoming a washout, I came to Lamplight...

Getting expelled would have left her unemployed, so joining Lamplight was the only option she'd had. At first, she was horrified. Going on a deadly Impossible Mission felt like it would be throwing her life away, and as she tearily told Lily at the time, she had planned on running away.

By all rights, Lamplight should have been hell on earth for Sara. And to make matters worse, all the other washouts on the team were still so much more talented than her. She had no place there.

But then I met people who accepted me...

There was the World's Strongest, who'd called her magnificent, there were people who'd become attached to her like little sisters, there were conniving friends who'd carved out spots for her in their plots to attack Klaus, and there were even older girls who'd mentored and helped guide her. Before Sara knew it, Lamplight had become an irreplaceable home to her.

I might not have a reason for being a spy—but I'm not going to let the others down...!

As her teammates' faces flashed through her head, Sara's legs moved faster still.

Eventually, she arrived at a tiny diner that had long since shut down. The door wasn't locked, and she threw it open with all her might.

The room inside had a small counter and a kitchen. The stove was off, and there was a young woman sitting atop it.

"Hmm?! You're that spy from earlier!"

It was Reirin.

She'd gotten injured in Erna's accident, and she was right in the middle of bandaging her leg. She finished winding the bandage, cut it off the roll with a pair of scissors, and stashed the bandage roll back in her *dogi*. She rose to her feet atop the counter.

"How peculiar! How did you find my hideout, one wonders?" Reirin furrowed her brow, then laughed once she spotted the puppy by Sara's feet. "Aha, I see! You followed my scent from the clothing scraps I left at the accident site! Ha-ha, how devilish. You're a clever one!"

"........."

"But at the same time, you never learn! To think you'd come fight me on your own after fleeing so shamefully earlier. So kind of you to seal your own fate!"

She lorded over Sara from her spot atop the counter and drew her fans. Her behavior was brimming with confidence. In her eyes, Sara was going to be a pushover.

"...I have one thing I'd like to ask you," Sara said.

"Oh?"

"Are you the guard who acts as the go-between for the Steel Urn Group and the Jewel Family?"

"Oh-ho. I'm surprised you knew." The corners of Reirin's mouth curled into a grin. "Right you are! That's me! Proud member of the Jewel Family Eight and liaison for the Steel Urn Group. So whaddaya want? You trying to get in touch with the Steel Urn Group? Because if you are, I'm the only one around these parts who's got an in with those rebellious shadow lurkers. If that's your game, just know that I charge a steep rate for my—"

"I'm here to train."

"...What?"

"I'm sorry you have to be part of this, but I'm going to catch you before my boss can. Then I'll make him say he surrenders in exchange for me handing you over." Sara adjusted her newsboy cap and looked straight at Reirin. "Please don't try to resist. I promise nothing bad will happen to you."

"...I feel like *someone's* being mighty impolite."

"Well, you were impolite first. It's time I got you back for that bump on Miss Erna's head."

Sara was pretty proud of how glib she was being. She'd learned the art of verbal warfare from watching Lily and Monika, and sure enough, she could see Reirin squeeze her fans so tightly that her fingertips went white. That woman was no hardened spy, so even Sara's psychological attacks were working like a charm.

Honestly, I'm scared to my bones, but...

There was no point worrying about how she might fail. She just had to do it.

After all, just how many mafia members had the Avian elite just torn through?

"If I can't beat someone like you, then I have no right to stand by the boss's side...!!"

You can do this, she told herself. *You're gifted, just the way Klaus said you were! Hold your head high like the magnificent prodigy that you are!*

Reirin rose to the challenge and leaped at her. "To think you would be this blind about how outmatched you are! You're a fool among fools!"

Sara immediately fell back and rushed out of the diner to an alley not far from where they fought earlier. The path curved back and forth, and it was dotted with myriad little hill roads and staircases. Between that and the signboards scattered all about, visibility in the area couldn't have been worse.

Sara raced down the road, probing for what her opponent would do next.

"You think you can get away?!"

Sure enough, Reirin appeared in front of her, cutting her off yet again. She couldn't have gotten there that fast on foot; she must have used her high-speed earth-shrinking technique.

However, Sara had come into this fight prepared. She took the paper bag she'd been concealing and hurled it at Reirin. Reirin swatted it away with one of her steel fans, but when she did, the bag tore and blasted her with its finely powdered contents.

"Ack! What is this, peppercorn?!" Reirin yelped, flustered.

A stinging aroma spread all through the alley. You could buy potent spices just about anywhere in Longchon, and by grinding them up, you could make yourself a quick and easy tear bomb.

Sara had successfully limited her foe's vision.

She wasted no time in drawing her gun, but Reirin quickly did a splendid somersault backward and hid behind a nearby building. Sara heard her confidently cry, "Sorry, but I could run through this town with my eyes closed!" However, Reirin's voice echoed off so many walls that Sara couldn't get a good bead on her position. "Is that all you've got up your sleeve?" Reirin went on. "If so, I'll settle this with my next blow! I'm in a bit of hurry—for some reason, my calls to HQ aren't going through!"

"...Your headquarters got taken out, actually."

"You're still lying, even now?! You truly are a deplorable one!"

Reirin wasn't listening to anything Sara told her. Her style was to ignore any battles of wits from the get-go and simply fight things out, no matter what. Annoyingly, that meant that any bluffs Sara tried to pull were unlikely to work. Sara renewed her resolve and tightened both her hands around her gun.

"Feel the wrath of my Jewel Family Eight secret art—all-out full-power earth-shrinking!"

The moment Reirin shouted, Sara felt her skin prickle as the hostility in the air rapidly swelled.

Something impossible was happening.

One moment, she heard footsteps from the south, but the next, Reirin came running at her from across the shops to the north. Sara spotted her to the east, and not seconds later, she saw her leaping atop a signboard to the west. The unbridled way she was moving made no logical sense, yet it was allowing her to close in on Sara all the same.

However—

"I know how you do it."

—Sara wasn't enough of an amateur to keep getting bamboozled by the same technique forever. She'd spent ages now training with teammates who came up with lies far cleverer than Reirin's.

"It's a pretty cheap lie. There's no such thing as earth-shrinking. I can track your smell from that pepper I used earlier, and that let me figure out the gimmick behind your movement."

Eventually, Reirin appeared directly in front of her and raised up her fans in a big, telegraphed attack.

Down by Sara's feet, her puppy Johnny let out a big bark.

"The secret behind your movement is a childish trick—the fact that you're a pair of twins!"

She fired backward.

Without turning her body, she swapped her gun to a single-handed grip. After taking it in her right hand, she shoved it under her left armpit and pulled the trigger.

"Gah—!"

A scream rose up from behind her.

Sara whirled around and found Reirin clutching at her bleeding shin. With the way Sara had shot, her reversed bullet had gone low instead of flying in a straight line. Sara had no intention of killing Reirin, of course, so that fact came as a relief. She took a big sniff, but she didn't smell any pepper. Her puppy didn't react, either.

Sure enough, there had been two Reirins all along.

"Your coordination was fantastic," Sara said. "So you had two people pretending to be a single woman? That's a wonderful technique."

By sheer coincidence, what the Reirins had pulled off was similar to the concept of liecraft Sara had been taught. A liecraft combined a unique talent with a synergistic form of deception, and the Reirins had paired their twin combo with just the right lie. That was how they fought—Coordination × Optical Illusions = Fake Earth-Shrinking.

"Urk..." Sweat streamed down Reirin's face. "I can't believe you saw through us..."

"I'm too old to believe in magic like earth-shrinking."

It had been far too implausible an explanation to be true. Now that Sara thought about it, Reirin had been relentlessly introducing herself as "a member of the Jewel Family Eight!" since they first met her. That must have been misdirection to distract from that fact that she was actually two twins.

Sara took a deep breath and aimed her gun at Reirin's forehead. "Surrender. You've got nowhere to run."

"You're not half bad!" Reirin scoffed. Even now, her triumphant expression never left her face. "But the thing is, the win is ours. Think about it—you've got two opponents. While you're here threatening me with your gun, all my sister has to do is attack you from behind."

"...You have a point."

"That's checkmate. You lose." Reirin grinned. "Now you have three seconds to lower your gun. Otherwise, my sister will cut you in half with her fans."

"..............."

Sara didn't lower her gun. It was obvious that if she did, the Reirin in front of her would attack her with *her* fans. Given the situation, though, it was impossible for her to deal with the imminent attack from behind the other Reirin was going to launch. However, she couldn't shoot the Reirin in front of her, either. She still needed to pump her for information.

Sara had lost.

Even after seeing through her opponents' trick, she still couldn't beat them in a fight. Plus, it was two against one, and these weren't the kind of people Sara could defeat by battling them head-on anyway.

She was weak.

That was why she needed something. She needed a type of deception all her own—one that would let her overcome that talent gap.

After counting down from three to one, Reirin smiled. "Come on, Reika! Attack her from behind, and—"

"There's a reason I'm not moving, you know. It's to lure you in," Sara said.

Then she quietly made her declaration.

"I'm code name Meadow—and it's time to run circles around you!"

Once again, a scream rose up from behind Sara.

Reika—Reirin's elder twin sister—had landed down in the alley to attack Sara, but a large hawk swooped down at her as though he'd been waiting for precisely that moment. His name was Bernard, and he was the pet Sara relied on most of all.

Bernard dug his talons deep into Reika's upper arm and jabbed his beak into the back of her neck.

"Wh-AHHHHHHH?! Where'd this beast *come* from?!"

The attacks didn't stop there—Aiden the pudgy pigeon followed up by body-slamming her, and Johnny the puppy diligently sank his teeth into her ankle. Sara's pets were all working together to gang up on Reika.

"Reika!" Reirin cried, but Sara shouted "I'd appreciate it if you didn't try anything!" and redrew her bead on Reirin's forehead to stop her from moving. "If you want to save your sister, then I'm going to have to ask that you drop your weapon."

".........!"

"I knew all along how little you two thought of me, so I put myself in danger so you'd charge at me without thinking too hard about it. Once you did, it was easy to have my animals surround you."

Sara had thought long and hard about how someone as weak as her could deceive someone, and in the end, she realized that she could *use her weak self as a decoy*. By intentionally placing herself in harm's way, she could get her opponents to lower their guard and give her animals an opportunity to take them down.

That was the new spy combat style Sara had just come up with— Rearing × Decoy = Human-Beast Pincer Attack.

By using it, she'd completely locked down the twins' movement.

I can fight. I can fight, too...!

Now all she had to do was extort them. Her hawk, Bernard, was far stronger than she was, and he was capable of tearing right through a person's carotid artery. At this rate, she was about to rack up her very first solo victory, but then—

"Huh...?"

Sara's thoughts got interrupted.

Her side was wounded. Unable to withstand the pain, she crumpled.

"It... It hurts...?"

When she saw the object that had just fallen in front of her, she realized where the attack had come from.

It was a crystal ball.

Reika must have thrown it during her battle against Sara's animals. Her fans had been blocking Sara's view of what she was holding, so Sara hadn't known to dodge it. Now that she thought about it, though, this wasn't the first time the twins had performed an "invisible" attack.

That was another trick in the twins' toolbox—using their iron fans to obscure their crystal projectiles.

Sara collapsing meant Reirin was free to move again, and she drove off the animals that were swarming Reika. Realizing that the situation had turned, the animals withdrew and returned to Sara's side.

""You're a crafty little rascal! This is how you spies like to fight, then? Laying twofold and threefold traps? We'll have to keep that in mind!"" the twins said in unison, verbally pounding the nail into Sara's coffin as she lay on her hands and knees.

Sara had no more moves left to play. She was out of schemes, and even though her hawk, Bernard, was pecking at her to urge her to flee, the pain in her flank was too bad for her to do even that.

""Now it's time for your punishment!""

The twins raised their fans in perfect harmony.

"Here's a question—have you ever heard of restraint?"

Then Sara heard a different voice come from behind her.

Reirin's and Reika's eyes both went wide, and Sara turned back. There stood a blue-haired girl—Monika—looking well and truly exasperated. She scratched the back of her head in annoyance. "I know I told you to be more confident, but that doesn't mean you should go picking solo fights against mafia members. What's with the sudden burst of motivation? You hitting that age where you're just itching for a brawl?"

Sara gasped. "Miss Monika, what are you doing here?"

"Lily and the others were freaking out. 'Erna went missing! She must be lost!' So I went out looking. Imagine my surprise when I found *you* here."

Reirin and Reika stared daggers at the newcomer to try to gauge how strong she was. Despite the intensity of their gazes, though, Monika remained cool and undaunted.

"So Rearing × Decoy, huh? That's the liecraft you came up with?" Monika must have been watching from somewhere.

Sara nodded, and with a "Hmmm," Monika sank into thought before finally delivering her verdict. "........................No dice."

Sara had received a failing grade.

She slumped her shoulders and let out a little groan. She'd worked really hard on that, too.

"Ultimately, a liecraft is a mirror of who you are. You take your experiences, your beliefs, your tics, your habits—everything about your life—and you come up with a form of deception all your own." Monika gave her a small smile. "Using you as a decoy is out of the question. You're not nearly as weak as you think you are."

After observing the conversation, Reirin and Reika eventually determined that Monika was a powerful threat. They backstepped with the exact same timing.

""We see, we see! Reinforcements, is it? Intriguing!"" they said as one. ""In that case, we'll bring all our might to bear! Remember, you're on our home turf. You're about to regret having spoiled our moods!""

With that, they simultaneously fled behind signboards.

The omni-directional noise of their footsteps sounded out even faster than before. They hadn't been using their full strength back when they were fighting Sara. They were blisteringly quick, and they circled Sara and Monika like a pair of predators hunting their prey.

"Well, that's a shame," Monika said flatly.

"Huh?"

"I wanted to practice my liecraft, but they're too weak for that. There's no point using a skill like that on a pair of shitters I don't even need to trick," Monika complained. It was a hard proclamation to believe, but Monika wasn't the sort to lie about something so trivial. "I'll be fine just going with the usual. Here you go, Sara. As a special treat, I'll show you my ability—creepshot."

With that, she pulled out a set of mirror shards and scattered them up into the air. They gleamed like powdered snow as they fell back to the ground.

"I'm code name Glint—now, let's harbor love for as long as we can."

Monika's eyes began twitching finely back and forth. It was like she was checking every one of the reflections. Actually, there was no "like" about it—with her astounding calculation abilities and precise movements, that was exactly what she was doing. On closer inspection, there were a couple of concave lenses mixed in with the mirror shards, too.

Sara had spent a long time working by Monika's side, so she understood what Monika's ability was. No, perhaps the word *ability* didn't do the full breadth of her capabilities justice. When Monika combined her mirrors and lenses, her expertise was downright superhuman. Creepshot was a skill that allowed her to *observe anything and everything within a set amount of space*!

Eventually, Reirin and Reika leaped out in unison. ""Eat dirt!""

However, Monika didn't twitch. She'd seen it all. The twins had been staying behind cover, but Monika had been tracking their every move.

A series of dull *thunks* echoed out in succession.

Monika's knives had struck Reirin and Reika straight in their temporal regions. That much was clear from the way their bodies crumpled. They sank to their knees simultaneously, then slowly keeled over.

The fight had been as quick as it had been decisive. Monika's strength was in a whole different league than Sara's.

"Well, that handles that. Now, it'd be nice if we could just pump them for intel straightaway—"

Monika shrugged, then turned her gaze from the downed sisters.

"—but sadly," she continued with a grim smile, "Klaus is already here."

Sara turned her attention over in the direction Monika was looking.

There stood Klaus.

Beside him, Erna was looking over at them with a worried look in her eyes. The two of them had come there together.

"Sara," said Klaus, who seemed to understand exactly what had happened. "You tried to fight them on your own? That was very brave of you."

Sara felt a tremble in the back of her throat.

She wanted to say *No, it wasn't*. She felt like she might cry. In the end, she hadn't been able to win. She was weak. She was inexperienced. Her skills were fatally lacking. She had lost to one of the same mafia members that Avian had been able to mow through with ease, and the liecraft she'd worked so hard to design had been a flawed dud. If Monika hadn't shown up and saved her, she would have died.

"Magnificent."

When Klaus's gentle gaze fell on her, though, she couldn't help but feel a sense of accomplishment.

Once the business stuff was all finished, Monika read Sara the riot act.

"Okay, seriously, what the hell were you thinking? What kind of imbecile takes an idea they just cooked up and does their test run in a live battle? I'd expect that from Lily, sure, but *you*? And plus, Rearing × Decoy... No. That gets thirteen out of a hundred. Your spot isn't on the front lines, remember? I don't ever want to see you pull a stunt like that again. For now, no working solo until you can at least complete that assignment I gave you."

She was laying on the criticism thick, and Sara had no rebuttal to any of it. It was hard to blame Monika for being mad after what Sara had done.

However, the taste of satisfaction still lingered in Sara's mouth.

She felt like she'd improved a bit. She still had a long way to go, but she was making forward progress. Monika's voice was a fair bit gentler than usual, and that was all the proof she needed.

In the end, the sun had already *started setting* by the time Monika released her. Sara was curious as to how the mission had gone, and her pets needed a walk anyway, so she headed over to the Lamplight base.

The villa sat atop a small hill on Longchon Island, and Sara was sweating profusely under the sunlight as she ascended the hill's precipitous slope. The higher she got, the better the view became. Just beyond the age-worn aluminum fence, she could see the rows of buildings lining the harbor as well as Longchon's turquoise sea.

Halfway up the hill, she discovered a small table. There was a fortune teller sitting at it with a sign that read CRYSTAL DIVINATION.

Isn't that what I saw this afternoon? Sara thought, thoroughly disquieted. She took another look at the fortune teller.

It was Erna.

"Reirin has my respect."

Sara froze. "Whaaaat...?"

For whatever reason, Erna was wearing a Ryukese-style cheongsam dress. Its fabric was bright pink, and she'd altered its hem to be adorned with frills. She was also going for some sort of tiger motif, as there was a pair of yellow ears on her head and a yellow-and-black-striped tail extending out from her backside.

She held up a crystal ball. "I'm going to become the best fortune teller in all of Longchon. When my targets come to visit me, I'll tell them that good fortune can be found on a train platform. Then when they arrive at the platform I tell them about, I'll deviously push them onto the tracks. It'll be the birth of Erna, the assassination specialist feared the world over."

"..................................."

Sara had no clue what to say to that.

"........"

"........"

"........"

"........"

Erna took her tiger ears and hurled them against the ground. "I can't keep doing thiiiiiiiiiiiiiiiiiiiiiiiiis!"

"She's gotten even more lost than before!"

Erna's face was bright red, and she began lashing out. It was plain to see how embarrassed she was. She crouched down and began rolling around on the ground, not caring how dirty she was getting.

Sara rushed over, hugged her, and helped her back to her feet.

"Now that I think about it, you never got a chance to try out your liecraft, huh?"

"No. We kept running into trouble. And then you went on that rampage, Big Sis Sara..."

"Urk. I am sorry about that."

"I get how you feel, though. You wanted to get stronger as fast as possible so you could beat Avian."

"That's right. Ah, but we can't afford to be so reckless." Sara patted Erna's head. "Miss Monika gave me some advice. She told me that a liecraft is like a mirror of who you are. Why don't we head back to the base for a bit, take a breather, and work together to come up with some ideas that suit us?"

Sara had been worried for a while now about how rashly Erna was acting. The way she'd strolled so casually into mafia-controlled territory had been really careless.

"...But I.............."

Still holding her crystal ball, Erna took a few unsteady steps. Her eyes swam with anguish.

Her lips twitched. "...don't like who I am..."

"What?"

"I hate myself... This whole mess we're in is all my fault."

Erna ran her hand along the aluminum safety fence and let out a pained groan.

That was the second time Sara had heard her say that. She was still beating herself up about her screwup back at the cotton mill.

It feels like there's something more going on with her, though...

Fear crept its way into Sara's heart as she headed over to Erna. "That wasn't your fault, Miss Erna. I heard about what happened, and the mission only went south because you got caught up in that weird explosion midway through. It was just bad luck. Let's go get some rest, okay?"

Erna shook her head in frustration. "True, that was unlucky..."

Down by her feet, Johnny let out a small bark.

Sara said nothing. "........."

"But I can't just shrug it off like that." Erna bit her lip. "I'm the one who gave Avian that opening to move in on us. I'm terrified to imagine what it'll be like if we lose Teach. That's why I—"

Erna squeezed down hard on the fence to try to contain her tempestuous emotions. And when she did, the fence warped.

Sara gasped.

From there, it felt like she perceived everything in slow motion.

The weathered aluminum fence, bending from the ground up. Erna's body lurching forward along with it. The thirty feet plus of cliff. Erna, falling as though sucked down by some force. Her crystal ball glinting in the sunlight as it quietly rolled away. The wind blowing. The smell of the sea. The stone steps down at the bottom of the cliff. Erna's widening eyes. Sara's own outstretched hand.

Erna's lips twitched. "How unlucky..."

The puppy barked so loudly it was practically screaming.

Sara had immediately thrust out her hand, but she was too late—and Erna fell down the cliff.

Chapter 3

Unlucky

There was something Sybilla had once pointed out.

"Y'know, I feel like Erna came off as way more mature back when Lamplight was just startin' out."

At the time, all the girls had been playing a board game. Their training had worn them out so badly that none of them wanted to move, so they decided to play a game instead. They spread the board out atop the table they usually used for their strategy meetings and munched on sweets as they played. It was interesting to see how disparate their play styles were. There was Lily, who focused more on keeping everyone engaged than on actually trying to win; there was Sybilla, who played largely on intuition but was a fierce competitor nonetheless; and there was Annette, whose strategy was inscrutable but who somehow always managed to shift the tides in her favor.

Erna was sulking about being in last place, which was what had inspired Sybilla's comment about her having seemed more mature back when they first met.

"That's not it," Erna replied. "People with social anxiety just throw up a bunch of walls when they talk to new people, so they seem older than they really are. Also, for the record, it's really embarrassing to having people say, 'Huh? *That's* what you're really like?' after I worked so hard to come out of my shell."

"Well, hey, sounds like you're talkin' to us just fine," Sybilla said.

In truth, Erna agreed with Sybilla. She was pretty sure she'd been way more poised when she first joined Lamplight, and she didn't quite know where along the line she had become the group's comic relief.

"Wait," Lily said delightedly, "does that mean we've won your trust, then?"

"Yeep…" Erna could feel her face going red. "Y-yeah, that's right."

The others all looked at her with tenderness in their gazes. That made Erna even more embarrassed, and she looked down bashfully.

This feels really nice.

It wasn't the first time the thought had crossed Erna's mind. Just as Thea had once pointed out, Erna had a needy side. She herself realized how childish she was for her age, and sometimes, she could hardly stand how attention-seeking she felt when she called the others Big Sis. *Stop being so manipulative*, she would say to herself.

That was precisely why she loved her teammates so much—they accepted her for who she was. And the person who was truest of all about that was—

"You're playing a board game? That's a new one."

Speak of the devil. No sooner did she imagine his face than Klaus himself showed up in the room.

Without missing a beat, Lily said "You wanna play too, Teach? Heh-heh-heh, we'll beat you around the board and back" and called him over to the table.

Once Klaus joined in, the energy in the room rose even more. Upon realizing that the game only supported eight, he made a decision. "Erna, let's you and I play as a team."

Erna, delighted by the proposal, raised her fist in the air. "I'm in!"

Lamplight had accepted her, and she loved them for it.

After all, Erna loathed herself so very much.

There was a strategy meeting going on in Klaus's base about the joint Lamplight-Avian mission.

As it turned out, their most frequent visitor from Avian was Qulle, which earned Klaus some dubious looks from the locals. "Looks like the wastrel's got himself a new girl…" However, their misunderstanding actually worked in his favor, so Klaus decided to ignore them and simply put up with it for the remainder of his time there in Longchon.

At the moment, both of the teams were dealing with the same problem: the information leaks Din was suffering from their embassy in Longchon. Their goal was to figure out the exact specifics of which embassy officials the local mafia had paid off, who it was that was buying Din's intelligence on the black market, and what foreign spies were involved in the whole situation. Lamplight and Avian were doing as Klaus instructed and conducting an undercover investigation, and Qulle and Thea were talking in the study.

"So how did it go, Thea? Were you able to get anything out of that mafia member?"

"Oh yes, Reirin sang like a bird. As we suspected, the Steel Urn Group was behind the whole thing. Qulle, can I ask Avian to pin down the specifics?"

"You got it. This is good, this is good. It feels like all the details of the incident are finally coming into view."

"Indeed they are. We even managed to track down that classified document's location."

The two of them put together their plan with brisk efficiency. By all accounts, Qulle's role in Avian was much like Thea's in Lamplight in that she organized the team's intel and handled their command and control.

The two of them had been running the investigation together for the past week, and in that time, Thea had found herself impressed on more than one occasion. After coming from the highly teamwork-oriented Lamplight, it was novel seeing how much discretion Avian gave to its members on the ground. And Qulle found it invigorating as well, often commenting things like, "Wow, you really plan things out that finely?" and "You guys have backup plans for every eventuality, huh."

The more time the two COs spent together, the more they learned from each other.

On the flip side, though, there were times when the mood got tense.

"Say, Qulle, would you mind if we put Avian in charge of tailing this target? You were able to get some really detailed data on that op three days ago. That was code name Lander who did that, right?"

"Yeah, that's no problem. I'll let him know."

"He's lying low now, right? Where's he staying, a café or something?"

"Oh, I can't remember. More importantly, do you think we could get that Glint of yours to help out? It sounds like you all trust her a lot, so I have to imagine she's really good."

"Hmm, that might be tricky. She doesn't really play well with others."

What was happening was, they were both fishing for information.

None of the Avian members except Qulle and Vindo had shown their faces, and in turn, Lamplight had successfully kept all specific information about Grete, Monika, and Sara a secret. It was an established fact that the two teams were going to butt heads at some point, and they both wanted to get ahold of any intel that might give them an advantage. As such, both Thea and Qulle spent their time trying to bait the other into overplaying their hand. However, neither of them was willing to cede an inch, and no careless slips of the tongue were forthcoming.

When Thea realized that any further conversing would be pointless, she headed over to the blackboard. That was where they'd hung their big map of the area around the Longchon coast.

"Let's go over everything one last time," she said. "This next big op will be the final part of our mission in Longchon. The day after tomorrow, Avian and Lamplight will be stealing back the classified document from its location in the Longchon Walled City. Each team will be working independently, and as soon as anyone gets ahold of the document, the mission will be complete."

"Right. No matter which team gets it, Avian or Lamplight, we're golden."

"And you're prepared for things to get a bit rocky?"

"Of course. Friendly fire is simply going to be unavoidable, so any level of violence short of outright homicide is on the table."

Naturally, Qulle knew exactly what Thea was implying with her question. It was no mere mission that would be taking place that day, and during the op, each team had the green light to attack the other. Both of them were going to be actively trying to crush the other one.

Thea smiled. "I think we can both agree that Teach deserves to work with only the finest of subordinates."

Qulle licked her lips. "But of course."

With that, the terms of Lamplight and Avian's battle were set. The starting time was ten PM tomorrow night. Violence was allowed. Sabotage was allowed. The location was Longchon's massive apartment complex block. The wager was Klaus. And their task was simple—steal back that document!

"Are you sure about this, though?" Qulle cheerfully asked once they finished laying out the specifics. "I hear one of your team members got wounded. Is she going to be okay?"

"………"

Apparently, Avian knew all about Erna's fall. However, perhaps that much was inevitable. One of their members must have spotted Sara when she came rushing in pale as a sheet two evenings ago shouting about how Erna had fallen off the cliff.

"Well, she certainly got a little too into her training." Thea smiled. "It's nothing to worry about, though. It wasn't life-threatening, and as a matter of fact, it wasn't even that serious of an injury."

"Oh, is that right? That's so good to hear."

"Isn't it? It's not a great situation, though."

Qulle cocked her head. "How so?"

"Like I said, the whole reason she got hurt was because she was training too hard. And that wouldn't have happened if a certain few someones hadn't butted into our mission and tried to steal our boss. You know, up until the incident, some of our members couldn't even learn liecraft because of how scared of you they were." Thea glared at Qulle. "But now we've made up our minds—we're going to crush you people into the dirt."

Qulle glared back, not faltering in the slightest. "There's this phrase called 'misdirected anger.' Ever heard of it?"

Vehement sparks flew between the two teams' COs.

Over in one of the base's bedrooms, Lily was helping Erna remove her clothes.

"And now for my homemade salve!"

With that, she pulled out a bottle of ointment. As of late, Lily had taken to practicing making pharmaceuticals in addition to just poison. Mixing compounds was a particular specialty of hers, and the quality of her medicine was increasing by the day. She might not have shown it often, but she actually took her work pretty seriously.

After loading her hand up with ointment, she lathered up Erna's left arm, poked her right cheek, carefully lathered up her left shoulder and back, poked her left cheek, then poked her right cheek a second time.

Then, finally, she gave both of Erna's cheeks another poke for good measure.

"I feel like that was more cheek poking than necessary," Erna protested.

"I'm pretty sure you're imagining things." Lily sealed up the jar, then gave Erna's body another once-over. "The silver lining is, it doesn't look like it's going to leave a scar. It'll still take a while to heal, but at least you have that going for you."

"Yeep…"

Erna hadn't been *gravely* injured in her fall, but that wasn't to say that her wounds were light, either. Her body was banged up all over and covered in black and blue. She was going to make it, but she was pretty pathetic to look at.

"For now you should spend the rest of the day taking it easy. It hurts pretty bad to move, right?"

"Yeah. It really does…"

"Then your only job is to rest up," Lily said gently. "Doctor's orders, okay?"

At that point, a new voice piped up. "I think she's a numbskull, yo."

As Lily had been applying Erna's ointment, Annette had been lying on the other side of the bed. "Only a total nincompoop would let herself get injured twice in a row like that," she declared, readying her extendable grabber and zigzagging it out to poke Erna in the back.

"Yeep?! That's where I'm hurt!"

"My assault begins now."

"C-cut it out! Johnny, stop her!"

Erna took the black puppy lying by her feet and tossed him at Annette. Johnny landed on Annette's belly and started licking her neck. Annette kicked her legs back and forth. "That tickles, yo!" she cried.

Erna snorted triumphantly. "Big Sis Sara lent him to me. From now on, I can have *him* protect me."

The puppy's eyes flashed smartly from atop Annette. It was clear to see how seriously he intended on taking his job. He understood full well just how kind his owner Sara was.

"She can be almost overprotective, that Sara," Lily said with a grin. Then she spoke up as though she'd suddenly recalled something. "Still, I can't deny that you've had a heck of a string of bad luck."

"Yeep."

"If you wouldn't mind, can you explain to me how your condition works again? It's not just a penchant for misfortune, right?"

Lily had heard the story, albeit just once. Erna's true, warped desire was that she pursued punishment. Losing her family to a fire had trapped her with a catastrophic case of survivor's guilt. Subconsciously, she sought out misfortune in order to finally find relief.

However, there were a lot of things about that explanation that Lily didn't fully buy.

"It's hard for me to talk about it," Erna mumbled sadly. "If I do, it means I have to talk about my family. It's not a happy story."

".........."

Lily could sense the somber, pained emotions lurking behind those words. She sat down beside Erna and squeezed her hand. "Could you try? Take as much time as you need."

Erna gave her a small nod. "To start, I was born into a family of aristocrats. The aristocracy's been abolished, so we were only nobility in name, but we were still pretty wealthy and well-known. But because of that, there were a lot of cruel people who had it in for us."

Lily had had an inkling that something like that was the case, but this was the first time Erna had told her outright. There had always been something sophisticated about the way Erna carried herself, and it made sense that it was because of her upbringing. She'd clearly been raised with great care.

Erna feebly went on. "We had a tradition of always spending Christmas together. Mom and Dad would buy loads of wine, Big Bro would get some party poppers, Big Sis would bake us a cake… That day was no different. I was eight years old, it was Christmas, and late that night, someone threw a Molotov cocktail into our living room."

"Oh no…"

Molotov cocktails were just about the easiest weapons for civilians to produce. In contrast with their simplicity, though, they were brutally powerful. People had even used them to stop tanks back in the Great War.

"By the time I knew what had happened, the fire had already spread, the whole mansion was burning, and the only person who escaped before the whole place burned down…" Erna gave her head a sad shake. "…was me."

Lily gasped. "Why would someone do that?"

"I don't know. There were no witnesses, and the perpetrator was never caught. The police said that whoever did it was probably jealous of us for being rich."

"Ah," Lily replied.

Lily knew all about how chaotic things had been in Din after the war. People across the nation had fought and scrabbled over what little money there was, and looting became rampant in the urban areas as people with no job prospects came together and formed gangs. Back then, simply being rich was reason enough for people to want you dead. The world they'd been born into was a world awash in pain, and the tragedy that had claimed Erna's family was just one more example of that.

Johnny let out a small whine from within Erna's arms.

Erna looked down in anguish, and Lily gave her hand a squeeze.

"Ever since then, I—"

"Yo, hold it! We've got an eavesdropper in the hallway, Sis."

That was when Annette spoke up.

Lily gasped, rushed over to the door, and threw it open.

Vindo was standing just outside the room. He was leaning against the wall with his hands in his pockets looking as smug and confident as could be. "In my defense, I wasn't *planning* on eavesdropping." He gave them a look with no small amount of contempt in it. "I was waiting here in the hallway for Qulle, and I happened to hear someone carelessly running their mouth. I just came a little closer because it sounded interesting, that's all."

Lily shot him a pointed glare.

Ever since their missions got merged, Vindo and Qulle had spent a lot of time stopping by the base. They were clearly trying to harvest information about Lamplight.

"Yeah, people usually call that eavesdropping." Lily dismissively waved her hands at Vindo. "Plus, whose fault do you think it is that Erna got herself injured like—?".

She tried to push him back out the door.

"Lay not thy hands on Brother Vindo's personage."

When she did, a voice came down from the ceiling, and a string wound its way around Lily's outstretched hand. By the time she tried to shake it off, it was already too late, and the first string was joined by several others. By the end of it all, she couldn't so much as wiggle her fingers.

In the blink of an eye, Lily had been completely restrained.

A beat later, a girl landed on the ground beside her. She'd been hiding above the ceiling. She was short of stature but carried herself with great poise. Her dark-red hair was long and straight, her androgynous facial features were strikingly clear-cut, and the gaze she leveled at Lily was composed in its dignity.

"Who're you…?" Lily asked.

"I am Lan, vassal of Avian. 'Tis a pleasure."

Lily had heard the name before. It belonged to code name Cloud Drift, third-place scorer on the graduation exam and one of the two people who filled out the middle of Avian's ranks.

Lan gave her fingers a bored shake and released the strings binding Lily's arm. Then she strode past Lily and stared at the girls gathered in the bedroom. She let out a sigh. "To think that Lamplight was home to such runts. 'Tis a disappointment, I daresay."

Erna and Annette tilted their heads to the side in confusion. It took them a moment to understood what Lan meant.

Annette's mouth contorted malevolently. "Yo, did you just call me a runt?"

Her fingertips twitched, and her skirt rustled. One of her inventions was just begging to be unleashed.

"Cease this chicanery."

However, Lan was faster. With a single wave of her hand, she stopped Annette in place. Her technique was blisteringly fast, and the strings extending from her fingers snaked around Annette's arms almost like they had a mind of their own.

"I need but halt thine actions, and thou'rt no threat to me."

Annette's eyes went wide. She froze. "......!"

Lan had stopped her before she could activate any of her prized inventions. She'd been completely neutralized.

Lily was just as flabbergasted at Lan's display of talent, too.

"Cut it out, Lan," Vindo interjected. "We're not here to pick fights over petty nonsense."

"Hmph. I had every intention of standing by, and had they not provoked—"

"Besides, you're pretty damn short yourself."

"At least I've more height than those runts!" Lan cried. But after a displeased "As thou will it, Brother Vindo, so shall it be done," she did release Annette from her strings. With that, she turned around and strode off toward the villa's entrance. "Sorry about the fuss," Vindo said before following after her.

The Lamplight girls could do nothing but glare silently at the Avian members' backs.

They'd been completely derailed from Erna's story.

After leaving the Lamplight base, Vindo and Lan boarded a boat and returned to the Longchon mainland. Midway there, they realized that they'd forgotten to tell Qulle they were leaving, but they decided it wasn't worth worrying about and bought some *shengjian bao* and fried chicken. When they got to their downtown apartment building, Vindo checked to make sure they were alone, then karate chopped the top of Lan's head with all his might.

"That hurts! Verily!" She squatted down with tears in her eyes.

"Don't go revealing your tricks to our opponents like that," Vindo scolded her.

"'Twas but some harmless fuuun," Lan protested, clutching her head.

"…Also, why are you talking like that?"

"'Tis mimicry. There come times when spies must falsify their speech patterns."

"All you're going to do is make yourself more conspicuous."

Lan lent Vindo no heed, instead choosing to mutter "Thee, thy, thou" to herself as they ascended the stairs.

Vindo didn't press the issue.

Avian's members changed their appearances and accents on the regular as a safeguard against the fact that one of their countrymen had leaked info about every spy in the Din Republic. To this day, there is still a lot of uncertainty about how much of the top academy students' info had been exposed as part of that.

"I do say, 'tis most wonderful," Lan murmured happily. "'Twas a harsh road we've walked. Taking that expedited graduation exam, being put in a team, immediately getting sent to the front lines, losing our boss, having to complete missions all on our lonesome… And thou didst fight the hardest of all of us, Brother Vindo. But now our reward is at hand."

"………"

"We shall have the finest boss there is, then undertake missions harder than any other. 'Tis the greatest honor a spy can receive."

"Don't get ahead of yourself," Vindo replied. "It's not a done deal yet."

Lan's smile stiffened. "True enough," she said with a nod right as they reached their apartment.

"We're back," they said as they went in, to which they got a number of replies. Everyone else was already gathered there, even Qulle, who'd returned as well.

All in all, there were four other people crammed into the tiny apartment. Some were sitting atop the bunk bed, whereas the others were lying sprawled directly on the floor.

"Ooh ♪," one of the young men cooed delightedly when Vindo began doling out the paper-wrapped *bao*. "These are from that Hyakuben restaurant, aren't they? ♪ You know me so well, Vindo. I'm always out eating with the ladies, so it's been forever since I got to dig my teeth into something so macho and garlicky. ♪"

The man's name was "Lander" Vics.

Vics was a handsome young man with a face as childish as a boy's.

He was generous with his smiles, making it wholly unclear whether he was complimenting Vindo or being snide.

Beside him, there was a woman wrapped up in a blanket with a languid look on her face.

"Reeeally, Vics? You went on another date today? Must be niiice. I want someone to pamper me. I want moneeey. Does anyone want to give me some money?"

Her name was "Feather" Pharma.

Pharma's hair was disheveled from over three months of neglect, she was a little chubby, and her mouth hung dazedly half-open. It was like someone had taken every unkempt feature they could think of and packed them all into a single woman.

She leaned against the legs of the young man who'd been standing stoically in the corner of the room.

"Come on, Queneau, provide for meee. Shower me with gobs and gobs of cash. If you do, there's loads and loads of benefits. Serving me is the best joy there is, you know? Findom, they call it."

"...Nay. Not interested," her counterpart bluntly replied.

His name was "South Wind" Queneau.

Queneau was wearing a white mask that obscured his entire face. He was tall and big-bellied, making him look almost like a large bell. Between that and the mask, he had an almost ursine energy to him.

Unsurprisingly, having the whole team together like that was a recipe for quite a hubbub.

"...Nay," Queneau said again. "And you all should turn her down, too."

"Whaaat? But I can't dooo anything without money," Pharma protested.

"C'mon, Queneau ♪," Vics agreed. "You should know that I can never say no to a lovely lady. ♪"

"By the way, what is this 'findom' thou doth speak of?" Lan asked.

"Ooh, Lan, are *you* interested? It's a world brimming with love and dreams," Pharma replied.

"I'm interested! ♪" Vics piped up.

"...Nay," Queneau repeated. "Nay."

"Hmm, hmm. Ah, I see! Ha-ha-ha, thou'rt debauched. Debauched, I daresay!"

The cramped room resounded with the youthful sound of their voices. Over on the bed, Qulle stared off into space. "Why do you guys always have to be so crass? I miss Lamplight…" However, her protestations failed to dampen the conversation.

Together, the six of them—Vindo, Qulle, and the four noisy ones—made up Avian.

At that point, a no-nonsense voice cut through the room. "I hate it when things get noisy." Vindo clapped his hands together. "Shut up—we need to get our strategy meeting underway."

With that, Avian ate their *bao* and began going over their plan. The room that had been so loud just moments before was silent now save for the sound of Qulle's voice. The others had been chattering away since the moment Vindo walked in the room, but now their lips were sealed, and their expressions shifted from their age-appropriate smiles to the hardened faces of spies who lived in a world marked by strife.

The reason they were able to change gears so quickly was because they were elites through and through. They were always ready to shift their full focus should the need arise.

Qulle quickly rattled off the pertinent information, and the others committed it to memory. Then once she was done explaining everything in brief, she gave them her outlook on the situation. "If things go smoothly, we should win this. That said, we still need to be careful. Mr. Klaus might have been looking after them, but the fact remains that our opponents have completed multiple Impossible Missions."

"…Aye," Queneau muttered.

"In particular, they have a girl called Glint who could be big trouble. Monika, I think." As Qulle spoke, she pulled out a document. On it, she'd listed out all the intel they'd gathered on Lamplight's members over the past week. They hadn't gotten ahold of anything truly decisive, but by keeping an eye on which Lamplight members handled which tasks, they'd gotten a decent idea of how strong each of them was. "We don't have any details on her, but her teammates clearly think really highly of her. We should put two people on her."

Baffled cries rose up from the others.

"Twooo people? When we're already at a numbers disadvantage?" Pharma said sluggishly.

"We'll be fine with just one. ♪ You're giving her too much credit ♪," Vics jabbed amusedly.

However, Qulle didn't change her marching orders. A tension filled the room. Everyone turned and looked at Vindo, their leader. They wanted him to make the call.

Vindo made his call without a moment's hesitation. "There's no way we're putting two people on her."

The others smiled, satisfied with his answer.

However, he went on. "That'd never be enough. I'm sending three of you after Glint."

Every member of the team stared at him in blank shock. Naturally, they had their pride, and they were confident that their skills were the real deal. What reason could he have for assigning three of them to take on a single ex-washout? All told, there were only six of them. His plan involved sending half their personnel after a single opponent.

"Art thou sending three to get Glint out of the fight quickly, then?" Lan asked, her eyebrows arched in confusion.

"No," Vindo replied sharply. "Even with three people, you're still going to lose. Your job is to buy as much time as you can before that happens."

"If thou dost say so, then believe it I must, but..." Lan crossed her arms in dissatisfaction. "What basis hast thou? And once we contain Glint, what wouldst thou have us do about the other seven?"

"A hunch. And we'll take our other two members and have them deal with one Lamplight opponent each."

"That doth leave five of them unaccounted for."

"I'll handle the rest myself."

Vindo made it sound simple, but the plan was unbelievably lopsided. Every Avian member glared at him, Lan included. Vindo's words made it clear how little he thought of his teammates' abilities. He was basically telling them not to get in his way while he took care of everything. The others had all graduated from their academies with top marks, and his comments were wounding their pride. However, none of them could rebut his unilateral declaration.

"If you've got complaints about that, then back them up with results," Vindo said almost tauntingly.

The thing was, Vindo really was in a league of his own. Even amid a group of elites like Avian, he still stood head and shoulders above the others. And ever since they lost their boss, he'd been learning and growing with no end in sight.

"I've got this under control. Lamplight has a weak point, and all I have to do is attack it."

Eventually, they concluded the strategy meeting by deciding to adopt Vindo's plan as is.

Each pair of eyes on the team was filled with a burning readiness to fight.

◇◇◇

The same night Avian was holding their strategy meeting, Lamplight was holding one of their own.

It had been a good long while since the eight of them had all gotten back together for a discussion like that. Lately, most of the team's strategy meetings had consisted solely of Klaus, Thea, and Grete coming up with plans and relaying them to the others afterward. As the girls argued and debated, they were all struck by a strange sense of nostalgia.

It reminded them of their training, back when they'd all gotten together to discuss how they were going to take down Klaus. The days and months they'd spent doing that had been truly fulfilling—and if Avian defeated them tomorrow night, Lamplight was going to lose them forever.

Each time the girls imagined that happening, their voices took on a little more fervor.

Once they'd settled on their plan, Klaus called them over for a follow-up meeting.

The girls sat in a circle around him on the living room sofas. That was the way they'd done it back in Heat Haze Palace, and that was the way they intended to do it in Longchon, too.

"This next operation will likely mark the end of our mission in Longchon, but it's taken on a very different form than the ops that came before it," Klaus told them. "Technically, our mission is to investigate the intelligence leaks from our embassy, but I don't think any of you much care about that part anymore. Professionally speaking, I'm not sure how I feel about that, but I'm going to choose to overlook that bit. Sometimes, the job takes us in unexpected directions."

The girls nodded.

The only thing that mattered now was surpassing Avian. The mission was nothing more than a means to achieve that end. Their hearts were united in a single goal—completing the mission before Avian and proving that they deserved to continue working with Klaus.

Klaus nodded as well. "Besides, all we have to do is steal a single document. I could do that with my eyes closed."

"Well, you don't have to put it like that!" Lily cried.

"However, I'm sitting this one out. I'll just be watching to see who wins between you and Avian."

The girls agreed that that made sense. If Klaus took part, that would defeat the entire point. They needed to beat Avian all on their own.

"I don't have a strong sense of what the academy environment is like, so to be honest, I have a difficult time understanding your trauma associated with it. In my opinion, you shouldn't get hung up on their narrow-minded opinions. But if the wounds they inflicted on your hearts left you with as many sleepless nights as you claim, then I have just one thing to say to you," Klaus declared. "Win. Take those inferiority complexes of yours and turn them on their heads."

His words lit a fire under the girls, and they all replied with a resounding "Yes, sir!"

With that, the meeting was over.

Lily was the first to rise to her feet. "Teach," she said. "You'd better watch close. I bet it'll feel reeeal good."

"What will?" Klaus asked.

Lily grinned. "Seeing your students crush a bunch of cocky elites into the dirt."

It was one of her characteristically smug grins, and it fit the team to a T.

"Magnificent," Klaus replied.

After the meeting's conclusion, Klaus called one of the girls back. "Erna, how are your injuries? Don't go pushing yourself, now."

Erna was still covered in bandages. "It still hurts, but sitting this out would hurt more," she answered.

"I see," Klaus said softly. "...Well, once the battle is over, I have something I want to talk to you about."

Erna tilted her head in curiosity. However, Klaus said nothing more. He just gave her a look tinged with a hint of sadness.

Then, twenty-four hours later, the battle between Lamplight and Avian began.

The stage for their battle was a region known as the Longchon Walled City, or as the government called it, the Longchon Illegal Housing Zone.

The Longchon Walled City had originally been constructed as a fortress to protect the country from foreign foes, but when the Fend Commonwealth colonized Longchon, they demolished the fortress and left nothing behind but a massive plot of land that was eventually populated by refugees from all across the Far East. After the Great War's end, people came to Longchon in droves in search of stability as they fled civil wars and colonization, but with no work to be found there for people without proper passports, many of them ended up settling in the ruins of the Longchon Walled City.

That was how the apartment complex got started.

Over time, the area's population grew and grew, and as it did, they started building housing on top of housing. Eventually, the fortress grew so large the government could no longer control it, and the complex ended up being home to thousands of people who had nowhere else to go. The unregulated construction was so dense that it took on a sort of mystique, with rumors sprouting up about how going in meant you could never leave and how residents who got lost simply starved to death. In the end, people took to calling it by its old name once again—the Longchon Walled City.

By that point, it was the single largest concrete city in the world. Some said its buildings went as tall as twelve stories high; others said fourteen. In truth, nobody knew the actual number. It also had its own economy, with everything from restaurants in gross violation of food sanitation laws, to back-alley doctors, to stores full of contraband foreign goods, to shops that sold illegal heavy weaponry and narcotics, to gambling dens and brothels. And the Steel Urn Group mafia controlled it all. Not even the police dared set foot in the city, so the Steel Urn Group was free to govern by their own set of laws and rule over the Longchon Walled City's desperate populace with an iron fist.

The leaked classified document they were looking for was somewhere in that city.

The spies had decided on a starting time to begin their infiltration.

Once they set foot inside, the mafia lookouts would spot them and go into high alert. Considering how insular the Longchon Walled City was, sneaking in by disguising themselves as residents would be too time intensive. Instead, they'd decided that the better play would be to sync up their timing and charge in all at once to steal the document by force.

The two sides' starting positions were as equal as could be. At ten PM sharp, Lamplight entered the city from the south, and Avian went in from the north. With that, the two spy teams' battle quietly began.

Thanks to its commander, Thea, and her trademark negotiation skills, Lamplight was able to rent out a one-room apartment ahead of time. She'd tempted one of the Longchon Walled City's residents with her honeyed words and managed to buy them off. The room was barely long enough for a person to lie down in, but it was going to serve her just fine as their operational headquarters. Thea hung up the map she'd procured in advance (although its accuracy was dubious at best), then installed the large radio setup Annette had put together. That was where Thea was going to relay orders to her teammates from. Staying in constant contact via radio was the only way they were going to avoid getting lost.

Klaus, who'd accompanied them up to that point, gave the girls a small nod. "I'll be off, then. I'll be keeping an eye out to make sure nobody gets injured too badly."

"Much appreciated."

Merely having Klaus in the same room as Thea was liable to give her an unfair advantage. Given that their goal was to defeat Avian fair and square, Klaus had a duty to leave. However, he stopped in his tracks the moment he first set foot outside the door. "The problem is, in a place this big, there's no real way of knowing who's going to get knocked out or where."

The Longchon Walled City was such a labyrinth that not even the people who lived there knew its entire layout. Watching everything that went on in the entire city was a feat beyond even the mighty Klaus.

"Oh?" Thea said, sounding rather surprised. "But, Teach, isn't it obvious who the first dropout will be?"

"Hmm?"

"Someone in Avian is about to go down, and that's just a fact. If you're worried about anyone, they're the ones you should check in on."

"Well, someone's confident."

"Why wouldn't I be? A certain someone told me in no unclear terms that she was going to be taking one member of Avian down, guaranteed."

"Oh," Klaus replied, sounding audibly impressed. That there was a bold statement indeed. Lamplight was in a veritable maze, and what's more, they were going up against Avian. To think that one of their members had spoken with such confidence. Who could it have been?

When Klaus looked back, Thea gave him a smile.

"All I did was turn her loose."

And what a brilliant smile it was.

"In any battle with you on the line, the power of love's going to multiply her strength a hundredfold."

It was twenty-five minutes in—barely any time at all—and the two teams were about to have their first skirmish.

Qulle found the Longchon Walled City to be a daunting den of vice.

Yeesh. I could get totally lost if I zoned out for even a second in here...

Together, the mass of unlicensed building additions created a city as sprawling as it was labyrinthine. Buildings had been built with no regard for their neighbors' heights, so it was all too easy to walk across a building's third floor only to inexplicably find yourself on the fourth of another, or to go up a flight of stairs from the third floor and discover that it went directly to floor five. The air in the seemingly endless concrete world was stagnant, and the smell of mold wafted from every nook and cranny. When Qulle went a little deeper into the city, she reached an area with no windows whatsoever. All she had to slowly guide her onward was what little light streamed in from the open rooms.

Plus, the buildings weren't the only things designed to obstruct intruders. There were the residents, too.

...I guess they've already figured out we're outsiders, huh.

She was being careful to avoid the residents whenever she could, but because of the way the city was set up, it was impossible to tell where people might be watching from. She could hear the inhabitants start muttering to each other about having spotted some unfamiliar faces. They were unlikely to harm Qulle and the others directly, but eventually, that information was going to make its way over to the mafia.

If we'd had more time, we could have disguised ourselves as residents or bribed enough people that it wouldn't have mattered, but with how closed-off this place is, it took everything we had to gather what little intel we did.

That said, what was done was done. Besides, Avian and Lamplight were operating under the same conditions.

Qulle stopped in front of a closed-up dental clinic and strained her ears, gathering in sound from a vast range and accurately capturing the voices of the residents who were still awake. On the upper floors, the Steel Urn Group mafia was all flustered. They'd just learned that there were some unidentified strangers roaming around their complex, and they were scurrying to and fro to protect the classified document.

Good, things are going smoothly.

Once she had a decent idea of where the document was, she sprang back into motion. Her gait was far lighter than it had been before.

Honestly, I'm not too concerned about Lamplight. Most of them aren't worth worrying about.

Looking at the recent data, Lamplight had given the lion's share of their work to Klaus and Glint, and their strategy for their Impossible

Mission had probably revolved around those two as well. In Qulle's eyes, the others were largely inconsequential.

If everything goes like it should, Mr. Klaus will be our boss by tomorrow night. I can't wait.

Qulle was on cloud nine—both from how proud she was as a spy, and from how besotted she was as a maiden who'd found a lovely new prospective suitor.

She thought back to the day when she got to go on a mission with him. The Greatest Spy in the World was far more dashing than she'd imagined. He came across as curt, sure, but once she got a chance to chat with him, she'd discovered that he had a considerate nature and a great sense of humor.

Once she learned that, a wonderful vision had come to mind.

I wonder if Mr. Klaus is seeing anyone right now, or if—

"I hear she went this way! The jade-haired chick's over here!"

An angry shout shook her from her reverie. It wasn't just one person shouting, either. Several people were. Loads of them, in fact.

"What?" Qulle gasped.

She hid herself in a storeroom, more on instinct than anything else. Something weird was going on.

She strained her ears again and sorted through the shouts one by one.

"Thief!" "That sneaky bitch. She took my wallet." "She stole my IOU." "That's it, she's dead meat." "You screw with one person in the Walled City, you screw with all of us." "If anyone finds her, make sure you catch her." "I hear she's got jade green hair and big-ass glasses." "I hear her name's Qulle." "Don't let the chick with the big glasses get away!"

Qulle shuddered.

"Wait, wait, wait, wait, wait, wait, wait!"

Waterfalls of sweat began gushing from every pore on her body.

She hadn't done anything wrong, yet somehow, she had earned the Longchon Walled City's ire. What's more, dozens of its residents had formed a posse and were trying to hunt her down.

But wait, why are they so riled up? And why are they zeroing in on me? Should I take them all out? No, no way. They're civilians, and besides, there's too many of them!

This was just supposed to be a mission about stealing a document from the mafia, so they'd assumed that the city's residents weren't going to get involved. The locals weren't liable to help them, but they weren't going to harm them, either. None of the spies would be stupid enough to make enemies out of the Longchon Walled City's thousands of residents.

There was little in the way of law and order there. If the locals caught her, they could very well end up killing her.

Qulle squeezed herself as far back in the storeroom as she could go. A group of angry men noisily rushed past. She strained her ears, and once the sounds had died down, she quietly slipped out of the room.

Right as she did, someone stepped out of the room directly across from hers. "...Qulle, are you all right? Looks like things have taken an unexpected turn."

"Vindo!"

It was Avian's leader. At that moment, there wasn't a single person she would have been happier to see. She rushed right on over to him. They needed to share their intel to figure out what the hell was going on. He walked toward her in turn, and Qulle felt the stress drain from her expression.

A moment later, though, it dawned on her—something was off. Vindo would never walk that noisily.

By that point, though, it was already too late.

"I'm code name Daughter Dearest—now, let's fill this time with laughter and tears."

The wrong voice came out of Vindo's mouth.

Vindo—or rather, the person Qulle had thought was Vindo—tore off his face to reveal Grete's face beneath it. The needle she brandished without a moment's delay glinted in the dim Walled City hallway.

She plunged it into Qulle's arm.

Qulle crumpled to the ground on the spot. It felt like her entire body was on fire.

"Lily concocted this poison herself. You won't be getting up anytime soon."

"Rrgh... Gah...!" Qulle's vision went bleary. It hurt even just to breathe.

As Grete grabbed her by the collar and dragged her toward an empty room, Qulle finally realized that Grete was the one who'd set up the whole thing. She'd disguised herself as Qulle, brazenly stolen from everyone she could, and worked the locals into a rage.

No way... She was never able to weave lies that elaborate back at the academy!

The two of them had gone to the same academy, and tucked away in the back of Qulle's memory, she remembered what Grete had been like. Back then, though, Grete had been a pathetic washout. She had a good head on her shoulders, but she was so frail she could barely function. She was a total novice, and even her talent with disguises was rendered all but useless by her androphobia. Qulle couldn't begin to count the number of times she'd knocked Grete to the ground during their combat training. She could have sparred Grete a hundred times in a row and not lost a single bout.

So why? It's not like I'm weak or anything!

She was flabbergasted.

The room Grete dragged her to was small and abandoned. The floor wasn't level, making it ill-suited for anyone to live in. Due to the haphazard way it had been constructed, the Longchon Walled City was full of awkward little crevices like that one.

Once they were inside, Grete dumped her unceremoniously on the ground. The poison coursing through Qulle's veins was so potent she couldn't so much as properly lift a finger.

"...It's been a long time, Qulle," Grete said as she calmly looked down at her. "Back at the academy, I suffered plenty of defeats at your hand. You were the best around, and I'm ashamed to say I spent my nights burning with jealousy. I knew that it was sensible people like you who got loved by others, not hideous, gloomy people like me..."

Grete's voice was gentle and calm, but there was a fire in her every word that burned with an unimaginable intensity.

"But now...even I have someone I refuse to relinquish!"

Grete's tone and gaze sharpened, and Qulle bit her lip.

What could have happened to her while I wasn't watching? What in the world made her like this?!

That was just the thing—Qulle hadn't been watching.

She hadn't seen the explosive way Grete's skills had improved after she came to Lamplight and fell in love with Klaus. And she hadn't seen the way Grete's affection and her desire to help shoulder her beloved's burden drove her to hone those same skills she'd let wither back at the academy.

In a battle with Klaus on the line, there was no way Grete wasn't going to rise to the occasion!

"You can rest easy. This room is safe. That said, if I told the locals where you were, I can only imagine the ways they would punish you…"

Grete softly leaned in toward Qulle's immobile body.

"Now, would you be so kind as to tell me about Avian? In detail, if you don't mind."

A cold pang of despair ran through Qulle at the barely veiled threat.

With that, Grete's ingenuity claimed the first victim in the Lamplight-versus-Avian battle.

Over on the second floor in the northern side of the Longchon Walled City, Grete returned from her solo op and made her way over to Erna and Lily's hiding spot. She looked downright invigorated as she gave her report. "I was just able to coerce some information out of Qulle. Now we should have a rough idea of the Avian members' personal information and current locations. She also said that the document is likely still on the Walled City's upper floors. And naturally, I also made sure that Qulle herself wouldn't be going anywhere."

"Slow down, girl, we only just got started!" Lily cried in shock.

Beside her, Erna's eyes went wide as well.

I can barely believe that Big Sis Grete did all that…

Erna had been confused when Grete wandered off on her own just as the battle began, but now she'd returned having achieved fantastic results. According to her story, she'd taken out Qulle—the fourth-ranked academy student—in the blink of an eye.

Even considering the way Qulle had stabbed them in the back and how personal the stakes were for Grete, she'd still accomplished more than anyone could have possibly asked of her.

"Still, we'll need to double-check the intel she gave you to make sure it's all true," Erna said.

She had a point—there was a very real chance that Qulle had fed Grete misinformation. However…

"…No, I think we can count on its veracity. From what I saw, I find it hard to imagine she was lying," Grete replied.

"Huh?"

"She was trembling like a baby."

"What did you do to her?!"

"That said, you do have a point. Just in case, we should go get in touch with Thea and cross-check what we can."

"You're being kind of scary today, Big Sis Grete!"

The three of them had come all the way to the Longchon Walled City's north side, and Thea was back down to the south. With how dense the city was, radios couldn't connect directly from one side to the other. That said, Lamplight had chosen to use radios this time around. They normally avoided them outside of emergencies because of how easily they could be intercepted, but their alternative solution—Sara's homing pigeon—was a little unwieldy. At the moment, Annette was installing radio repeaters throughout the complex. Their plan was that, over time, they would extend their range to cover the entire city.

The girls headed south through a bare concrete corridor. Fortunately for them, the residents were all busy searching for Qulle, so getting from point A to point B was a piece of cake.

"Hey, Erna," Lily said as they walked. "Isn't he heavy?"

"It's actually not too bad, once you get used to it," Erna replied. Erna was currently wearing Sara's pet puppy on her head. His nose twitched ceaselessly, and he let out a little *"yarf"* as though to announce his presence. "Big Sis Sara lent him to me as a bodyguard."

"Still, you're injured. You should really be taking it easy."

"No, no, it's fine. Running with him on my head is a breeze."

The puppy barked again. *"Yarf!"*

Rather than press the issue any further, Lily turned her attention back to running. When they got to the middle of the Walled City, their radio linked up with Thea's. They slipped behind a staircase forcibly joining a third floor to a fourth and extended their radio's antenna.

After Grete succinctly relayed the news, they got a satisfied-sounding reply back. *"I read you, loud and clear. I'll pass the information along to the others. You never disappoint, Grete. I knew it was the right call, letting you go in first."*

"…I couldn't have done it without your words of encouragement."

Apparently, deploying their strategist Grete onto the front lines had been Thea's idea. After recognizing how motivated Grete was going to be, she'd chosen to believe in that. Looking at the results, it had definitely been the right call.

Erna turned her thoughts toward their next moves.

At the moment, we're up eight to five. If we devote all our resources to searching for the document, we could win this without having to get into any more fights…

Thanks to Grete's efforts, their prospects were looking good.

However, all that soon changed.

"Ah! Where did you come from—?"

A disquieting cry crackled through the radio. Then the signal went dark. The last thing they heard was the sound of the radio being destroyed.

Grete, Lily, and Erna looked at each other. All of them could tell exactly what had just happened—Thea had been attacked.

It was forty-five minutes in, and the situation was starting to deteriorate.

Lily quickly stowed away her radio. "We should go help her. It's not far." The others nodded. "Yeah, I agree." "As do I…"

At the moment, they had no way of knowing if it was Avian or the mafia that had attacked Thea. If it was Avian, then at least her life wasn't in any danger, but the same couldn't be said of the latter.

The three of them rushed southward. The corridors on the southern side of the city were highly populated, so it was impossible to get through them without bumping into at least a few residents. As the girls made their way onward, they braced themselves for their faces to get exposed to the locals.

"I have an idea," Grete proposed. "After this, we should fabricate another twenty or so crimes for Qulle's rap sheet. The more we rile the locals up, the easier it will be for us to move around."

"Have you no mercy?!" Erna cried.

As an aside, Grete had been positively bursting with hostility ever since Sara told her about how she "saw Qulle and the boss sharing a chummy conversation." As far as Grete was concerned, whatever happened to Qulle wasn't her problem.

The only reason they found such a direct route to their headquarters was because of Grete's intellect. The Longchon Walled City's lifeless concrete walls could disorient even the most battle-hardened of spies.

Lily and Erna followed Grete out into a wide, open space. They must have made it down to the bottom floor, as the ground beneath them was nothing more than bare earth. This was the Longchon Walled City's so-called main street. It was about seventy feet wide, which was pretty darn big by the city's standards, and it was lined on both sides by restaurants with crudely written signs advertising congee, noodles, and fish meal dumplings. When they looked up, they could see the quarter moon peeking out from above the veritable web of clotheslines.

Grete stopped in her tracks. "Erna, could I ask you to be on your guard?"

"Huh?"

"They lured us here," Grete said, biting her lip. "And it's the perfect spot for an ambush...!"

On hearing that, Erna understood what Grete was getting at. From their enemies' perspective, the best course of action would be to let Lamplight know that one of their members was in danger, then round up the rest of them when they came to help.

Sure enough, Grete's prediction was right on the money.

"Behind us!"

No sooner did the words escape Erna's mouth than a figure leaped at them. The girls dodged to the side, but Grete's reaction was a fraction of a second too slow. Lily pulled her by the arm, but that wasn't fast enough, either.

The figure was blisteringly fast. It called to mind a beast hunting an herbivore.

The dull side of a knife struck Grete clean in the back of the neck.

"Hmph. And here I was hoping to take all three of you down in one go."

Before they could react, the figure backed off and came to a stop. His entire body moved with a monstrous, springlike acceleration. He could go from zero to one hundred or one hundred to zero at the drop of a hat. By the time they realized they were under attack, he'd already retreated to safety.

The figure grinned. "Well, at least I took down the single biggest pain in our ass."

Lily ground her teeth. "Vindo…!"

Erna shuddered as well. It was Vindo—the one person they'd been desperately hoping to avoid.

Grete crumpled like a puppet with its strings cut, and Erna gently caught her as she fell and set her down softly on the ground. "Big Sis Grete…," she mumbled.

Vindo made sure to continue maintaining a distance of about fifteen feet as he readied a knife in each hand and glared at the girls. "I just lost contact with Qulle. Do I have you people to thank?"

"Oh, who knows?" Lily shot back.

Vindo covered his face with one hand. "That's so like her. She's weak, but she thinks she's hot shit." When he lowered his hand, the girls caught a glimpse of the wrath broiling in his expression. "Well, that's fine. That'll be the splash of cold water that some of the others need."

Lily let out a provocative laugh. "What, that's your excuse?"

"You'll understand soon enough." Vindo slowly twirled his knives. "If anyone's underestimating their opponents, it's you."

Lily and Erna gasped in awe.

"Flock" Vindo was the single top performer out of the academies' entire 3,098-student body, and now he was ready to show them what he could really do.

For that mission, Lamplight had split into four groups.

First up was Monika, who'd been tasked with proactively getting in Avian's way. They knew she was the only one with the skills to straight-up overpower the elites, so her job was to root out Avian's members and hunt them down.

Then there was Lily, Grete, and Erna, whose priority was to hunt down the document. Grete could disguise herself as any of the locals, Lily was nigh unbeatable in enclosed spaces, and Erna's abilities truly shone in a place as accident-prone as the Walled City. As the three people who synergized best with the operating environment, theirs was the group the rest of the team operated around.

Next up were Sybilla and Sara, who were on flex duty. Their job was to take instructions over the radio and adapt to whatever roles the team needed from moment to moment. Sybilla's athletic abilities let her get to wherever she needed to go, and Sara had an abundance of ways she could help out in all sorts of different situations. The two of them were the perfect people for the job.

Finally, Thea and Annette were in charge of comms. As Annette installed radio repeaters, Thea stayed in touch with the others to relay information and orders.

Now, all across the complex, the four groups were coming head-to-head with the enemy.

The first people to reach the room Lamplight was using as its operating headquarters were Sybilla and Sara. Just like Lily's team, they got worried and rushed over when they abruptly lost contact with Thea.

Thea was sprawled on the ground in the middle of the room. She'd been bound from head to toe in rope and left lying on the floor. Her eyes were open, so she was definitely conscious, but the gag in her mouth was keeping her from saying anything. She'd obviously been attacked. Based on what they could see from the doorway, though, she didn't have any external wounds, and there wasn't anyone else in the room.

"Hold on, we're comin'," Sybilla reassured her.

"Wh-who did this to you?!" Sara asked.

The two of them hurriedly rushed into the room. The moment they set foot inside, Thea's and Sybilla's gazes met.

DON'T

A word rushed unbidden through Sybilla's mind. She reflexively froze, then shot Thea a questioning look.

TO YOUR LEFT

Sybilla immediately raised her fists and moved to cover Sara.

A young man came charging out of the room's refrigerator. "Ooh, you noticed me? Good going ♪," he said in an annoyingly friendly tone.

That handsome, boyish face belonged to "Lander" Vics. He stretched one of his long legs out wide and fired off a roundhouse kick.

"So you're the one who took out Thea?" Sybilla asked as she blocked it. "I can't believe you found her so fast."

"How could I not? ♪ Rushing straight to a lady's side is what a gentleman does. ♪"

Vics was a man who liked to get physical. Sybilla could tell as much from the force behind his kick. When it came to close combat, though, she was no slouch, either. She had a special talent—a knack for theft that allowed her to steal anything within arm's reach. All she needed to do was steal her opponent's weapons. Once she seized all their weapons for herself, she could beat just about anyone.

Those were the thoughts driving her as she reached for Vics—

"...Oh? Tell me, what'd you just do there? ♪"

—but she came up empty.

Vics was unarmed. Sybilla couldn't spot a single weapon anywhere in his clothes.

Maybe he prefers to fight barehanded, she hypothesized. If that was the case, she could just use her own knife to overpower him—

"I'm code name Lander—and it's time to get smashing. ♪"

—but he gave his arm a big swing.

In his hand, he was holding the cudgel he'd just produced *as if out of nowhere*.

The attack caught her completely by surprise, and she hastily brought her knife up to block it.

"——!"

From the look of it, Vics hadn't even committed that hard to the attack. However, it was enough to send Sybilla flying all the same. It felt like she'd just gotten blasted away by a windstorm. She hurtled backward, sending both her and Sara spinning. They didn't stop until they crashed into the wall.

"I don't enjoy using this on women, you know. ♪"

"...Where the hell's all that power of yours comin' from?"

Vics's slender frame was hiding more strength than Sybilla would have thought possible. She'd practically blacked out just blocking that single hit. She looked his way, but the cudgel was already gone, and Vics's hands were empty again. He was just standing there cheerfully grinning.

"Hey, you can take a hit. I love that. That just gives us more time to enjoy ourselves. ♪"

"Hey Sara," Sybilla said, ignoring Vics's nonsense, "didja catch where he pulled his weapon from or where he stashed it just now?"

Sara gave her a scared little shake of the head. "I—I didn't... I don't see it anywhere..."

She didn't know what had happened, either.

Vics had *produced a cudgel out of thin air* and caught them totally unawares. Now Sybilla had no idea what his reach was. She knew she needed to watch out for his monstrous strength, but not knowing how he was going to use it put her at a serious disadvantage.

Is that cudgel the only weapon he's got? And if he's got others, where's he keepin' 'em...?

If nothing else, she knew the name of the technique he was using to toy with them: liecraft. That was how spies fought—by using lies to multiply the strength of their abilities.

"This time, I'm coming at you for real, okay? I want to put up better results than Vindo. ♪"

Vics reached toward Sybilla as though flaunting how empty his hands were.

"Lander" Vics was the second-ranked spy out of the academy student body, and now he was standing in their way.

Meanwhile, Monika let out a big yawn from atop a Walled City rooftop as she stood beneath the waxing moon. She viewed the complex's lights. As far as the eye could see, she observed dirty, moss-ridden concrete and tiny windows with clotheslines and radio antennas sticking out of them.

Monika was on the highest roof in the whole city. Her hair swayed in the damp sea wind. Up there, she was free from the musty stink that permeated the complex. Instead, she smelled the aroma of grilled fish. Someone down in the city was having themselves a late-night snack with their booze.

After standing there for a while, she felt hostility begin coiling almost palpably around her neck. She stooped down to dodge the attack, and something passed over her head. Then she used the city's myriad clotheslines as stepping stones to descend to a different roof one floor down.

"Ah, thou hast dodged my string. Most impressive." A petite girl appeared atop the roof Monika had just been on. There were a number of strings dangling from her fingers. "I am 'Cloud Drift' Lan. 'Tis a pleasure."

"'Thou'? ''Tis'?"

"Hmph, yet more unjust criticism. I thought it a right fine dialect."

"Well, you're clearly an idiot," Monika said dismissively. She turned her gaze away from Lan. "There's two more of you, yeah? The fatso and the weirdo in the mask. I can see you, you know."

It was an angle that should have been impossible to cover from Monika's position, but thanks to the mirrors she'd set up ahead of time, she could see her hidden foes just fine. Once she called them out, two more spies showed themselves as well.

"'Fatso'? That's so mean…," pouted the plump "Feather" Pharma.

"…Aye," said "South Wind" Queneau. He was once again wearing an all-white mask, rendering his expression unreadable.

Counting Lan, there were three of them, and they had Monika surrounded. Lan smiled as she readied her strings, illuminated by the moonlight shining down from the northern sky; Pharma had both her guns trained on Monika and was hemming her in from the south; and Queneau was standing tall and empty-handed atop a roof two floors down to the east.

"So three against one. That was Avian's plan, right?"

Monika heaved a sigh from her rooftop position amid the other three. She, too, was privy to the information Grete had squeezed out of Qulle.

"…If thou knewest that, then why expose thyself so?" Lan asked, looking visibly puzzled. "Thou wast so conspicuous, 'twas like thou wast asking to be surrounded."

"Yeah, it's easier this way. All I had to do was stand around, and a trio of shitters came and threw themselves at my feet."

The moment the provocation left Monika's mouth, Lan sprang into action. She stowed her strings, drew her automatic, and fired off a shot all in the same motion. Her target was the antenna sticking out beside Monika, and the bullet sent the antenna flying straight at her.

As Monika dodged the shot, she let out a confused grunt. She could have sworn that Lan's weapon of choice was those strings, yet she wasn't using them in her attack.

"Victory lies not within my sights," Lan said.

"Huh?"

"Brother Vindo declared it to be so, so thus it must be. Defeating thee is beyond us, even as three. Long since have we discarded any notions of triumph."

Behind Monika, Pharma and Queneau went back into hiding. They made no efforts to all attack her at once.

Monika laughed mockingly. "You're seriously not gonna come at me? Cowards."

"Thine insults mean naught. Lying is basic custom for us. This dialect is but one example," Lan said, returning Monika's laugh with one of her own. "Why should I show thee my full strength? We falsify our might, falsify our teamwork, falsify our abilities, and wrap it all in liecraft upon liecraft. How willst thou fell three elites who've abandoned all pride and all chance of victory in the name of buying time?"

"........."

"Come, Dame Prodigy, dance with us. Dance with us as thy teammates crumble and fall."

After gleefully making her proclamation, Lan drew another bead with her pistol.

"Cloud Drift" Lan had been ranked third on the graduation exam, "Feather" Pharma had been ranked fifth, and "South Wind" Queneau had been ranked sixth.

Together, the three elites began running circles around Monika.

It was seventy-five minutes in, and now Avian and Lamplight were both going for the throat.

◇◇◇

Down on the main street in the middle of the Longchon Walled City's ground floor, Vindo was leisurely holding a knife as he stood across from Erna and Lily. He wasn't offering them the slightest of openings. If they tried to pull their guns on him, he would close the gap and slit their wrists in the blink of an eye.

Erna and Lily exchanged a glance, then took the best course of action available to them: fleeing. There was no specific need for them to defeat Vindo. The only thing that mattered was stealing back the document before Avian did, so the smart thing to do was to run away. Luckily for them, their Walled City battlefield had escape routes in abundance.

The two fled back inside as fast as their legs would carry them.

"That's not a bad call, you know." Vindo's voice echoed out calmly from behind. "Or at least, it wouldn't be if you could actually outrun me."

They could feel a wave of hostility approaching.

Erna and Lily fought tooth and nail to hinder Vindo's path as they fled. They knocked over buckets full of drainage water and hurled every discarded PVC pipe they found back at him. However, Vindo deftly batted their obstructions away with his knives without so much as slowing down. They could feel him gaining on them.

"Erna, in here!" Lily shouted before tugging her teammate into one of the complex's apartments. It was a cramped single room just barely big enough for two people to live in, and though it showed signs of being inhabited, its residents were fortunately nowhere to be seen. As the two of them rudely barged in, Lily offered an oddly conscientious "Sorry for the intrusion" to no one in particular.

The problem, unsurprisingly enough, was that the apartment was a dead end. They had nowhere left to run. Vindo charged into the room and launched a merciless knife thrust at them.

Lily clamped her hand over Erna's mouth.

"I'm code name Flower Garden—and it's time to bloom out of control."

Poison gas came bursting out of her ample chest.

Erna recognized that attack. It was Lily's go-to move—spraying a paralytic that she herself was immune to. The technique's effectiveness hardly felt fair.

"........."

Vindo immediately gave up on his knife attack and dodged to the side. However, he was a step too slow. By the look of it, Lily's poison hit him head-on. He held out for a brief moment, but it wasn't long before his knives tumbled from his hands. He collapsed onto the ground.

"Heh. You picked the wrong girl to mess with," Lily said proudly. "When Wunderkind Lily's on the job, not even elites stand a—"

"Run!"

Erna yanked on Lily's arm.

Not a moment later, a knife grazed Lily's throat.

"Good call."

As soon as Vindo finished collapsing, he'd sprang right back up and lashed out with yet another knife.

It was just like they'd been warned. Vindo's liecraft—Instakill Counterattack—involved using his incredible springlike movements to take his opponents down the very instant they thought they'd won. Pretending to lose was his signature move.

As soon as he landed from his leap, he fell to one knee. "...Looks like I breathed some in after all."

He could easily have been acting. As soon as they got close, he might well launch another counterattack. As long as Erna and Lily weren't sure one way or the other, they had no choice but to flee. They rushed out of the room and dashed down the Longchon Walled City hallways once more.

After climbing a ladder that felt like it might break at any moment, they arrived in a corridor whose walls were covered in cracks and tears. By that point, they had no idea what cardinal direction they were moving in. They passed a couple of locals who gawked at them in bewilderment, but Erna and Lily paid them no heed.

As soon as they found an empty apartment, the two of them slipped into it. It, too, had clearly been lived in, and its floor was adorned with a plain rug. Erna quickly scanned the room's layout. The sink was heaped full of kitchenware, and there was a large closet about seven feet from the entrance. Once again, whoever lived there was fortuitously absent.

Erna and Lily hid against the wall and focused all their attention on listening. However, they didn't hear the sound of Vindo's footsteps.

"...Wait, he's not coming after us?" Erna asked.

"Maybe...," Lily muttered. "Maybe the poison actually worked."

"Huh...?"

"I mean, it's worked on Teach before," Lily continued, sounding vexed. "But with just the gas, he'll be back up and moving in no time. We had the perfect opportunity, and we blew it."

"____"

At that, Erna realized the blunder they'd made.

Vindo *had* gotten hit by the gas after all. Prodigy or not, there was no way he could have defended against an attack he didn't see coming. That last counterattack of his must have taken every ounce of strength he had left. In truth, though, he'd barely been able to move.

He'd *pretended to pretend to lose.*

That was how skilled spies fought—by using lies and deception to get out of tough situations. By using liecraft, Vindo had led them around by the nose and gotten them caught up in his pace with the one technique Lamplight had never been able to learn.

"C'mon, let's not beat ourselves up about it." Lily patted Erna's head. "At least now we know something. They might be elites, but they're still human. They can be beaten just like us."

"...Yeah, you're right."

"Let's not run; let's take him down. It shouldn't be long before he comes after us."

".........."

Upon hearing Lily's words of encouragement, Erna steeled her resolve.

If they left Vindo to his own devices, there was a real danger that he would work his way through Lamplight one member at a time. They probably didn't have a single person who could stand up to his surprise attacks. If they wanted to fight him with the advantage of having an ambush on their side, then this was the only chance they were going to get.

It was time for them to take down the greatest spy in the entire academy student body.

"I have a plan," Erna said. "We can use the puppy I borrowed from Big Sis Sara. He'll be able to warn us when Vindo gets close."

"Ooh, so it's finally *his* time to shine."

"Then we go for Vindo's eyes. I have this souped-up flashlight that Annette made."

"Got it. Annette really can make anything, can't she?"

Erna helped the puppy down from her head and gave him the knife Vindo had dropped to sniff. Meanwhile, Lily took the flashlight from Erna and flipped it on and off to make sure it worked. It emitted a blast of light so powerful it made the whole room look like it was midafternoon.

Now they had one of Sara's pets and one of Annette's inventions. Erna was ready to finish the job, and she was going to use the tools her Specialist squad teammates had given her to do it.

Lily nodded in admiration. "Got it. So after that, how're we gonna finish him off?"

"We'll throw whatever we find in the room at him!"

"That's your plan?!"

At that point, the puppy's nose twitched. That was their signal that Vindo was there.

Lily blasted the flashlight at the room's entrance, and Erna took a frying pan, a stainless steel bowl, and a cutting board from the sink and hurled them.

As Vindo charged in from the hallway, he swatted away the kitchenware and closed in on Lily. He was moving so fast all their efforts to blind him were for naught.

However, that was precisely the opening Erna had been waiting for.

"I'm code name Fool—and it's time to kill with everything."

She yanked the rug with all the force her legs could muster. And when she did, *the closet toppled over.*

For Erna, spotting a piece of furniture that was primed to tip over was child's play, and that was precisely what the large closet behind Vindo did.

"_____"

Even the great Vindo was caught flabbergasted. His eyes went wide, and Lily took full advantage of the opening.

"This time, you're mine!"

Without a moment's delay, she fired off her next blast of poison gas. Once again, it hit Vindo head-on.

Erna clamped her hands over her mouth, already certain of Lily's success.

There's no way he could avoid breathing in the gas...

When people fell victim to unexpected disasters like that, their natural reaction was to gasp. That would give Vindo a big lungful of poison. Plus, even if Lily's poison wasn't enough to take him down on its own, he also had Erna's disaster to contend with. Out of everyone in Lamplight, Erna was the one who'd spent the most effort forging her bonds with her teammates.

That was the one thing Lamplight had that Avian lacked—the time they'd spent together with Klaus.

Together, we've spent ages training against Teach...! Erna encouraged herself.

The poison gas and the falling furniture attacks bore down on Vindo in unison. Erna's head was telling her that they'd won, and her heart was soaring at the sight. She couldn't help but react that way—despite knowing exactly what Vindo's liecraft was.

"I hope you enjoyed that daydream of yours."

All of a sudden, Vindo vanished. The next time the girls spotted him, he was standing beside Lily like he'd been there the whole time. They gasped in shock.

"You already showed me that attack once. All I have to do to beat it is not breathe."

Vindo slammed his knives into Lily's shoulder and neck. "........." She choked as the air rushed from her lungs and she crumpled to the floor. The still-lit flashlight fell from her hand and rolled over by Erna's feet.

"It was simple," Vindo said, sounding almost bored. "I knew that if I let the poison hit me, you two would try to fight back. It saved me a load of time."

He'd *pretended to pretend to pretend to lose.*

The whole thing had been part of his plan. He'd intentionally fell for their attack, analyzed their techniques, and used that knowledge to win the follow-up fight.

"Big Sis Lily..."

Lily had been bested just like Grete before her, but that wasn't the only thing that had shocked Erna. There was also the matter of Vindo's movement.

"Just for the record, if you people think you're the only ones who've gotten special training, you're dead wrong."

Hearing Vindo's words caused the blood to drain from Erna's face.

It wasn't because she'd never seen that footwork before. It was because she *had*. Vindo's movement had been so blisteringly fast it bordered on teleportation, and Erna recognized it in an instant. It was the same footwork as Klaus's—the movement he'd used during the climax of his battle against Purple Ant back in Mitario.

The question was, where had Vindo learned it from?

Erna was horrified. Her teammates were dropping like flies, and now she was all on her own. Klaus wasn't coming to rescue her, and she had no idea where the rest of her team was. Their comms were down, so she had no way of calling for help. And with how labyrinthine the Longchon Walled City was, there was no way anyone was just randomly going to come save her.

A pair of words spilled from her lips. "How unlucky..."

"...What the hell are you talking about?" When they did, Vindo shot her a confused question. "'Unlucky'? Please. All of this happened because *you* screwed up."

"What...?"

"What, you think you have a penchant for misfortune or something?"

"............................"

Erna didn't understand what he was implying, so all she could do was go silent.

"You seriously don't get it?" Vindo let out an exasperated sigh. "Well, you don't. You're just an idiot. You can trace the whole situation you're in back to your own blunder."

"......"

"When you Lamplight people botched your mission, it gave us an opening to steal your boss. But the question is, where'd you botch it? And the answer is, it was that fire in the cotton mill office. That was where you got burned, and your mission went south."

"............"

"And you know what started the fire? It was the goldfish bowl that *you* moved."

"_____"

"It's called a burning lens. The curved glass took the setting sunlight and gathered its heat on a single spot. That was what set the carpet on fire. It smoldered as it ate through the oxygen in the room, but when you opened up the door, the backdraft effect lit it right back up. That was what caused the explosion you got blasted by."

"_____"

"Honestly, I should be thanking you. You blowing yourself up made my job a million times easier. It's pathetic, the way you live your life dragging your teammates down with your stupid mistakes. Lamplight has a weak point, and it's you," Vindo declared.

"I'll say it again: You're not unfortunate—you're a fool who *brings* misfortune down on your team."

It was ninety-two minutes in, and Vindo's biting words had just smashed Erna's heart to pieces.

Chapter 4

Ideals and Reality

Klaus watched over the battle from the middle of the Longchon Walled City. As he'd expected, both sides had put hunting down the document on the backburner in favor of trying to knock out the competition directly. Fierce battles were being waged all across the complex.

Klaus moved nimbly across the Walled City in order to keep tabs on both sides. Just a moment ago, he'd spotted Vindo taking down Grete. Afterward, Lily and Erna had fled, and Vindo had given chase.

Ah, that makes sense, Klaus thought as he watched in admiration. *I wondered why Vindo's mission success rate was so strangely high, but looking at that footwork... One of Inferno's members must have taught him the secret to shifting his center of balance.*

Now that he'd seen Vindo in action, he finally understood how the young man had gotten so strong. Just like Klaus, he'd learned the ropes from someone truly talented.

Once Klaus was done observing, he descended to the main street. The others had left Grete there unconscious. None of them had had the bandwidth to get her to safety.

When he approached her, her eyes fluttered open. "...Boss, is that you?"

"Are you all right? I'm taking you somewhere safe."

Klaus moved around to her side and scooped her up. As soon as he did, her face went red. "What...?" she stammered, followed by an

"I—I...," but eventually, she went limp and leaned gently against Klaus's body.

"I'm sorry, Boss... I lost..."

"You took one of them out, didn't you? You did well." Klaus had already gotten Qulle to safety, and she'd told him all about what Grete had accomplished. "You can rest easy now and leave the rest to the others."

"In that case, would it be all right if we stayed like this a little while longer...?"

"Be my guest."

Grete softly squeezed at Klaus's clothes. They'd been so busy with missions lately that Klaus hadn't been able to make much time for Grete. He didn't mind indulging her a bit here.

He carried her inside.

"Those movements of Vindo's...," Grete said as he did. "I couldn't help but notice how much they resembled yours, Boss... Do you have any idea why that might be?"

Apparently, she'd noticed it, too.

Klaus nodded. "It's an Inferno technique."

"It is...?"

"That footwork belongs to a woman named Gerde. Her code name was Firewalker, but I called her Granny G. Vindo must have met her somewhere and learned the technique from her."

It wasn't that odd, once you thought about it. Inferno's work took them all over the world, so there would have been plenty of opportunities for something like that to happen. "Hearth" Veronika had met Thea and passed her spirit along to her, and "Firewalker" Gerde must have passed her technique along to Vindo in much the same way.

Inferno's memories seem to be living on in all sorts of unexpected places...

Gerde's secret technique was a form of footwork involving sharp acceleration and deceleration—zero to one hundred, one hundred to zero. She liked to use it while rapidly firing off rifle shots, and even once she hit her sixties, she continued using it to dive straight into firefights. Back in her youth, she worked for the army and racked up results that left scores of men in her dust. Eventually, she became one of the scariest geriatrics in the world.

Klaus had mastered the technique, too, of course. He knew just how effective its speed was at overpowering one's foes.

"Not many are even capable of learning it, and Granny G rarely taught it to people. She must have really taken a liking to Vindo. It wasn't often that anyone measured up to her standards."

"...Is there any way to counter it?"

"That's a hard ask. In places like this with lots of cover, things often devolve into close-quarters combat. If Vindo is combining Granny G's footwork with those knife skills of his, he could probably give Corpse a run for his money."

"........."

Grete's eyes went wide at Klaus's evaluation. At the same time, though, she doubted he was exaggerating. Corpse was an assassin who'd traveled the world doing covert ops at Purple Ant's behest, and while spies from all across the globe had struggled to best even one or two Worker Ants, Corpse had managed to beat a whole dozen of them.

Here in the Longchon Walled City, Vindo's skills might well be on par with his. Lily's and Erna's prospects looked grim. At this rate, their defeat was all but assured.

"Ultimately, what decides the contest is going to be whether any of you are capable of explosive improvement."

They hadn't had nearly enough time to train, and Klaus hadn't been able to help them much. However, he'd given them the one secret they needed in order to turn the situation around—liecraft. If even just one of the girls was able to master it, they would stand a fighting chance against Avian.

Grete spoke up. "........Don't worry, Boss."

Klaus looked down and saw her smiling assuredly in his arms.

"This mission taught me something," she prefaced her statement. "All of us love Lamplight with our whole hearts, and the thought of losing one of our own is rousing us to action. For better or for worse, our bonds of *camaraderie* are strong."

"You have a point," Klaus agreed. Perhaps it was the sort of solidarity you only saw in washouts at work, but whatever the reason, the girls had grown dependent on Lamplight. Klaus cared deeply about the team, but the girls' feelings were stronger still. Even the ever-timid Sara had taken on a member of the Longchon mafia in order to improve their chances against Avian. The girls always had a way of unlocking their potential at the oddest of times.

"When that person is you, Boss, the feeling is that much stronger. And the injury Erna suffered because of all this only adds to the pile. Everyone is firing on all cylinders, Lily and Sybilla in particular."

"..."

"I believe in the others. I believe they're going to pull through."

Grete's tone was soft, but her declaration was confident and firm.

"You have a point," Klaus replied concisely.

She was right. They were just going to have to believe in Lamplight— and trust they were capable when their backs were against the wall.

"I'll say it again: You're not unfortunate—you're a fool who brings misfortune down on your team."

Vindo's words pierced Erna deep in her heart.

Her throat stung. Her legs trembled. Her eyes welled up with tears. She knew it was pathetic, but all she could do was hang her head.

Vindo was on the verge.

He'd almost figured out the huge secret Erna was keeping.

Erna simply stood there in the dank, musty room. She'd forgotten all about fleeing. She envisioned mold growing all throughout her body and eventually rotting her away completely. Oh, if only it were that easy. Sadly, though, her heart kept on beating, and her vital activity refused to cease. Pathetic as she was, she was still alive.

"...You're dead wrong."

Then a voice came from a wholly unexpected direction.

It was Lily. Vindo's knife strikes to her shoulder and neck should have knocked her out, but she'd returned to her senses and was back on her feet.

"You're tenacious, Silver, I'll give you that." Vindo narrowed his gaze at her, impressed. "In your spot, any normal person would've gone down ages ago."

"Oh, I've never been better. Your attacks are nothing compared to how bad Monika's fists hurt when I spilled water on her book."

"...That's an odd analogy."

"And that time I doodled on Sybilla's face? Her punches hurt a dozen times more than your knives."

"...Why do you make your teammates hit you so much?"

"The point is, you're nothing." Lily stood tall and proud and glared at Vindo. "Those weakling words of yours ring hollow. The insults you're throwing at my teammate aren't even worth listening to."

Once she was finished tearing Vindo a new one, Lily strode over and planted herself between him and Erna.

All Erna could do was stare helplessly at Lily's back. Lily was normally such a jokester, but now there was something almost radiant about the figure she cast from behind, and her fists were trembling.

She's furious. And it's on my behalf.

Erna felt a heat bubbling up at the back of her throat. If the situation hadn't been so tense, she probably would have started crying.

"Damn, you really let me have it," Vindo said with the slightest of smirks. "All I did was point out the truth. It's like I said—*everything* that happened, happened because of her mistakes. And I'm not just talking about during the mission."

"...What do you mean?" Lily asked.

"That fall she took not long before this competition. She had a big fight coming up right around the corner, and she got injured. What do you think? You really believe that she fell because she was scared of us?"

Vindo's voice was ice-cold.

"Well, she didn't. It was heat. I checked out the fence, and it showed signs of heat damage. It wasn't a great fence to begin with, and that combined with the heat made it easy for the fence to warp. And it had the same root cause as the last one—converged light."

He dispassionately went on.

"I've got an eyewitness who says they saw a kid sitting there for ages *with a crystal ball.* The crystal ball was focusing the sunlight against that fence that whole time. All it took was a little weight, and the aluminum fence bent over."

"........."

"Normally, having that many accidents happen in a row would be unlucky, yeah. But see, spies don't get to make excuses like that. All those screwups are on her. She's her own worst enemy."

Lily's expression was pained. She tried to come up with a rebuttal, but no words came out. Then she glanced back at Erna.

Her eyes were swimming with doubt.

Erna wanted to scream.

Stop it.

She wanted to yell at the top of her lungs.

Please, stop exposing all of my shame.

"And while I'm at it, how about I make one more reveal?" However, Vindo offered her no such mercy. He raised a finger. "This is partially conjecture, but I'd bet that fire she was in as a kid was her own fault, too. The thing is, her story didn't check out. The fire started at night, then spread unnoticed and burned her whole house down. The only survivor was a single girl. There were no witnesses, and the culprit never got caught. Do I have all that right?"

"I don't get it. What's the problem—?"

"Then do tell me—*How did she know it was a Molotov that started the fire?*"

"………"

Lily's eyes went wide. Now she saw it, too.

The most basic style of Molotov cocktail was simply a beer bottle filled with kerosene or gasoline and topped off with a piece of cloth. Once you tossed one, the only evidence it left was cinders and broken glass. Even if you used the scorch marks to figure out what room the fire had started in, it was difficult to identify an exact source. However, Erna had stated confidently that the fire had been started by a Molotov cocktail.

"What's more, she said her parents bought loads of wine that afternoon. Even if they found an unidentified bottle in the burned-out living room, how could a girl that young be sure it was from a Molotov?" Vindo said. He went on. "Here's what I'm thinking. The only person who could have known it was a Molotov was the survivor. In other words, she must have been there when it landed. But that still leaves mysteries. If she saw the fire start, she could easily have gone and woken up her family. Molotovs are powerful, but not powerful enough to burn down an entire aristocratic mansion in the blink of an eye. It begs the question, then, why did her family die? There's only one logical answer— *little Blondie there fled all on her own.* The fire itself might have been man-made, but her family's deaths were caused by her own blunder. That's my theory."

"........................"

Erna couldn't move. It felt as though every drop of blood in her body had just frozen solid. Words were failing her, too. Vindo had used his keen intellect and arrived at a story exceedingly close to the truth. It was like that harsh gaze of his was peering right into her heart. Erna was worried her legs were going to give out under her. It took everything she had just to stay upright—

".........And?"

—yet beside her, Lily was totally unfazed.

"Is there a point to all these selfish little theories of yours?"

"...Look, you're the one who asked."

"Maybe I did, maybe I didn't. Who cares?"

"Look, I'm just looking out for you. Spies who live like fools can only ever fight like worms."

Vindo flicked his arms and produced a new set of knives from within his sleeves. He held three of them clenched within the fingers on his right hand and another two between the fingers on his left.

The man was ready for war.

"You should cut her loose sooner rather than later. Want me to do it for you?"

"You and me are never gonna see eye to eye, are we?" As soon as Vindo's voice turned murderous, Lily sprang into action. She pulled out a rod from behind her back and held it in front of her. It was metallic and looked oddly bumpy. "Time for Deluxe Annette Weapon Prototype #72," she roared. "Destr—"

"You think I'm going to lose to some pathetic prototype?"

However, Vindo was faster. He didn't even give Lily a chance to use her weapon. After using his brutally quick footwork to close in on her, he smashed the backs of his knives into her wrist, her neck, and— for his finishing blow—the side of her head.

Lily's body toppled over to the side. "Erna...," she barely managed to say. "I'll buy you some time. Run for it..."

Erna choked down her desire to burst into tears and fled past Lily. Lily had put everything on the line to secure an escape route for her.

"You're not going anywhere, Blondie."

Vindo's arm extended toward her from behind.

He's going to get me.

Right as fear seized her, though, Vindo's arm froze.

Erna glanced back to see that Lily had caught Vindo by the leg. There was barely any light left in her eyes, but even so, she was grabbing him so tight her nails were digging into his skin.

"God *damn* it, you're hardy." Vindo raised his knives aloft. "Will you please just go down already?"

A heavy sound echoed through the room. Vindo must have struck her with the butt of one of his knives.

The despair-inducing match results of Vindo vs Lily had just come out.

I'm sorry…Big Sis Lily…!

As Erna raced down the Longchon Walled City hallway, each step felt like it was tearing off a little piece of her heart.

It was 115 minutes in, and the battle was still raging.

Over in the "Pandemonium" Sybilla and "Meadow" Sara vs "Lander" Vics battle, the handsome Vics had been totally composed the whole way through. After trading a few blows with Sybilla to gauge her strength, he put together a plan, then made full use of the Walled City's many corridors and repeatedly dashed from hallway to hallway.

The reason for his composure was simple—Avian didn't actually care that much about Lamplight.

If I'm being honest, the only one we're actually interested in is Mr. Klaus. ♪

Lamplight's members harbored deep inferiority complexes about the elites, but the reverse was far from true. Avian held no particular feelings toward their washout counterparts one way or the other.

Vics smiled.

They get props for finishing those Impossible Missions, but at the end of the day, Mr. Klaus did all the work. ♪ *Sure, they're no normal washouts, but they're not anything special, either.* ♪

As a result, all Vics had to do was play it smart. Just as he'd predicted, Sara had been unable to keep up with the battle and got left behind.

After dashing down a few more corridors with Sybilla in hot pursuit, he reached a dead end. There was a small safety railing there and nothing more. Sybilla and Vics cleared the railing in unison and leaped outside of the Longchon Walled City altogether.

Now that we've both got room to maneuver, all that's left is to dive into the world of battle. ♪

Vics's unique talent was his superhuman strength. His build looked slender, but his latissimus dorsi muscles were gigantic, and their abnormal size allowed him to generate a huge amount of power. When Vics threw punches, he always made sure to put his back into them.

On top of that, his lats were even big enough to conceal his weapons. By making it look like he was unarmed, he was able to catch his foes by surprise.

Superhuman Strength × Concealment = Bottomless Brawn.

That was the liecraft Vics had devised. If his opponents didn't know his weapons' reach, he could leverage his immense strength to make each block a knockout!

"___!"

Vics took the whip he'd retrieved from behind his back and gave it a big swing. This time, he'd chosen a medium-range weapon with a completely different reach than his fists or his cudgel.

Sybilla just barely managed to dodge back in time. Those were some serious reflexes she had.

"Where the hell'd you get that whip from?!" she yelped.

"Oh, who knows? Hmm... ♪ Should I go for a spear next?"

"Wait, you've got a *spear*?"

"Wouldn't you like to know? ♪ Ha-ha-ha, make sure you keep your eyes fixed on me!" Vics chirped, poking fun at his bewildered foe.

Naturally, the weapons he hid in his lats had to be small, and he could only hold a maximum of four at a time. At the moment, he was armed with a cudgel, a whip, a pistol, and a pair of brass knuckles. There was no way he could have actually fit an entire spear back there, but by that point, Sybilla would have believed just about anything.

Vics's score was the second best out of all the academy students, and he had the skills to back that rank up.

Now the two of them had arrived at a completely empty lot. Someone was probably prepping it to build out the Longchon Walled City even farther, as the bare earthen ground was neat and tidy.

Looks like she specializes in theft, but that's not gonna work on me. ♪ I guess I'd better go ahead and settle this with my next attack. ♪

As long as he had his strength, Vics was confident he could emerge victorious from any close-quarters fight. And as far as deception went, he could tell that he had Sybilla well and truly flummoxed.

"All right, let's do this. ♪ If I don't hurry it up, Vindo's gonna beat me to the punch. ♪"

He stowed his whip back behind his back and replaced it with his brass knuckles. They were the perfect weapon to take advantage of his monstrous strength, so they were his go-to when he wanted to finish a fight.

He lowered his center of gravity and got ready to put Sybilla down with a counter.

"........."

However, she didn't attack him.

Instead, she sulkily pursed her lips and lowered her raised fists. "... Vindo, huh? So you're sayin' I don't even register to you."

"Hmm? Yeah, not really. ♪"

"Well, that's a fine how do you do. I guess that's just how it is, huh? You guys are elites. No sense payin' attention to us little people," she muttered. "You're pissin' me off, man."

Upon seeing her reaction, Vics couldn't help but let out a laugh. "Ha-ha-ha. ♪ Y'know, there's something that's never made sense to me. ♪"

"What's that?"

"See, it's funny. ♪ I don't know why, but losers always get hung up on meaningless evaluations and ratings. ♪ What school you went to, what your grades were like... That kind of stuff bores me to death. You'd think that losers would want to just ignore those rating systems altogether, but instead, they start obsessing over tiny changes and differences. ♪ It's like, don't you know there's a whole world out there? ♪"

It was a mystery Vics had been grappling with for some time.

During his time as an academy student, grades had been the furthest thing from his mind. He knew about spies who were leagues stronger than him—people like Hearth, the Greatest Spy in the World; people like Ouka, the honorable spy whose nationality was a mystery; people like Calico, the strongest counterintelligence agent in all of Lylat; and people like "Flock" Vindo, a rookie from the same generation as Vics who'd immediately distinguished himself. When Vics compared himself to any of them, it filled him with a mortifying sense of inferiority. So what if he was an "elite"? Academy grades weren't worth the paper they were written on.

"Her name was Erna, right? That chick who wanted so badly to reach our level that she got in an accident while she was training. ♪ She got fixed on arbitrary metrics, got tunnel vision, and screwed herself over. That's pretty pathetic, if you ask me. ♪"

While he was at it, he decided to add in a little taunt. Using his flippant attitude to throw his enemies off their game was one of Vics's signature moves.

"..."

Sure enough, Sybilla went flush with rage. She was so furious the air around her seemed liable to catch on fire.

Once again, Vics got himself ready to fire off a counter.

"...Maybe you've got a point," Sybilla quietly grumbled. "Fact is, we do get hung up on little things. From your perspective, the stuff we care about probably seems trivial."

"Oh yeah. ♪ It couldn't matter less. ♪"

"Can you really blame us, though? All the shit you're sayin' might be true, but every time I think back to those cramped academy dorms, I get this ugly pain in my heart. Maybe if I'd been able to become a badass adult, I could laugh that shit off, but guess what? I wasn't. And my buddies weren't, either!" Sybilla leaped. "You piss me off, asshole—bad enough to make me pull out a technique I'd just as soon never use."

".........?"

Vics wasn't quite sure how to describe what he experienced next.

It felt like a blank spot had just drifted through his mind. All at once, he stopped being able to perceive the girl in front of him. *Who was it I was just fighting?* All the information about her in his head vanished like a candle being blown out.

Then a moment later—there she was.

"——!!"

Vics immediately leaped away to put some distance between himself and Sybilla. Then he got to work analyzing the strange sensation that had just violated his brain.

…Did I seriously stop being able to perceive her for a second? There's no way. But at the same time, that's the only explanation.

He looked over at Sybilla. She was cracking her knuckles and radiating the quiet rage of a person preparing their next move.

That's probably the secret behind her "theft" skill… She erases herself from her opponent's perception, then steals their stuff. It's just about the best ability a pickpocket could ask for. But no matter how you slice it—

Vics gulped.

—this girl'd be even better at killing people!

It was all too easy to picture.

What if she took those fingers so capable of withdrawing a wallet from an interior pocket and dug them ever so slightly into soft flesh? What if she filed her nails down like knives and stabbed them into someone's heart? Doing so would have been beyond most pickpockets, but not Sybilla. She had the raw strength and combat instincts to pull it off.

Where the hell did she learn a trick like that…?

Vics felt a slight chill in his bones. That was when he noticed that, once more, he couldn't perceive Sybilla. By the time he could see her again, she was already in melee range.

"Here's the thing, though. For all our faults, there's a guy who thinks we're magnificent."

With that short declaration, Sybilla swung her knife.

This was going to be a problem. If she was too up in his face for him to trick her, then obviously, he couldn't use his liecraft.

"Watch close. I'm gonna show you how a lame-ass washout fights."

Vics only barely managed to block her attack with his cudgel.

Clearly, he was going to have to revise his assessment of her skills. Like it or not, this called for a massive change of plans.

As Vics reevaluated his opinion of Lamplight, Vindo was experiencing some unexpected emotions of his own.

When Erna fled, it had locked in a leader-versus-leader battle between

Vindo and Lily, and the battle had ended almost as soon as it began. Vindo had won in overwhelming fashion.

He hadn't given Lily a single inch. He'd made sure to overpower her before she could so much as arm herself. Using his trademark knife skills, he struck her in the head. Then, after thinking back to how quickly she'd recovered the last time he knocked her out, he hit her head again even harder.

All the strength flooded out of Lily's body. She'd made a valiant attempt to brace herself, but her legs went limp all the same, and she toppled to the ground face-first.

Vindo glanced at the ground to make sure Lily was actually down for the count.

...After a hit like that, not even she could get up again.

His attack had been so strong that if he'd used it against a civilian, there was a very real chance it could have caused a brain injury. He was a bit worried he'd overdone it, but at the same time, it wasn't like he could have afforded to pull punches.

His job was to eliminate Lamplight's members, but they were proving to be far more tenacious than he'd expected. Now that Erna had fled, he was going to have to give chase. He turned toward the hallway.

"...Hold it right there."

The moment he did, though, he heard an all-too-familiar voice.

"_____!"

He looked back, hardly able to believe his ears.

Lily was bracing herself against the wall to drag herself back to her feet. That was enough to baffle even Vindo.

What's this girl made of? She shouldn't be able to move. Any normal person would have passed out ages ago...

As far as he was aware, she didn't know any techniques for shrugging off attacks. Every blow Vindo had dealt her had struck true. It was the same knife technique he'd used to knock out scores of enemies, soldiers, mafia members, and enemy spies alike. When Vindo attacked someone, he rendered them utterly immobile.

The fact that Lily was still standing could only mean one thing—her mental fortitude was beyond the beyonds. It was a silly explanation, but it was the only one that made sense. The girl was just tough as nails.

"What the hell even are you?" said Vindo.

"I'm Wunderkind Lily," Lily hoarsely replied. "...And my specialty is buying time."

"All this, just for the blond... You really care that much about your teammates?"

"Who knows...? Maybe I just love the way protecting them makes me feel..."

"You and I are never going to understand each other, are we?"

"Nope. I hate...your guts, too..."

That there was her limit.

Midway through her mumbled stream of verbal abuse, she keeled over forward and passed out atop the cold concrete floor.

Seriously, what is that girl made of...?

In terms of spy skills, she couldn't hold a candle to Vindo. If their positions had been reversed, though, Vindo knew that there was no way he could have gotten up that many times in a row to buy time for his allies.

What are they all made of...?

Despite being comprised of nothing but washouts, Lamplight had successfully completed multiple Impossible Missions. And sure, their recent missions had been marred by successive failures, but they'd put up a surprisingly robust resistance in their battle against Avian.

Vindo couldn't make heads or tails of how intensely they were struggling.

He sucked in a deep breath, held it for a moment, and let it out to center himself.

"It doesn't matter. Either way, I'll do what needs to be done," he muttered to himself. He started thinking about how he was going to chase down Erna.

Then, as he turned his back on Lily, he spotted someone unexpected walking down the corridor. It was Klaus. He gave Vindo a steely look.

"........."

It felt like a chill had just run through the air itself.

Apparently, Klaus was going around and getting the knocked-out combatants to safety. Despite his professed neutrality, everything about his demeanor was practically bubbling with resentment. Fair fight or not, he couldn't stand seeing his teammates get hurt.

"There's no point holding this against me, Bonfire," Vindo said before

Klaus had a chance to say anything. "This is what the Republic needs. It's important we find out who's better so the stronger team can work under your command. It's for the good of the motherland."

"I understand that. I don't need you to spell it out for me."

Klaus strode past Vindo and gently felt Lily's bleeding forehead. Then he wordlessly wrapped a bandage around his subordinate's scalp. His expression was hard, but his fingers moved with a decided softness.

As he continued applying first aid, he spoke. "It does beg the question, though—why do you want to work with me so badly?"

"………"

"You were the one who gave that bold order to send three people after Monika, weren't you? Your judgment is sound, and I watched you fight just now. You aren't the kind of man who needs to work under someone else's command."

"…That's my call to make."

Klaus pressed the issue. "Why do you want me so badly? The way I see it, Avian is a perfectly fine team already."

However, Vindo didn't understand what he was getting at. He had no idea what kind of future Klaus had in mind.

"…I'm just paying off a stupid debt," Vindo briefly replied before striding on past Klaus.

There was no need to tell him, he'd decided.

Klaus didn't need to know that the reason Vindo had set his sights on him to fulfill "Firewalker" Gerde's final wish.

Vindo met the spy known as Firewalker on two separate occasions.

The first was a chance encounter—and an indirect one—during the Great War. There, a younger Vindo bore witness to a miracle.

Vindo was a tender ten years of age at the time, and his hometown was under Galgad occupation. Their rule was horrific, and his town descended into a state of exploitation and murder. The Galgad soldiers confiscated what little rations there were, and they mercilessly killed any who tried to stand up to them. Both of Vindo's parents had been shot dead when they begged the soldiers for food.

Vindo stared through the window as they buried his parents in a hole far too ignoble to be properly called a grave.

I'll kill them!

Tears welled up in his young eyes as he chanted the words inside his head like a curse.

I'll kill them all, every last one of them...!

He wouldn't find out until later, but a full 20 percent of his town's population ended up dying at the Imperial army's hands. It was there that a lust for vengeance took root within his heart, accompanied by a tormented realization of his own powerlessness.

In the end, it was someone else's hands that carried out his revenge.

A strange rumor began circulating through the Galgad-occupied town.

I hear the army had some classified information leaked. Apparently, there's a spy hiding in the town.

There were other rumors, too.

Whenever the Imperial army takes territory, there are these five monsters that show up there.

There's a man with a katana and unmatched combat skills; there's an old woman sniper who charges full speed through battlefields like nobody's business; there's a pair of twin brothers—a games master who's won a thousand battles in a row and a fortune teller who can see the future; and there's a mysterious woman with hair like a raging inferno.

Those five can make the impossible possible.

A week later, the Allies launched a surprise attack on the Imperial forces there. For a town drowning in despair, their arrival was like a beam of light shining through the darkness. Before long, the Imperials' position started falling apart, and the soldiers starting scrambling to be the first to get the hell out of there.

It was like magic, and it moved young Vindo's heart.

Later on, he would discover that it was a spy who made that magic possible.

The second time he met her was during his time in the navy.

After witnessing the miracle of espionage work driving back despair, Vindo set his sights on joining the Naval Intelligence Department.

And graduating from the naval academy with outstanding grades was exactly what he did. Having a job where he got to travel the globe doing intelligence work was also exactly what he wanted.

During his travels, he ran into a striking-looking old woman on a street corner in the Fend Commonwealth. The woman was pretty darn conspicuous. Her tank top and jeans left her brawny muscles bare, her grizzled hair was tied back behind her, and she had a pair of sunglasses resting on her forehead. It was almost inspiring, the way she smoked three cigarettes at once and pounded down beer out of a large mug in broad daylight.

As Vindo was giving her a long, hard look, she suddenly turned and glared at him.

"You there, sonny. You're a spy, right?"

She'd found him out in a heartbeat.

As Vindo stared dumbfounded, the woman went on. "You've still got the stink of soldier on you, greenhorn, and I can feel your thirst for revenge from over here. What're you, Naval Intelligence? You punks haven't learned a thing. Well, someone had better teach you something. All right, sonny, c'mere."

Without even giving him her name, she simply laid on the criticism and dragged Vindo off to her basement apartment. Whenever he argued back, she would throw him against the ground and stick a gun to his head.

Then, after all but kidnapping him, she subjected him to three days and three nights of hellish training down in that same basement.

Every time he tried to flee, she would grab him by the throat and haul him right back. Vindo was so out of it by the end of the training that he couldn't actually remember any of the specifics. All he knew was that he emerged with several broken ribs.

On the third night, after Vindo threw up for the fifth time, the old woman finally released him. "That's pathetic is what it is, kiddo. Little Klaus only threw up three times getting through that regimen. Well, it is what it is. You're better now than you were before. You've still only just started learning to control those emotions of yours, mind you."

The woman had been merciless from start to finish. She still hadn't introduced herself, but over the past three days, Vindo had deduced that she was nobody to be trifled with. The list of people with skills like hers had to be a short one.

"...During the war, you ever go to a town called Melatock?" he asked.

"Hmm?"

"I was there, and I watched with my own two eyes as spies screwed with the Imperials' intel and left their bastard soldiers without a leg to stand on. I'm wondering if you were there, too."

The older woman scratched her head in disinterest. "I couldn't say, really. It's hard to remember that far back. But sure, I might've worked there."

Vindo gasped, and his heart stirred. Sure enough, the woman across from him was one of the legendary spies who freed him from that hell.

"Well, I was one of the civilians you saved." He gave her a deep bow. "Thank you, really. You're exactly the kind of spy I want to be like."

"..............." After thinking for a long time, the older woman licked her dry lips. "I see, I see. So you owe me one. In that case, I'm going to go ahead and be a bit selfish."

"Hmm?" Vindo looked up. He had an ominous feeling about this.

"Drop that naval nonsense and come join the Foreign Intelligence Office. Its existence isn't public, but your bosses will know the name. Just tell them that 'Firewalker' Gerde sent you, and they'll square you away right quick. That's where the *real* spies work. With your skills, you'll be through and done with the academy inside a year."

"If that's where the skilled spies are, then I'd be happy to join, but I'm not sure I follow..."

"Then I'm gonna need you to lend Little Klaus a hand."

"Who?"

"He's a young'un, like you... Hell, you might even be the same age. He's called Bonfire. You remember that, now. You stay in this world, and you're bound to find him someday."

Vindo didn't recognize the code name, but he made sure to commit it to memory. Whoever this Bonfire was, he was clearly important to her.

She narrowed her eyes, like she was gazing far off into the distance. "...Little Klaus is awful at relying on people, you see." There was a certain sadness to her words. "I've got to foster more talent before these old bones run out of life in 'em. At this rate, he's gonna end up alone.

Sigh... The work never ends when your subordinates are as much of a handful as mine."

With an exasperated "That boy, I swear," she shook her head and left.

Harsh as her words were, though, her voice had the warmth of a grandmother fretting over her grandson.

Vindo's expression softened as he reminisced on his run-ins with the older woman.

Two years had passed since he'd followed her instructions and transferred over to the Foreign Intelligence Office. Since then, he'd blitzed his way through his academy and joined the front lines of espionage work. It was there that Avian's old boss Sky Monk had told him the rumors about Bonfire.

The story was, Gerde was part of a team called Inferno, and everyone on the team except Bonfire had been wiped out. Vindo never got to have his reunion with Gerde, but he'd long since mastered her technique. He'd taken his burning lust for revenge and locked it deep away, only sublimating it into a liecraft that let him launch immediate, explosive counterattacks.

"Don't you worry, Firewalker," Vindo said. "I'll drive off the flies buzzing around your grandson and crush Lamplight until there's nothing left."

That was the secret to his fixation on Klaus—a desire to do right by the woman who'd given him hope all those years ago.

Two hours had passed since the teams infiltrated the Longchon Walled City.

The city had initially seemed like a labyrinth, but as it turned out, it was pretty manageable if you took it one section at a time. After fleeing from the room Lily had gotten injured in, Erna took a long detour, then made her way back to the same room. She glanced inside, and sure enough, Lily was gone. Klaus must have come and picked her up or something. Erna quickly closed the door.

From there, she left the room, headed down the hallway, and sank to the floor. She couldn't walk another step. Her lungs hurt so bad it felt like they were going to burst.

In all likelihood, Vindo was still close by. He'd been working to elim- inate Lamplight's members, and now that he'd taken out Grete and Lily, Erna was the only one left. Right now he was probably on the hunt for his final prey.

As Erna tried to catch her breath, something fell off her head and onto the floor.

It was a black puppy, Johnny.

"...Oh, that's right. You're still here, too."

She scritched the puppy's chin, and he licked her fingers, almost like he was trying to console her.

"Big Sis Sara..." As the puppy helped Erna calm her nerves, she thought about the Lamplight member she so dearly adored. "...I'm not scared. I'm not scared anymore...," she whispered.

"*Yarf*," the puppy barked sadly.

Erna stroked his fur and turned her thoughts back to the past.

When was it I first became a slave to misfortune?

After her family passed away in a fire, she became fixated on a pecu- liar notion—the notion that it wasn't fair that only she got to live. At her family's funeral, seeing the attendees mourning their deaths made her want to run away and hide, and when the attendees gently told her to be strong on her family's behalf, the words rang like a curse in her ears. All she was in their eyes was a pitiable little orphan.

At the same time, though, she realized something. The more *misfor- tunate* she was, the more *sympathy* people would show her, even though she was a wretched child who'd survived all on her own.

She hated herself for even letting the thought cross her mind.

How did I feel when I joined my spy academy?

She recognized what a horrible person she was, and being drawn to misfortune was her way of punishing herself. However, she still wanted people to console her. That made her that much more drawn to misfortune, and she threw herself into situations where it was liable to occur.

Eventually, word of the ex-aristocrat girl who showed up at the scene of accidents with nigh miraculous frequency made its way to the spy academy scouts, and when they offered her a spot, she had no reason to turn them down.

She wanted to become a spy and save loads of people to do her late family proud—or at least, that was what she told them. However, not even she herself was sure if that was really true. Perhaps she only said that because she wanted someone to compliment her, she mused.

.........The question was, who?

Why was I so alone at the academy?

She was inarticulate, gloomy, secretly a teensy bit prideful, and overly prone to accidents. However, that was all just details. The actual reason was it was because of how twisted her personality was.

Why did I keep getting drawn to misfortune?

Because she knew. She knew that every time she got unlucky it gave her an excuse she could give both to herself and to others.

After all, it would mean it wasn't her fault.

If she was unlucky, it wasn't her fault she got bad grades. If she was unlucky, it wasn't her fault she had no friends. If she was unlucky, it wasn't her fault that everyone hated her. If she was unlucky, it wasn't her fault that she couldn't be a good girl and make her dead parents proud. So what if she was cowardly and dishonest to her core? Her misfortune was delivering a commensurate punishment, so it was fine. It wasn't her fault. It wasn't her fault. It wasn't her fault. It wasn't her fault. It wasn't her fault. It wasn't her fault. It wasn't her fault. It wasn't her fault.

She might have been a pathetic washout, but that was all just bad luck, so it wasn't her fault.

She loathed the way she chose to live her life.

But at the same time, she had a young man who'd saved her and a group of teammates who'd accepted her with open arms.

◇◇◇

Johnny the puppy twitched his nose to let Erna know that someone was coming. She looked up with a start.

Vindo strode out of the long hallway's shadows.

He twirled his knives in his hands as though getting a feel for their weight. As a sort of tic, he juggled three of them into the air at once like an acrobat.

Finally, he clutched them between his fingers and looked up as well. "Found you, Blondie."

"......!"

Erna brimmed with resolve as she rose to her feet. Retreat wasn't an option. This time around, she was going to have to face him.

The two of them squared off in the silent, abandoned corridor with about fifteen feet between them. The light bulb dangling from the ceiling let off a feeble glow.

Erna could hear gunshots coming from off in the distance. Some of Lamplight's and Avian's members were probably duking it out, but the shots were coming from far enough away that there was no way anyone was going to come save her.

She focused every nerve in her body and glared at Vindo.

"Here's some friendly advice," Vindo said detachedly. "Surrender now. I get no joy out of bullying weaklings."

"..........No way."

"I swear, you people just don't know when to quit." Vindo combed back his hair with his hand, visibly annoyed. "In that case, I guess I'd better take it easy on you. I'll bring you down with my bare hands."

"Take it easy"?

By the time Erna reacted to the phrase, Vindo was already closing the gap. He dodged the bottle Erna hastily threw at him, and a moment later, he was right in front of her.

Erna pulled out the lead pipe she'd been hiding behind her back and swung it down with all her might.

Vindo tilted his body backward to evade the blow. He dipped so low he nearly hit the floor. It almost looked as though he'd fainted. Then, in an instant, he sprang back up from his defeated-looking position.

"I'm code name Flock—and it's time to gouge clean through."

His knife-hand attack struck Erna square in the gut. Spittle flew from her mouth, and she couldn't breathe as her body jerked into the air, then tumbled across the ground. Her mind went fuzzy for a second, but she snapped out of it upon vomiting and ending up on her hands and knees in a puddle of her own gastric juices.

Vindo had completely overpowered her without even using his knives. She hadn't been able to so much as put up a fight. For him, beating her had been like taking candy from a baby.

"That should about do it." Satisfied with his work, Vindo brushed off his hands. "Now just go to sleep so Bonfire can come pick you up. Enjoy that kindness of his. This'll be your last chance to do so."

".........."

"Don't worry. It's not like you're saying good-bye to him forever. Just accept your powerlessness, go back to your academy, and pour yourself into your training. Right now that's your place." His tone left no room for rebuttal. "And while you do, Avian will protect you. I'll protect you, and I'll protect our nation."

Vindo's voice rang loud with pride. His dignity and patriotism came through, clear as day.

A sharp pain ran through Erna's heart. She'd seen it time and time again at her academy. Deep down, *that* was who the elites really were. Sure, some of them were greedy and arrogant, but the vast majority of the top students were like Vindo and had a strong moral compass to go along with their talents. Erna couldn't count the number of times she'd seen their faces brim with confidence.

"You're so cool...!"

The words spilled from her mouth, and tears spilled from her eyes. Her opponent's words had gouged at her heart, and his blows had stung her body, but her true feelings tumbled out all the same.

"I want to be like that, too... I want to live my life like you do!"

She was so jealous. Vindo was everything she admired. Everything she yearned for. She wanted to become a valiant, courageous spy like him.

How many times had that wish crossed her mind back at the academy, she wondered? How many times had she resented its refusal to come true?

She wanted to be a strong, talented spy. She wanted to live a life trusted and relied on by everyone she met. She wanted for people to have great expectations for her—and to meet those expectations by saving her nation from peril. She wanted to be someone who could deftly deceive her foes and confidently tell those weaker than her that she would protect them.

She wanted to be one of the elite.

"I just wanted...to become a spy...who Mom and Dad...and Big Bro...and Big Sis would be proud of from up in heaven..."

Ah, she thought as realization dawned on her. *That* was who she wanted to have compliment her—the family she would never see again.

In the end, though, I couldn't do it.

I was never able to become the ideal spy I wanted to be.

Her weakness left her drawn to misfortune, and bit by bit she strayed from the path of righteousness. She grew to love disasters for the excuses they gave her for her ever-falling grades, and before she knew it, the people at the academy started seeing her as a washout and handling her with kid gloves.

"They wouldn't care," Vindo said curtly. "Not everyone has it in them to be strong. That's why it's up to us strong people to protect weaklings like you. Now, yield."

"I can't do that!"

Erna fought through the pain racking her body and stood up. She panted as her lungs frantically tried to take in as much oxygen as they could, but she stood on her own two feet all the same.

"I couldn't become a cool spy... And the only way I know how to live is one that I hate... But even so, despite all that, I've had good things happen to me, too... Lamplight is the one thing I can't give up on," she declared. "And so I decided to accept myself for the shameful, horrid, uncool person that I am."

Confusion flitted across Vindo's face, and Erna quietly smiled.

She was about to show him something.

She was going to show him the twisted way a washout who was unable to become an ideal spy fought!

She was going to show him a way of life so uncool that an elite could never even conceive of it!

"I'm code name Fool—and it's time to kill with everything."

She opened up the door beside her and immediately leaped out of the way.

The door led to the empty room she and Lily had just fought Vindo in. Under normal circumstances, opening it up wouldn't have done anything. But this time, flames blasted out of it.

Vindo was standing right in front of the door, and flames billowed directly toward him. He tried to leap to the side as quickly as he could, but there was no way for him to make it in time.

The raging flames assailed him.

"____?!"

Vindo screamed when the fire hit him, then rolled across the floor to put out his burning clothes. The Longchon Walled City was made of concrete, so there was little danger of the fire spreading and creating a huge conflagration. After it finished scorching the area around the room, it was going to die out in no time.

Vindo managed to put out the fires on his body, but not before suffering some serious damage. He groaned in pain as he clutched at his burned right leg. He wasn't going to be pulling off any more of his fancy footwork any time soon.

"Why...was there a fire there...?" Vindo's eyes went wide, and he glared at Erna. "When did you set it up? Back when we fought, you didn't have any sort of bombs on you!"

He must have checked her for weapons when he attacked her with his knives earlier. It was the work of a consummate professional.

He clicked his tongue. "How could you have set that fire while you were fleeing?"

"With a burning lens. I used that stainless steel bowl I threw to focus the light from the flashlight Big Sis Lily dropped and set the rug on fire. Then, when I opened the door just now, it triggered the backdraft effect."

The Longchon Walled City's expansions had been uncoordinatedly slapped together out of concrete. Plenty of its concrete rooms had terrible ventilation, and a locked room with poor airflow was precisely the right kind of environment for the backdraft effect to take place.

"You told me all that yourself," Erna matter-of-factly declared.

"No," Vindo snapped back in irritation. "The time line doesn't add up!"

"But..."

"I didn't tell you about burning lenses until after you two lost control of that flashlight. Up to that point, you couldn't have known they existed. If you did, what was up with those accidents you caused?"

He had a point. Before their current showdown, Erna had gone through a pair of accidents. There was the backdraft effect from the burning lens fishbowl at the cotton mill, and there was her fall caused by the aluminum fence warping under the converged light from her crystal ball.

Vindo had determined that both events were caused by Erna's negligence. In his view, they'd only happened because of her ignorance regarding scientific concepts like burning lenses. The thing was, though, he'd stopped one step short of the truth. If not for the one fatal misconception he was operating under, he would have gotten there.

"They weren't mistakes; they were on purpose," Erna replied.

"Both of the accidents happened *just the way I engineered them to.*"

"...The hell?"

"It was all intentional. I felt that I had to, so I *caused the fire and let myself get hit.* It was the same thing with my fall. I intentionally put my weight on the part of the aluminum fence I'd weakened *and made myself fall off the cliff.*"

That was the truth behind the two accidents: Erna had actively caused them both. Everyday danger or not, there was no way that so many focused-light-related accidents could happen one after another—not unless someone was consciously making them occur.

However, Vindo hadn't been able to reach that truth. No reasonable person could possibly understand the mindset of someone who willingly threw themselves into disaster—and that was precisely why Erna had known it would work. Intentionally creating misfortune and using it to fool everyone was a combat style that was hers and hers alone.

Accidents × Starring in Her Own Productions = Catastrophe Creation.

That was the liecraft Erna had devised.

"Are you...," Vindo said, dumbfounded. "Are you insane?"

It was unclear if the look in his eyes was one of fear or disdain.

There was no way he could comprehend why Erna had willingly caused those accidents. Nobody who lived their life untwisted could possibly understand her.

And so she replied. "I've known there was something broken about me for a long time," she said with a casual coldness. She gave Vindo a smile that didn't reach her eyes. "Good-bye."

The trap she set off for good measure was a simple one. The fire had spread to the lumber piled carelessly in the hallway, and with how badly the planks at its base were smoldering, the pile was starting to lose its balance. All Erna had done was cut the wire holding the wood up.

A pile of burning planks came toppling down toward Erna and Vindo. Erna yanked her body to the side, just barely managing to avoid the misfortune she'd called forth, but with Vindo's injured leg, there was no way for him to do the same.

"………"

The planks landed and crushed him under their bulk.

A wave of black soot struck Erna head-on. As she wiped her face clean, she started making her way down the hallway. Her joints were killing her. She needed to find somewhere safe to rest up.

"Let's go," she said to Johnny the puppy, then scooped him up in her arms from his spot by her feet. He obediently leaned against Erna's chest. Feeling his warmth helped settle her nerves a bit.

Once Erna had covered a little bit of ground, she turned and looked back. Vindo hadn't gotten up yet. She'd really taken him down.

"………"

She stopped for a moment and thought.

If Vindo had passed out, his life might be in actual danger. It *was* Vindo she was talking about, so she was sure he'd avoided any fatal injuries, but she was still a bit concerned about his safety. That said, she also didn't want to carelessly approach him and end up eating one of his counterattacks. Plus, she was worried that some of the locals might get caught up in the fire…

D-did I take things too far?

Erna started fretting. Regrettably, holding back hadn't really been an option.

"…I get it now."

Then Vindo's voice smashed right through her train of thought.

"＿＿!"

Vindo shoved the piled-up planks aside as he rose to his feet. There was something slower and more relaxed about his movement now. Like he was flaunting how confident he was.

He gave his knives a flick, and the gale force from that alone cleaved a path through the smoke hanging in the air. His wind also blew away the last smoldering bits of fire.

"Good, I can still move," Erna heard him mutter to himself in satisfaction. He looked at her, blood streaming from his forehead. "I underestimated you," he said. "No, that's not it. My read on you was completely off."

His right leg was burned, his body was covered from head to toe in cuts, and there were bluish patches of internal bleeding visible through the hole in his shredded jacket. Yet still he was standing.

Erna ground her teeth.

All that…? All that, and it wasn't enough to beat him?!

Her self-inflicted injuries had ostensibly made him complacent, Grete and Lily had fought tooth and nail to let her escape, and she'd lured him in and caught him right in the middle of one of her trademark accidents. Erna had put everything she had on the line. And yet even so, she'd failed to bring Vindo down.

"Now I get you," he said proudly as he wiped the soot off his clothes. "I've heard of a mental disorder like that, where someone who's otherwise healthy injures themselves to garner sympathy from others. Munchausen's syndrome, it's called. You've got something like that; you just fake accidents instead of illnesses."

"………"

"I bet it started with that fire that killed your family. Did you set that, too? No, I guess not even you would go and burn your whole family to death. That fire probably *was* an accident, but you went and passed it off as arson by taking an empty bottle and throwing it into the burning building yourself. Then you told the police you'd seen someone sketchy. Go on, tell me I'm wrong."

Erna bit down on her lip. "I thought not," Vindo said, nodding to himself. "Your motive was simple—*you wanted to elicit as much sympathy as you could.* Your family was a bunch of former aristocrats, and everyone else was jealous of them, right? You knew the world would grieve more for an act of arson by a cowardly villain than a simple hearth fire that happened to get out of control. You lied for the sake of your dead family."

It was like his words could see right through her.

"But that just made you hungry for more. All you had to do was make yourself unfortunate, and people would shower you with pity. You couldn't stop. You sought out misfortune, and you were drawn to accidents. In the end, you even started causing them yourself."

"..........."

"Deep down, that's who you are—a brat who loves the pathetic misfortune of her own situation."

After saying his piece, Vindo let out a long exhale.

Then, after a pregnant pause, he went on.

"It's sickening."

He looked at Erna like one would a pile of filthy garbage. It was a look she'd received countless times at her academy.

"You think…," she said. "You think I don't know that?!"

"But you haven't told your teammates, have you?"

"I…"

"You can't. Not if you want them to keep spoiling you with their kindness and affection when you run into misfortune." Vindo's voice echoed within her skull. "If they knew who you really were, they would find you repulsive, too."

Erna couldn't help but picture it. What would happen if they found out that some of her misfortune was of her own creation? Sara consoled her whenever Erna got into accidents, Sybilla and Lily doted on her, and Thea looked after her. How would they treat her once they knew?

Her body went limp, and the puppy she was holding fell to the floor.

"Guess I hit the nail on the head."

Vindo clutched his knives and approached Erna.

He's bluffing, the logical part of her brain told her. *He's too injured to move properly, and that's why he's trying to rattle me. Deducing people's mental states and using that to wage psychological warfare is just another weapon in his arsenal.*

Don't let him get to you, she encouraged herself. Vindo wasn't beaten yet. She needed to devise a new disaster. *None of that stuff he's saying matters right now!*

However, visions of her teammates' eyes full of revulsion flitted through her mind.

"I'm not scared…," she said. Down by her feet, the puppy barked.

Step by step, Vindo closed in on her.

"I'm not scared of the others finding me repulsive…"

"*Woof!*" the puppy barked loudly.

Vindo lowered his center of gravity a little.

"I'm not scared of that future you talked about, not one bit."

"*Yarf!*" the puppy howled.

Vindo took a running start and charged at her.

Erna squeezed her hands together as though in prayer.

"I don't care if the others hate me if it means I can take you down…!"

She had to will it into being.

She needed to put everything she had on the line and call forth a disaster so bad it would obliterate her enemy where he stood!

Erna leaped to the side and readied a bomb in her hand. As she did, Vindo swung his knives.

The puppy jumped up.

"YARF, YARF, WOOF, YARF, WOOF, YAAAAAAAAAAARF!"

"Yeep…?" "What?"

Erna and Vindo both froze.

The puppy was barking like there was no tomorrow. Something was getting him all riled up, and his cries were getting shriller and shriller. Erna was right next to him, and it got so bad her ears started hurting.

Neither combatant could do anything but stare at the puppy in bewilderment. The wind had been taken right out of their sails.

"So…" Vindo furrowed his brow. "What's the deal with the dog?"

"I—I don't know…"

Erna had no answer to give him.

She'd heard the dog bark a couple times since she borrowed him from Sara, but this was the first time she'd seen him so agitated.

Then a reply came from an unexpected direction.

"Oh gosh, I'm so sorry! I haven't finished training him yet!"

It was Sara.

She popped up from around the corner and gave them an apologetic bow. "I'm teaching him a trick like Miss Monika told me to."

She gave her cheek an embarrassed scratch as she came over, then scooped Johnny up and gave him a stern look. "She said it would be handy, so I should hurry up and make him learn it. The thing is: It's trickier than I expected, so I'm starting off by doing a test run on my teammates, but…he still gets worked up sometimes…"

"I…see?" Vindo replied, still perplexed.

Sara went on, excited to get a chance to talk about her pets. "According to Miss Monika, not all perspiration is made of the same components, and people have researched how to figure out people's emotion from their sweat. So I did a little experiment on Miss Erna. I've always been a bit worried about her, so I taught Mr. Johnny to react whenever she sweated in a *very particular way.*"

She happily made her reveal.

"Specifically, *the way she sweats when she lies.*"

Erna was shocked.

She racked her brain to think of all the times he'd barked. Sure enough, they all matched up with times she'd been lying.

In other words, Sara had known for ages. She knew that some of Erna's accidents were of her own creation. She knew that Erna had caused the screwup in the cotton mill on purpose, too. And even so, *Sara had stuck by her side.*

Erna felt the corners of her eyes growing hot.

As she stood there motionless, Vindo boredly flipped his knives into his hands beside her. "So?" He gave Sara a domineering glare. "You want a piece of me next?"

"Huh?" Sara's expression sank. "No, no, no, no, no! I couldn't; I could never! I'm not here to fight you! Miss Monika *just* finished lecturing me about how that wasn't my job!"

She rapidly waved her hands in front of her and scurried backward. Then, once she was all the way out of sight, she went on in a much more composed tone.

"That's why I brought some people way stronger than me when I followed Mr. Johnny's barking."

The assistants in question were standing on the other side of the hallway Sara had just disappeared down.

"You've got a lotta nerve, makin' our Erna cry like that!"

"Yeah, I hope you're ready. It takes a lot to tick me off, and you managed to do just that."

It was Sybilla and Monika—Lamplight's two heaviest hitters.

Vindo gritted his teeth in unconcealed frustration. "...Those idiots let you give them the slip?"

Sybilla was the first one into the fray. She closed the distance in a flash and hurled a punch at Vindo's face with a fierce "Eat this!"

The attack was straightforward to a fault, but Vindo no longer had the strength to properly react to it. He was able to block the punch itself, but the force from the blow still sent him toppling to the floor. After landing from the spill, he managed to get back on his feet, but then—

"A burning lens, huh? That's a clever idea." Monika looked at the scorch marks, then nodded as if something had just clicked. "But just so you know, bending light is *my* specialty."

A flash went off.

The camera Monika had produced gave off a blinding light, and after reflecting off the mirrors Monika had simultaneously strewn, it struck Vindo square in the eyes.

Her attack couldn't be dodged. It was quite literally as fast as light.

As the camera robbed Vindo of his vision, Erna started running.

"YEEEEEEEEEEEEEEEEP!"

Her body ached, but she fought through it and let out a howling shout to encourage herself as she charged. She poured everything she had into jumping at Vindo, then head-butted him with all her might.

Her head slammed right into his face.

At long last, Vindo's body finally went limp, and the man who'd stood above all the other academy students sank to his knees.

Chapter 5

Fool

"...What is this, a mob? How much of your team did you plan on sending at me?" Vindo quite reasonably grumbled after getting captured.

The moment he'd gone limp, Monika had wasted no time in tying him up with wires and tightly binding his wrists together. He was officially out of the fight.

Meanwhile, Sybilla and Sara kept watch over the perimeter. The commotion had woken up a number of the locals, and Sybilla and Sara had to feed them some lies while also stamping out the last bits of Erna's fire. Thanks to their efforts, the incident ended as nothing more than a minor fire scare. Erna had taken some basic precautions, but still, letting the fire get out of hand would have been bad news for everyone.

Erna watched them handle the cleanup, feeling rather surreal about the whole thing. The fierce battle had taken her all over the Longchon Walled City, but in the end, she'd successfully struck down the top-ranked student in all the academies.

By that point, it had been over two hours since it all began.

"I can't believe I actually lost," Vindo muttered lifelessly.

He stared up at the ceiling.

"..........................."

Then he turned his attention elsewhere.

He was surrounded by four Lamplight members: Erna, Sara, Monika, and Sybilla. When you considered the fact that he'd also taken down Grete and Lily, it meant that, all in all, he'd fought six different people. He hadn't been kidding about the mob thing. They'd basically just thrown sheer numbers at him until he went down.

Vindo let out a big sigh. "What are the others even doing?"

"That's a good question," Monika said with a nod. "Sybilla, Sara, what're you two doing here? I thought you were supposed to be fighting that Lander guy. You take him out already?"

Sybilla and Sara twitched in unison. ""——!!""

"...Yeep?"

Erna didn't like where this was going.

Monika gave the duo a vicious glare, and the two of them began sweating bullets.

"Y-yeah, uh, about that...," Sybilla falteringly replied, waving her hands to and fro. "His name was Vics, right? The guy was tough as nails... I had him pretty much dead to rights, but he got away. We figured there was nothin' for it, so we might as well join up with Erna..."

A buzzing sound rang out from Vindo's pocket. He was getting a call on his wireless radio.

Eventually, a pleased-sounding male voice came through.

"Hey, hey, hey! ♪ Lander here. I just picked up the classified document. Mission's all done. ♪"

"""""" .... """"""

It went without saying, but the whole contest had been about who could steal the classified document first. All their fighting had simply been a means, not an end in and of itself. Taking that logic to its extremes, the battle would end the moment anyone got their hands on the document, even if that person hadn't defeated a single one of their opponents.

In other words...

"WE LOOOOOOOOOOOOST?!" Erna screamed.

The battle between Lamplight and Avian was over, and Avian had emerged victorious.

◇◇◇

The first thing both teams did was leave the Longchon Walled City. They hadn't paid the mafia much heed during the battle, but it was technically a stronghold of theirs. There was no sense getting into any more fights with them than necessary.

As they left, Monika read Sybilla the riot act. "I swear to God, you two need to get your *shit* together!"

"Shaddap! What about the people Vindo took out solo, huh?"

At this point, they were all trying to foist off the blame. Whenever they lost, things tended to get ugly quick.

However, the truth of the matter was that the reason Lamplight lost was because they weren't strong enough. It wasn't any one person's fault. They lacked the raw firepower to deal with Avian's two big heavy hitters, Vindo and Vics, and no matter how they'd allocated their resources, it wouldn't have been enough to close that gap.

"Hey, Blue," Vindo said, cutting into their verbal battle. "What about you? Did you really manage to drive off Lan, Pharma, and Queneau that quickly? I thought I told them to do whatever it took to keep you pinned down."

The question was directed at Monika. She'd been boxed in by three elites. How had she broken through their ranks?

"Hmm? Oh, I only took out two of them. The 'thou' chick disappeared midway through. Once their formation fell apart, crushing them was easy," she replied coolly.

"Wait, Lan disappeared?"

"Yeah, I think Annette captured her and dragged her off somewhere."

The non-Monika Lamplight members looked at her quizzically. """"She did?""""

Annette had been in charge of expanding their radio network, but Thea had gotten knocked out pretty early on, and none of them knew where Annette had gone after that or what she'd been doing.

"Now that you mention it," Erna said, "she got really mad after that Lan lady called her a runt the other day."

"Ah," Vindo replied. "In that case, the two of them might still be fighting. Someone should go let them know that—"

He trailed off midsentence.

A shriek had just split the night air. Everyone strained their ears.

When they arrived at the Walled City's northern border, they discovered where the scream had come from.

"PRITHEE, FORGIVE MEEEEEEE!"

Lan was half naked and apologizing.

Her legs were folded under her, and she was scraping her forehead against the ground. It was a stance known in one of the Far East's isles as *dogeza*. Tears gushed from her eyes as she repeated her cry. "Prithee, forgive me!" Her outfit was burned onto her skin, leaving much of her body bare in the most unsightly way imaginable.

"You can plead all you like…"

Annette was standing triumphantly before her and wearing a radiant smile.

"…but it's falling on deaf ears, yo."

"I retract it all! 'Tis I who am the runt! So please, stop this! I beg of thee clemency! Actually, maybe I should cool it with the thees and the thous… Did it make it sound like I was being insincere? Because I promise, I wasn't. It's just a persona I was doing. Oh, I can't believe I ever said that. I know better now. Seriously, I'm so, so sorry. You're so tall, Annette. Taller than me! And you know what?! I bet you're just going to keep on growing! Heh, heh…"

She was talking a mile a minute and abasing herself with every word.

It was unclear what exactly had happened, but by all accounts, Annette had completely crushed her.

Then Lan spotted Erna and the rest of the onlooking spies. She ran over to Erna as fast as her legs would carry her and clung to her ankles. "I—I beseech thee, save me! That girl intends to k…to ki… Death would be preferable to what I've endured… She's a demon. A demon in human flesh… She took her electric drill and put it…put it in—"

"Yo!" Annette shouted.

Lan's entire body trembled.

"I'm feeling kind of thirsty all of a sudden."

"I shall purchase thee some tea posthaaaaaaaste!" Lan dashed off at full speed and vanished from sight.

The others dazedly watched her go.

"Annette...what did you *do* to her?" Erna asked.

Annette looked as pleased as punch. She laid her index finger over her mouth. "That's a secret, yo!"

In any case, the full breakdown of the Longchon Walled City battle was now clear.

LAMPLIGHT: Grete defeated Qulle.

AVIAN: Vics defeated Thea.

AVIAN: Vindo defeated Grete.

LAMPLIGHT: Sybilla fought Vics and forced him to beat a tactical retreat.

AVIAN: Vindo defeated Lily.

LAMPLIGHT: Annette trounced Lan. Completely gave her what for.

LAMPLIGHT: Monika defeated Queneau and Pharma.

LAMPLIGHT: Erna, along with three others, defeated Vindo.

AVIAN: Vics acquired the classified document and ended the match.

All the members of Lamplight and Avian who took part in the battle gathered together and were told the results once more.

Lamplight's members were despondent.

Lily's shoulders slumped, and Sybilla clenched her fists in frustration. Grete closed her eyes in pain, and Sara tried to console her. Monika and Thea were stone-faced. Erna and Annette stood motionless.

Over on Avian's side, everyone but Qulle exchanged high fives. It was a rare display, coming from them. Qulle looked none too happy about having been the first one to get knocked out.

"................"

Meanwhile, Vindo appeared to be brooding over something.

The morning after the battle in the Longchon Walled City, Klaus got to work writing up his report. The classified document Vics retrieved had contained a list of all the perpetrators involved in the Din embassy leaks, and once Klaus passed that along to the Ministry of Foreign Affairs, they could handle the rest. Before long, the Longchon police would be on their way to arrest those responsible. None of the list's contents were particularly shocking, but it was that kind of straight-forward intelligence and counterintelligence work that allowed their nation to thrive.

With that, their mission in Longchon was complete, and they'd helped Longchon by dealing a major blow to their local mafia groups to boot. The only thing left to do now was head home.

Klaus turned his gaze to the morning light streaming into his room and sighed. "...I can't believe we lost."

Saying it aloud made it feel terribly real.

Klaus felt conflicted about his subordinates' defeat. The girls themselves did all they could. In his eyes, the blame lay solely on him for his poor leadership skills.

It's frustrating. I can't help but wonder what more I could have done.

It was an odd feeling. In all his days, he'd never felt this specific sort of pain before. He hadn't been directly participating this time around, so it wasn't like anyone had defeated him personally, yet a dull ache rose up in his chest all the same.

As the Greatest Spy in the World, it had been a good long while since he'd felt such a stinging loss. He quietly clenched his fists.

Assuming he held true to his word, he was going to have to leave Lamplight and become Avian's boss now. He wasn't going to be the girls' boss anymore.

"........."

It wasn't going to be good-bye forever, not by any stretch of the imagination, but even so, the thought caused an indescribable sadness to well up inside him.

That aside, though, he needed to get some breakfast. He left the study.

The eight girls were waiting out in the hallway.

"Teach..."

He'd assumed that they would have all gone to sleep after their big battle, but clearly that wasn't the case.

The girls looked at him sadly with Lily leading their vanguard. Klaus could see guilt flickering in their eyes. As far as he was concerned, though, they had nothing to feel sorry about.

"Good morning, everyone," Klaus said in the gentlest voice he could muster. "That was some good work you did last night. For now you should give some serious thought as to what you're—"

"Here's your stuff, Teach."

Lily handed him a large briefcase. All his personal effects were shoved inside.

"Hmm?"

"Now c'mon, it's time for you to make a break for it! Before Avian shows up!"

Lily raised her fist in the air, and the rest of the girls all cheered. """"Yeah!""""

"Once we get you outta here, we'll be golden!" said Sybilla.

Grete nodded. "…I already have your trip booked, Boss."

"Then we can just tell Avian you ran off," Thea added.

"Look, I'm not happy about it," Monika said.

"I'm not giving you away to nobody, Bro!" Annette chirped.

"Me neither," agreed Erna.

"I—I…I feel the same way," said Sara.

One after another, they all urged him to flee.

"You people are shameless," Klaus coolly noted.

"Hey, sometimes you gotta get out while the gettin's good," Lily replied. That hardheaded determination was so very like her.

Clearly, none of them had any intention of honoring their deal with Avian. Klaus wished he could say he was surprised.

"…Sounds like *someone's* gotten some interesting ideas into their heads."

Not a moment later, a terse voice came from behind them.

The girls' shoulders twitched. "——!"

All six members of Avian were standing by the entrance, with Vindo leading the group.

"S-so uh…," Lily stammered, breaking out into a cold sweat. "I—I guess we're still on for that promise, after all?"

Vindo gave her an exasperated look. "Forget learning how to be decent spies; you need to worry about being decent *people*."

The girls began slumping their shoulders. At the end of the day, none of them had actually been planning on getting away with it. They may have been spies, but they did have *some* dignity.

"Hey, Teach." After biting her lip in anguish, Lily fixed her gaze straight on Klaus. "Wait for us, you hear? We're gonna get stronger, and someday, we're gonna steal you right back from—"

"Nah," Vindo interjected. "What do you say we just call the whole thing null and void?"

"Whaaat?"

"Our primary objective is looking out for our nation's interests," Vindo replied. "The team talked it over, and we decided that having Bonfire stay as Lamplight's boss is probably the right call."

The girls blinked in confusion, unable to process the unexpected turn of events.

Vindo went on in a decisive tone. "We admit it—you people are strong."

Behind him, the rest of Avian nodded in agreement.

"We may have won, but you took out more of us than vice versa, and a couple of us even lost one-on-one. We'd be lying to ourselves if we pretended those results proved we were better than you."

"I—I mean, sure, but...," Sybilla rebutted. "What're you guys gonna do? You're still out a boss, right? You got some other idea for how to fill those shoes?"

"What, you're actually *worried* about us?"

"Shaddap. Look, it sucks, but the facts are the facts. You all won, and you've got a right to take our boss. Why give that up?"

The corners of Vindo's mouth curled upward at Sybilla's question in an almost self-mocking way. He looked over at Klaus. "Go on, Bonfire. You tell them."

"Are you sure?"

"It was basically your idea, no?"

"Fair enough," Klaus said with a nod. "You beat us. I'm the Greatest Spy in the World, and you took my subordinates and ran circles around them to complete your mission. As you are now, your talents are already some of the best our nation has."

He gestured at Vindo.

"Code name Flock, I'm assigning you to be Avian's new boss."

"Very well. I accept the position."

The girls' jaws dropped.

Vindo stuck his hands in his pockets and gave them a haughty look.

"This is the best option for our nation. Now Lamplight and Avian can protect Din on two fronts."

Klaus had been considering this outcome since the moment he first saw Vindo's raw skill. Vindo was the kind of man who should be leading a team. He had talent that could make him a world-class spy someday, and working under Klaus's command might well have hindered his growth. Just as Vindo had said, this was the option that would do the most good for the Republic.

"Together, we're going to turn this world on its head. Try to keep up with us, ladies of Lamplight."

The other Avian members spoke up in agreement.

"Ooh, this is going to be fun. ♪ We'll be the two pillars of a new era. ♪" "The Empire shan't know what hit it." "Yeah, let's do this together." "Lamplight's so strooong. Watching you all moved me." "...Aye."

Vindo strode over to the girls and whispered in Erna's ear. "Hey, Blondie."

Erna's eyes went wide. "Yeep?"

"Don't worry too much about that stuff I said back in the Walled City. I'll be expecting big things from you."

Erna could feel her throat tremble. "........."

Having finished what he set out to do, Vindo offered them a final "... Once we get back to Din, we'll at least stick around for some of your training. Make sure you get those skills of yours up to snuff," and turned to go.

"""""""""   """"""""""""
....

The girls were still dumbstruck.

Avian was on a whole different level than they were, and they'd made sure to demonstrate it through to the very end. They were decisive, strong, and most of all, badass—the very picture of the elites Lamplight's members had envied for so long.

At the same time, though, the girls were satisfied with that. If they were going to look up to anyone, then those were the kind of people they wanted it to be.

"Hey, Avian!" Lily called out to the departing team.

The rest of the girls figured out what she was getting at, and they all gave Avian a thumbs-up. Their voices rang out in spontaneous unison.

""""""""Magnificent.""""""""

Vindo laughed. "That should go without saying."

Now that the mission was over, the girls had no reason to stay in Longchon. After booking boat tickets home, they spent the rest of their time there enjoying themselves.

They started out by getting ready to vacate their base, but once they'd finished packing up all their luggage, they made sure to go see all the sights they didn't get a chance to check out during the mission. Lily stocked up on foodstuffs like mooncakes and *jiàng*, Thea stocked up on cosmetics containing oils made from flowers that only grew in the Far East, and Monika went around taking photos. Meanwhile, Sybilla took Grete along as she handed out candy to the local children she'd been forging fast friendships with. Whenever the girls had downtime, they always made sure to live it up.

As for Erna, she went along with Sara and Annette to the local market. However, it didn't take long before Annette said "I'm gonna go buy some fun junk, yo!" and vanished into the hustle and bustle of the crowd, leaving Erna and Sara alone together.

"So, Big Sis Sara," Erna asked quietly. "You knew that some of my accidents were my own fault...?"

"Hmm? Yeah, I did."

"...And you don't hate me?"

"Why would I? I mean, there are a lot of times when you get into accidents for real, right? It's hard to tell the difference, so I usually just accept it all at face value...," Sara replied like it was really no big deal.

She did have a point—not all the misfortune Erna ran into was of her own creation. There was the misfortune she was subconsciously drawn to, there was the misfortune she noticed and actively avoided, there was the misfortune that was just honest bad luck, and there was the misfortune she deliberately caused. Plus, Erna's heart was unstable enough that the lines between the various categories got blurred.

Sara's friendly smile didn't falter. "Sometimes, it's really cute when you go rushing headlong into Miss Annette's traps and come crying to me afterward. I'm like, 'Oh, she wants me to dote on her.'"

"I-it's embarrassing to have you spell it all out like that…"

"On some level, I'm sure the others have all realized it, too. So don't worry. We could never hate you, Miss Erna," Sara said gently. Then she hurriedly backpedaled a bit. "Oh, but you have to promise not to put yourself in *too* much danger, okay? That's a big no-no."

She squeezed Erna's hand.

It was like the way one would comfort a child, and Erna offered her a mumbled "Thank you."

Then she heard Annette noisily shouting for them off in the distance. Apparently, she'd stumbled on an interesting find. "You don't have to be so loud," Erna shot back, then headed over Annette's way.

On the night of their final day in Longchon, Klaus came to Erna. "Would you care to join me on a little excursion?"

She had no particular reason to turn him down, so the two of them headed out.

The destination Klaus had in mind was the night market on the Longchon mainland. There were over a hundred stalls, each billowing with steam. The smell of fish-based spices wafted through the air, and standing before the stalls offering all manner of fish-paste delicacies caused Erna's stomach to start rumbling.

As far as she could tell, Klaus taking her there had nothing to do with work. On his invitation, she enjoyed the Longchon night to its fullest by helping herself to some fried *shumai*, then buying a glistening yellow egg tart for dessert.

Once they were done at the market, they walked a bit and came to the sea. They sat down on one of the benches that had been put there for people to watch the night skyline from and gazed at the city's lights.

"The accident at the cotton mill and your fall on Longchon Island."

"Hmm?"

"I take it you engineered both of those?" Klaus calmly asked. Upon hearing the slight hesitation in his voice, Erna realized that that was what he'd invited her out to talk about.

"I did," she admitted. "I burned myself on purpose and screwed up the mission."

"Before I ask why, would you mind if I told you a story?"

"...Okay."

"A woman named Gerde once taught me that just barely getting by was the most dangerous thing you could do. Now I know just how brutally true that is. For a while there, Lamplight was messing up missions one after another, but Monika and I had been picking up the slack and forcibly dragging us across the finish lines. It wasn't ideal, but things certainly could have been worse. So I decided to wait and see how things would play out, and I kept letting you all fail."

"........."

"Furthermore—and it was Grete who taught me this—Lamplight's bonds of camaraderie are strong, for better or for worse. When it looked like you were going to lose one of your own, that feeling of uneasiness drove you to rapidly improve your skills. When your battle against Avian was right around the corner, and you had every reason to be nervous, it hardened you all up like nothing else."

Then he put those two concepts together.

"You put yourself in harm's way to *instill a sense of urgency in your teammates*. Am I wrong?"

"...That's right."

Erna gave him a small nod. Back at the cotton mill, she'd been terrified that if Lamplight kept screwing up their missions, somebody on the team was going to die. After that, her body had more or less moved on its own. After adjusting the goldfish bowl to create a burning lens, she waited for the alarm to ring, pretended to panic, and charged into the room and let the backdraft effect she set up burn her.

"I figured that if I got hurt, the others would take things more seriously..."

A thought had crossed her mind.

At this rate, an unspeakable tragedy is going to take place.

If the alternative is someone dying, then I should get myself hurt right away.

"And I figured that if I got hurt, the others would get really mad on my behalf..."

What she'd done was about as far from cool as it got, but as soon as Sara had told her that a person's liecraft was a mirror of who they were, she knew she had to accept it. That was the way Erna fought.

I'll do whatever it takes to protect Lamplight.

She was willing to throw herself into a fire.

She was willing to dive off a cliff.

She was willing to put herself through whatever misfortune it took to protect the place she called home.

Even that second accident, the fall, had been designed to raise morale by firing up her teammates' rage.

"In other words, you engineered this incident from start to finish," Klaus said matter-of-factly. "Your screwup at the cotton mill kicked it all off, and the Avian threat forced Lamplight to rapidly get stronger. Then, right before the showdown, you injured yourself again to turn the others against Avian even more. And finally, by the end of the battle, Lamplight had improved enough to earn Avian's respect. That was a hell of a job you did."

"...That's all just hindsight. I had no way of knowing we would run into Avian like that. That was just actual bad luck."

"No, no. What I'm saying is, this entire mess was my fault."

That wasn't what Erna had been expecting at all. "N-not at all," she hurriedly disagreed, but Klaus was undeterred. "By all rights, that was supposed to be my job. If I'd been more proactive about pushing you all to improve, none of this would have happened. As your teacher, I failed you." He gently placed a hand on Erna's head. "It's not just you all; I need to improve as a teacher, too. I see that now. I'm sorry, Erna. I promise I'll never put you in a position where you have to make that call again."

She could feel his warmth through her hair. It was a wonderfully comfortable feeling, and she softly closed her eyes a smidge. "..............You're right."

"Hmm?"

"I'm bad. I'm weird, and foolish, and I charge headlong into danger."

"That you do."

"So you'll need to keep a real close eye on me."

"No problem," Klaus replied. "I wouldn't be much of a teacher if I couldn't handle a single problem child."

Erna slowly smiled and rested her head against his body. It felt so nice, having him call her a "problem child" in that gentle tone of his.

Erna hadn't been able to live up to her ideals as a spy. She was simply too great a fool. Even if their positions had been reversed, she doubted she could ever have become as badass a spy as Vindo. The only way she knew how to operate was cowardly and uncool. She farmed sympathy from her allies, appalled her opponents, and sacrificed herself. She loved failure more than success, tragedies more than comedies, and misfortune more than fortune, and in realizing that, she found a way to fight—a liecraft—perfect for a washout like herself.

Dad, Mom, Big Bro, Big Sis...can this be good enough?

She thought back to the family who would have wanted her to live on in their absence.

It wasn't anything to be proud of, but she was living her life as best she knew how.

On the day the girl gave up on her ideals, she had a thought.

I can call myself Fool.

She would never stop being stupid, and her broken, twisted heart was never going to heal. With that being the case, it would be best for her to pick a name that would make people want to avoid her. Then nobody would have to get hurt.

Plus, if people accepted her in spite of it, she could cherish them dearly. It would mean she had a place she truly belonged—a place more full of light and good fortune than any other.

Next Mission

A document came in two months after their mission in Longchon.

This is code name Moonwatcher, reporting from Fend Commonwealth Radio Site 2974.

"Flock" Vindo: KIA
"Lander" Vics: KIA
"Cloud Drift" Lan: MIA
"Glide" Qulle: KIA
"Feather" Pharma: KIA
"South Wind" Queneau: KIA

Avian has been deemed incapable of completing their mission.

A woman was dancing the rumba in a Fend Commonwealth dance hall.
The elegant way her dress swayed in step with the song's slow rhythm enthralled any and all who saw her. A double-digit number of pairs danced back and forth across the floor, but she commanded more attention than anyone else present. Her long, straight-necked

body seemed almost made for dancing, and there was a curvaceous beauty to the way she moved it. At first glance, it appeared as though she was merely following her partner's lead, but the more you looked, the more it seemed that the reverse was true and that she was using her allure to pull her partner's strings.

"You're in an awfully good mood today," said her dance partner.

"Oh, I suppose," she replied with a smile. "Something very nice just happened."

"Did it, now?"

"Oh, yes. I got to swat away some flies that had been bothering me."

When she smiled, her face looked like that of a teenage girl.

Actually, she might well have still been rather young.

Every so often, the world gave birth to a monster. And just as it had created the peerless spy that was Klaus, it had created another one in that very nation...

She grinned bewitchingly. "Tell me, do you know what the simplest way to destroy an organization is?"

"...What's this about destroying things?" the man asked. "That seems rather uncouth."

"I'll give you a hint. It's the same way that the greatest spy team in the world got laid low."

"You know, you say the oddest things sometimes."

"Oh, don't worry about it. A lady's secrets are best left unexplored."

The music stopped.

The woman stepped away from the man and gave him a merry grin. "The answer is, betrayal from within. It can destroy legendary teams and up-and-comers alike."

The man blinked at her in confusion, for he knew nothing. He had no idea who the woman he occasionally went ballroom dancing with truly was.

She was a spy for the Galgad Empire.

Her code name was Green Butterfly, and she was a member of the Serpent team.

* * *

With that, the curtain rose on a whole new spy game.

Eventually, news of Avian's deaths reached the Din Republic, and they dispatched Lamplight, their team that specialized in Impossible Missions, to pick up where their compatriots had failed. The stage for the next act was going to be the land of tea, royalty, and fog: the Fend Commonwealth.

That was where Serpent's prodigy child, Green Butterfly, was waiting for them.

For she had set a trap—a scheme, to kill the man who'd gotten in Serpent's way time and again. Just as betrayal from within had felled Inferno, she intended to destroy Lamplight the same way. Eventually, she would decide on one of the girls as her target.

Once the world's wheels began turning, there wasn't a person alive who could grind them to a halt.

Soon, Lamplight was going to be faced with a cruel task.

Of the eight of them, they would need to find the person who'd fallen into Green Butterfly's clutches—*the girl who was going to betray Lamplight.*

Afterword

I know that the Volume 5 afterword isn't the greatest place for it, but I hope you don't mind if I take a moment to talk about my writing process for Volume 4.

So I have this editor named Mr. O. He's been *Spy Classroom*'s editor since the very beginning, and thanks to his passion and drive, he's made tons of huge contributions to the series like giving the first manuscript its big post-award overhaul and helping produce the seven girls' character PVs. If it wasn't for him, *Spy Classroom* wouldn't be nearly the work it is today.

However, there's a heavy cross he's had to bear.

"When we unveil the girls on the official website, we're going to do everyone except Erna..." (said through tears of blood) ← Before Volume 1 came out

That's right—he was the one saddled with the decision of when to start making Erna's existence public.

The book won the Grand Prize in the Fantasia Taisho awards, so it had a pretty big advertising push behind it. However, it was hard to decide how much of the Volume 1 content to reveal, and he agonized pretty hard over how to advertise it. In the end, Erna got excluded from the character *PVs*, the Volume 1 frontispiece, and the character bios on the main website. All of them got made with everyone but her.

At the time, I recall him saying something about making Erna's existence public at around Volume 3, but then...

"The first book's still selling pretty well, so we should probably keep her a secret..." ← When Volume 3 came out

...he was forced to make another bitter decision, and Erna's big debut got pushed back again.

Note that around this point, there was a merch offering involving acrylic standees of the *seven* girls.

I figured I would do what I could and make Erna the protagonist of the booklet that came bundled with the special edition of Volume 4, but then...

"Turns out, I'm getting reassigned." ← While I was writing Volume 4 "?!"

...Mr. O got transferred off of *Spy Classroom*.

This must be her hatred manifest! How terrifying!

(In truth, it was just a regular old staff reassignment, and he wasn't getting demoted or anything bad like that. Also, as far as the way Erna got treated went, I always said "Well, it's Erna. Them's the breaks" and laughed it all off.)

The point is: I'm writing *Spy Classroom 5* under a whole new world order. Farewell, Mr. O.

Tomari, thank you for the illustrations, which were as excellent as ever. When I saw the rough draft of the cover, I was deeply moved. "It's finally her turn!" Furthermore, I would like to offer my deepest gratitude to my new editor, as well as everyone who went out and purchased this book.

Finally, a preview of what's to come. Like it said in the Next Mission section, the team is going to be confronted with a difficult challenge. There's one girl who has a particularly cruel destiny in store for her, and I hope I'm able to depict her emotional journey with sufficient care. Until then, that's all from me.

Takemachi

HAVE YOU BEEN TURNED ON TO LIGHT NOVELS YET?